A Touch of Poison

Aaron Kite

To Irene,
(And Joedog, of course...)
Hope you enjoy it!

Ack

FIVE RIVERS PUBLISHING

WWW.FIVERIVERSPUBLISHING.COM

'15

Published by Five Rivers Publishing, 704 Queen Street, P.O. Box 293, Neustadt, ON N0G 2M0, Canada

www.fiveriverspublishing.com

www.jessicaallainart.com

Edited by Lorina Stephens.

Interior design by Lorina Stephens

Title set in Mascara, designed by Rebecca Alaccari in 2004 for Canada Type.

Text set in Adobe Casalon Pro, developed by Adobe and based upon the original English typeface created by William Caslon in 1722.

Published in Canada

Library and Archives Canada Cataloguing in Publication

Kite, Aaron, 1972-, author

A touch of poison / Aaron Kite.

Issued in print and electronic formats.

ISBN 978-1-927400-59-3 (pbk.).--ISBN 978-1-927400-60-9 (epub)

I. Title.

PS8621.I835T69 2014   C813'.6   C2014-900524-5   C2014-900525-3

For Kalysta, who knows how freaked out I can get when you mention 'the bedbugs'...

Contents

Chapter 1

Even from way up in her tower bedchamber, Gwen couldn't help but hear the young maid's shrieks of pain.

Retreating to her room hadn't helped. The hundreds of thick grey slabs of rough-cut stone, the aging mortar that held them all together, the massive oak door that barred the entrance to the room — none of it seemed able to prevent the girl's tortured screams from reaching Gwen's ears. It was everywhere at once, and seemed the only thing she could hear.

Gwen sat on her bed quietly, hands clasped in her lap, her dress smoothed out over her legs. Her calm, placid expression belied the feeling of guilt and dread that sat like cold gravel in her stomach.

The screams ended briefly and then began anew, practically doubling in volume; Gwen felt her shoulders tighten even more. In fact, it felt as if her entire spine had been stolen and replaced with screeching violin strings. She brushed a stray lock of hair out of her face while sighing a bitter, anxious sigh.

She hadn't meant to touch that poor girl's arm. It had been an accident.

And besides, what was a castle maid doing wearing a sleeveless blouse in the first place? Sure, the day was hot enough for most everyone to eschew heavier clothing — Gwen herself was wearing a sleeveless gown today — but sleeves were part of the regulation uniform that applied to anybody who worked in the castle. How could Gwen have known she'd be sleeveless?

And it had happened in the library, of all places. So, in addition to having to explain about that poor maid's arm, Gwen would also have to try to explain what she was doing there to begin with.

It wasn't her fault!

No, even if that unfortunate maid was one of the new girls, this wasn't Gwen's fault. There were rules. If you didn't follow the rules and you ended up getting hurt, that was your own fault, wasn't it? *She* had to follow rules she didn't understand, and she was a princess! Did other people think the rules didn't apply to them?

"Gwenwyn!" a voice bellowed from somewhere beyond her heavy oak door.

Great. Now *he* was coming.

A moment later, she could hear the clomping of boots on the stone stairs leading to her tower bedchamber, and her stomach tightened further.

"I won't apologize. I won't!" she said softly, her words sounding frightened even to her own ears. "This wasn't my fault. If she'd been wearing sleeves like she was *supposed* to...."

Gwen took a deep breath and lifted her chin, focusing her gaze on the door and preparing herself. It was always necessary to put up a token front. Gwen had learned early on apologizing immediately was *never* a good idea.

She wondered what she should call him this time.

There was always *father*, spoken with heavy irony and disdain — that one always annoyed him. It was over six weeks since her last incident though, and with all the changes he'd made around the castle, she was more than a little afraid. Honestly, she had no idea how angry he was going to be this time.

Maybe it was best if she didn't use *father* on this particular occasion.

Highness might work. It really bugged him, but very rarely did he ever slap her for calling him that, even when she was all ironic about it.

Without even a knock of warning, her massive bedchamber door burst open with a speed that should have been impossible. A moment later her father stood there in her room, the dark nothingness of the stairwell looming behind his round face like a black halo, his thin curls of brown hair selves like a briar patch on either side of the simple iron crown he wore. He looked angrier than she'd seen in a long time, and his massive chest heaved from the effort of climbing up the stairs.

Gwen stood up from her bed as gracefully as she could and bowed from the neck, hoping the rest of her wasn't trembling as badly as her tummy muscles.

"Highness," she said. "This is a delightful surprise. I hadn't expected to see—"

"Do you want to tell me what *that* is all about?" Bryn bellowed, jerking an angry thumb over his shoulder.

As if on cue, another scream pierced the air. It was louder now that her bedroom door had been opened.

"I'm sorry, could you be more specific?" she asked.

Red-faced, Bryn took a slow, deep breath in through his nose, glaring hard at her as he exhaled. It was the sort of look that caused Gwen to decide she should forego the stalling and cut right to trying to explain what happened.

"It wasn't my fault!" she said quickly. "*She* brushed up against *me!* I didn't even see her, because the lights are so dim in the library! It was just her arm and a light touch, so she'll probably be fine. And besides, she should have known better than—"

"*You* should know better!" the king roared. "I warned you about this *months* ago! New servants, all of them! They wouldn't know, because they're not supposed to know! Nobody around here *knows better* except for you! This was *your* fault!"

"No, it wasn't! She wasn't wearing sleeves! They're all supposed to, even if they don't know why. You tell them yourself. Are mere servants allowed to ignore their king now? Anyways, now that she *does* know why, maybe she'll—"

"They're here *because* they don't know! That's the entire point, for the love of Eirene! Brand new staff, top to bottom, filled with servants who come from far enough away that they don't know anything about your condition, or that you—"

"—were regularly force-fed herbs as a baby by my ogre of a father, who ruined my life, and made it so every living thing I touch burns, and blisters, and dies." Gwen jutted her chin out at him just a little. "I've been meaning to ask; is this sort of like a fresh start for you? Are you finally properly ashamed of what you've done to your only daughter, and wish to hide it?"

Eons passed as the two of them stared at each other in silence. Gwen saw her father's fingers twitch, as though he contemplated fists.

"Only daughter," he growled, shaking his head at her ever so slightly.

This was going to be a bad one. Well, it was too late to take all those words back now. Gwen returned his glare, and tried to look as regal as she could with her insides acting all twitchy.

"*Only* daughter," he repeated softly, striding forward, his face now inches away from hers, closer than anyone else ever dared. "Your mother dies bringing you into this world, and you figure it's a mark of distinction, is that it? Willful, *evil child!* I raise you, feed you, clothe you, even after you *kill* your mother, and this is my reward, is it? A child who doesn't do as she's told, who can't remember anything, and who carelessly inflicts pain on others wherever she goes? What were you even doing in the library to begin with? I've told you more times than I can count that I don't want you going in there!"

"Well what can I say, *Dad?*" she shouted back at him. "Do you want me to continue the normal-little-girl act or not? I'm fairly certain that princesses in other kingdoms get things like tutors, and access to books! You may not actually give a damn about me, but at the very least you might try to give other people the impression you want me to learn! And if I did kill Mom, why does the crystal *I'm* holding glow just as brightly as everyone else's when we're attending service? Why am I still a princess, and not banished like some criminal? Why does Eirene continue to bless me?"

"And still she gives me back-talk, after everything I've done to—"

"Done? I didn't ask for any of this!" Gwen practically screamed at him, no longer concerned about damage control. "Am I supposed to be happy I'm like this? Gee, thank you, *Father,* for making it possible to accidentally kill people by brushing up against them!"

"Wicked child! A lesser man would have left you in the forest to die years ago!"

"You mean there's lesser men than *you?*"

Even as the words had left her mouth, Gwen knew that she'd gone way too far on that one. Out of instinct, she shut her eyes tightly and turned her head away from the hard slap she knew was coming.

She waited, tense and afraid, but nothing happened. After a few moments, she risked a tentative look out of one eye.

Bryn appeared relaxed, and was looking at her with a much softer, calmer expression.

"Aww, Pumpkin," he said, putting on a look of parental concern that practically oozed insincerity. "I haven't thought about this from your point of view, and that's not fair to you. My poor, sweet little girl."

Gwen eyed him warily, and her anxiousness increased tenfold. She really hated it when he got like this. In many ways, she'd almost prefer getting slapped.

"Can I get you something — make it up to you? Obviously with everything going on I've been neglecting my dear, sweet daughter." He rubbed his chin briefly and then snapped his fingers. "Wait, I know. I haven't bought my little princess anything for a while. I could get you a nice present! Would you like that?"

"I... don't need anything, Highness," she stammered, flinching slightly as another of the young maid's screams found its way into the room. "I'm very sorry for raising my voice. It's just that I don't think it's very fair to blame me for what happened, when—"

"Yes, I know. I was being terribly unfair just now, and I want to make it up to you. I feel just *awful*." His brow creased in thought, and a moment later his entire face was lit by a beatific smile. "I know just the thing! How about I get you another puppy?"

Gwen suddenly felt like she'd been punched in the stomach.

"There's a fellow in town, runs the tavern by the grain mill, who just got a litter of the most adorable floppy-eared puppies you've ever seen in your life," he continued, smiling mercilessly. "White and brown, mostly. We could go down there together, pick one out! Why, there might even be one that looks like...what was his name again? Ralph?"

Her legs felt weak. The bedroom threatened to spin.

"It was something like that, wasn't it? Ralph? No, wait," he smiled, a glint in his eye, "it was Rolf. I remember."

Gwen remembered too.

Rolf had been just a couple months old when her father had educated her, many years ago. He'd brought a bunch of puppies to the castle one day, let her name them all, and encouraged her to watch them romp and play in their pen for an entire week. Then, he'd asked her to pick out her favourite, and told her that one would be her very own to care for, and love....

And pet.

For a little girl who was never touched at all, the very thought of such a thing had made Gwen so happy that she'd cried for joy.

She was six. She hadn't known.

It was one of her earliest and most horrifying memories, staring down in shock at the poor, yowling puppy desperately trying to wriggle away from her, watching the terrified animal's back and neck begin to sizzle and smoke, the smell of burned dog filling her nostrils. And all the while, she'd heard her father's voice whispering in her ear in that sad, gentle monotone of his, *"Just look what you've done. You must be an evil little girl. Everything you touch suffers."*

It had been years since he'd brought up Rolf, though the poor, suffering animal often visited her in her nightmares, causing her to wake with a start, crying out and—

"Do you even remember Rolf?" he mused. "I wonder. You might have been too young. Poor little thing had been so energetic. So full of life."

It was too much. Gwen began sobbing quietly, her entire bedroom becoming a blur of light she could barely make out through the sting of fresh tears.

That was when the whole world flashed white and jerked sideways, and Gwen was knocked spinning onto her bed. Her cheek burned from where the rough brown leather of her father's glove had connected.

She felt paralyzed, unable to move her arms or do anything but lay there on the bed and wail silently, her occasional sobs mixing with the keening of the young maid downstairs.

"You think you'll ruin my plans?" Bryn roared savagely, his voice drowning out the cries of both girls. "Evil little wench! You think this time you can apologize for another of your little accidents and everything will be okay? Seventeen years, Gwenwyn! For over seventeen years I've worked for this, the only option your mother's death left me and this wretched excuse for a kingdom! Seventeen years of my life spent chained to this miserable, pathetic little castle. Seventeen years spent chained to you, oh daughter mine. I will not allow you to ruin everything I've worked so hard for!"

Gwen's cry of "I'm sorry" came out as two tearful wails. The pain from her jaw told some part of her awareness that he'd used a fist this time, and not an open hand.

"I've spent a small fortune, Daughter, to ensure nobody knows what you really are except you, Captain Anifail, and myself! Oh, and your precious lady-in-waiting, of course. Maybe I've let you have too much. Should I have sent Rhosyn away like I did all the other servants and staff? Would you like it if I sent her away as well?"

Gwen frantically shook her head, crying, only managing to mouth the word "no" at him.

"You deserve worse, you wretched little girl! There's a young woman down there," he said, a chubby finger jabbing at the stairwell, "who has painful blisters all over her arm and neck, impossible to hide. Even if she does manage to live, I have to fire her now...just like I have to fire all those other girls who brought bandages and water, the ones who came to help her after *you* touched her. Witnesses, all of them! Three at least, but as many as six young ladies may be leaving the castle tonight, without employment or references or anything but the clothes on their back. And then I have to take time out of my busy schedule to find replacements for them. All because of you."

She tried to protest, but something happened to the words as they made their way to her mouth, and they all came out as sobs and strangled noises.

"I know it's been a very hot summer, Gwenwyn, but I highly suggest you rethink your position on wearing sleeves and gloves inside the castle, despite the heat. Unless, of course, you don't particularly care about the new staff," Bryn said, turning away from her and towards the door. "I have a dangerous feeling the next servant involved in one of your accidents may lose something considerably more valuable than their job."

With that, he drew his slightly dingy ermine-lined cloak around him imperiously and swept out of the room, the monstrous oak door closing behind him with a resounding slam.

Gwen collapsed even further into her bed, wailing bitterly into her pillow, pressing it tightly against her face to muffle her cries.

Chapter 2

"Horrible," Rhosyn said darkly, shaking her head. "No, I take that back. It's monstrous! Gwen, how does someone who's even capable of stuff like that ever get to be king?"

"Well, I guess ruthlessness is part of the job," Gwen replied softly, stepping around a solitary yellow flower that was just beginning to bloom. The grass was green and lush for the entire length of the field, but the dozen or so horses stabled nearby kept the various grasses short and manageable through grazing, and they often left things like flowers alone. The grass provided ample food for the entire herd. In fact, some days it seemed to Gwen that there was nothing more to Rhosyn's job minding the stables than coming out of her cabin and taking them out riding, perhaps brushing out their manes from time to time.

"I'm serious, Gwen," said Rhosyn. "It's awful how he treats you! I mean, sure he's always been a monster, but it's never been this bad before, has it? With all the changes he's made, I don't even know what's what anymore. It's like he's gone insane!"

Gwen swiped at a stray clump of grass with her boot. "It's probably from worrying about all that stuff he's been arranging. There have been some big changes. And I was in the library too. You know how upset he gets about that."

"Don't you *dare* make excuses for him, Gwen!"

"Oh, I'm not. I'm just trying to understand what sets him off, though there never seems to be much point, does there? He's lost a bit of weight, looks jumpy and nervous all the time. He's quicker to anger now too, so I'd watch what you say to him, if you're unfortunate enough to see him."

"I've never held anything back when talking to him before." Rhosyn sent Gwen a sidelong grin. "Why start now?"

Gwen couldn't help but smile back. Rhosyn's conspiratorial grin always reminded Gwen of how they'd become friends in the first place.

"He still hasn't forgotten, you know," Gwen said. "In fact, just mentioning your name is usually enough to make him scowl, most days."

"He told me I'd been hired as your confidant, your lady-in-waiting, and that I should gain your trust. Then, a week later, he's demanding I betray that confidence and tell him everything we talked about? How could you ever trust me if I did something like that?"

"I think he's more upset that he believed all the tall tales you fed him, actually."

Rhosyn stood a little straighter and affected a demure expression. "Highness, Princess Gwenwyn is displaying all *manner* of strange behaviour! Why, just this morning she spent an hour apologizing to an apple before feeding it to one of the horses. And then later she lay in a field and began naming the clouds as they went by, holding small funerals and birthday parties for them. And then—"

Gwen giggled. "He got so mad when he found out."

"It's his own fault; he shouldn't have hired an orphan girl as your lady-in-waiting. If there's one thing I learned at the orphanage, it's that you never shared private talks with the keepers, or with anyone. And remember how bad things were back then, how unhappy you were? You needed someone to confide in so badly, and I wasn't about to let your father discover some new way to make you miserable."

"And as punishment, he sent you out here."

"I'd hardly call it punishment," said Rhosyn. "Given how miserly your father can be, I doubt he'd tolerate employing anyone whose only job was to be your friend. If I hadn't been assigned to the stables, he'd probably have me working as a chambermaid or some such thing anyway. And at least this way I don't have to be anywhere near your father when he loses his temper. It's not like he'd ever actually come out here."

"True," Gwen admitted.

"I do have to ask you something though," Rhosyn said, her expression and tone becoming serious. "You knew your father was getting edgy and irritable lately, what with all the changes he's been making and the repair work on the castle. And we both know he hates it when you go to the library, probably because he's afraid you might actually learn something. Being in the library, the accident with the maid, it almost feels like you did that on purpose, like you were trying to test the waters a little."

"I wasn't trying to get in trouble! Touching that maid was a complete accident—I would have been able to sneak out of the library unseen if it weren't for what happened to that poor girl." Gwen sighed, tugging on her gloves once more to ensure her sleeves were tucked away inside them. "I was in there because father had meetings all morning, and I thought I could use some of that time in the library."

"Use it for what?"

Gwen gave a light shrug. "I was looking through the herbology stuff again."

"You've been over that stuff more times than I can count, Gwen. He may be a monster, but he's not stupid. You mentioned he's already removed the more interesting books from the library once he found out you were poking around them. If there's a book that contains anything at all about that stuff he makes you eat with every meal, you don't think he's going to leave it lying around the library, do you?"

"No, but there are hints where this dull book refers to that dull book written by this boring fellow, things like that. I keep thinking one of these days I'll get lucky, find a hidden reference or something somewhere," Gwen said, shrugging once more. "Then, when I got tired of picking through those books, I found one that distracted me a little."

"Let me guess." Rhosyn cast her friend a reproachful look. "A fairy tale."

Gwen nodded, feeling foolish. "I hadn't read this one before, and I just couldn't seem to put it down. I was being stupid. It got me all emotional, too."

"Emotional?"

"Crying. It was such a beautiful story. I ended up staying way too long, and not paying attention when I should have been." Gwen looked thoughtful for a moment. "I remember I was feeling *very* emotional when the maid walked by, and I swear she barely even touched me, but," Gwen's eyes went wide and she lowered her voice to a whisper, "you should see what happened to her arm. One of the worst I'd ever seen! Do you think my touch gets stronger when I'm sad, or angry, or emotional?"

"Could be. Really, we don't know all that much about it, so we can't say one way or another."

"True," said Gwen. The two of them had only recently started researching Gwen's condition, covertly of course, and so far it had yielded them nothing. "I do feel awful about that maid though. I'm just glad she's going to be okay. Did you manage to slip her that brooch I gave you before she left?"

"Yes, I got it to her."

"Good. She probably still hates me, and it likely won't sell for much, barely any money at all, but...." Gwen sighed and shrugged at the same time.

"*Ah*," Rhosyn said warningly, holding up a finger, "I told you, don't go putting down the nice things you do, or shrug them off as nothing. Those are the echoes of your father talking; get out of that habit. You're a wonderful person Gwen, and you deserve to feel good about some of the things you do. I guarantee you gave her more than your father did."

"Yeah, I know. I'm not really thinking too straight. He brought up Rolf, and he hadn't done that in years. I guess I wasn't ready for him to twist that particular knife." Gwen shook her head, as though getting rid of unpleasant thoughts. "Bah, that's enough talk about that, I think. On to happier subjects!" Gwen gave Rhosyn a knowing smile and arched a solitary eyebrow. "Are things going well with a certain young man?"

Rhosyn frowned at her.

"C'mon, Gwen. Can we not talk about that? Please?"

"I want to know everything, you strumpet!" Gwen teased. "He came over to visit a couple of days ago, if I'm not mistaken."

"Yeah, he did."

"Well? What happened? Tell me!"

"Gwen, just reading a fairy tale in the library was enough to reduce you to tears." Looking uneasy, Rhosyn twirled a stray lock of hair with her finger. "I don't think that me talking about my relationship with Darin is a good idea."

"Oooooh." Gwen leered at Rhosyn, clapping her hands together gleefully. "It's a relationship now, is it?"

"Gwen—"

"Rosie, my life has been a tragedy for as long as I can remember. My mother died giving birth to me, my father hates me, and as punishment for everything, he's given me a condition that's like the realm's most lethal chastity belt. I've never been kissed, and I never will be. I wouldn't even have known what a hug was like if it weren't for you. You're my best friend — my only friend! I certainly dump enough of my life into your lap, and I don't do it just because it's your job to listen. It wouldn't be fair if you didn't get to share your life, or things that are important to you. Friends share that stuff. Especially the happy stuff."

"I just feel bad, like it's not fair," Rhosyn said.

"I understand what you're saying, and I don't care." Gwen gave her friend a knowing smirk. "Spill. Or I'll force the details out of you, make it a royal decree or something."

"Well," said Rhosyn, grinning like sun after fog, "I have been dying to talk about it."

Gwen looked at her and made an impatient get-on-with-it gesture.

"Okay, he came over the other day, right? He knew I looked after the horses, because I'd told him from before, and he was all excited to see them, but," Rhosyn's smile was mischievously amused, "he didn't know I could ride. He grew up on a farm, next to a ranch. Nothing but boys working it, and he never met a girl who rode horses before. You should have seen his face when I hopped up on Winter. His eyes practically fell out of his head!"

"I thought you said he was smart. How does he think someone could tend the royal stables and not know how to ride?"

"I think it was how he was raised, mostly. That, and I was a little vague on the details of my job when I first met him. I've found that if men discover that I work for the king, it's harder to tell what they're more interested in: me, or some of the perks that might come with me."

"Gotcha. So, you went riding?"

"Yup. Took Winter and Diego and followed the path up into the hills, stopped at the meadow you and I usually ride by." Rhosyn smiled and sighed. "He'd brought a picnic basket with him. We spread a blanket out, ate a little bit, and just lay there talking the whole afternoon. He's got this look in his eye whenever I'm talking, like he's hanging on every word I'm about to say. Gorgeous blue eyes."

"How long were you out there for?" Gwen asked.

"All afternoon. Would have been longer, except I'd already pushed my afternoon chores to that evening, and a few of them couldn't wait." Rhosyn smiled, giving her a knowing look. "He really wants to kiss me, I can tell. I think I've intimidated him a little, so he's not quite sure of himself or something. Sometimes when we were talking to each other, there'd be these gaps where we were just staring at each other, and I kept thinking, *Oooo, he's gonna do it now!*" She shrugged. "He didn't though, a perfect gentleman the whole time."

"Darn the luck, hey?"

Rhosyn laughed. "Well, I was a little disappointed. I mean, this wasn't our first date, but it was the first time we were alone together. Maybe I wasn't giving strong enough hints."

"I'm sure he'll come around, Rosie. He'd be crazy not to want to kiss you. Maybe he just didn't want to risk ruining the afternoon; it does sound romantic. I can picture it: the two of you, riding out on horseback to a secluded meadow, laying in the sun, hand in hand, just looking at each other and talking, and I'm sure you'll both make each other very happy, and—"

Gwen found she couldn't hold her tears in any longer, and the last of her words transformed themselves into a sob.

"Oh, hon!" Rhosyn quickly grabbed hold of Gwen's shoulders and pulled her close, hugging her tightly. "Oh, you see? I knew it was a bad idea."

"No, no," Gwen sniffed, forcing herself to smile and trying to laugh so it would be heard in her voice. "I do want to hear the details, Rosie. I'm just, I don't know. I'm all over the place today. But I'm happy for you, Rosie. I really am!" Gwen hugged her friend fiercely.

The muscles under Gwen's fingertips bunched up, and she felt her friend stiffen the tiniest bit.

In a panic, Gwen quickly pulled away and checked the clothing that covered her from head to toe, hoping desperately that she hadn't inadvertently touched her friend. Finding no exposed skin that could account for Rhosyn's reaction, Gwen looked at her, confused.

With her jaw clenched, Rhosyn slowly pulled the collar of her blouse away from her skin, uncovering an angry red circle at the base of her neck. To Gwen, it looked to be the size of a pinkie nail.

Or a teardrop.

"Oh, no no no!" Gwen cried out, aghast, her hand covering her mouth. "Not again! Oh, I'm so sorry Rosie!"

"You didn't mean it," Rhosyn said through gritted teeth, her free hand already reaching for the small jar of salve she always kept with her. "I've had plenty worse than that one. A bit soaked through my clothes, that's all. No big deal."

"It's always a big deal, Rhosyn! Oh, Goddess, why is it that no matter how hard I try I always end up hurting people?"

"Gwen, I know you try, and I know you care, so stop beating yourself up about it. I'm the one who hugged you, so it's just as much my fault that it happened. It was an accident." Rhosyn applied a dab of salve to the scarlet welt and spread it carefully. "So, no more talking about me and Darin, alright?"

"No, I'll be okay. I do want to talk about you two, because it does make me happy for you. Despite all evidence to the contrary." Gwen smiled wanly at her friend as she wiped another tear from her cheek. "It's that stupid fairy tale, I think. What I really need is to start avoiding books featuring a dashing prince, or that start with the words *Once upon a time.*"

Chapter 3

Gwen made absolutely certain her arms were properly covered for dinner that evening.

After her lengthy meeting with Rhosyn, she'd changed out of her riding clothes and into a heavy gown with a lace front, the sleeves of which were long, and finished in a point with a little loop of cloth through which she put her middle finger. Very, very long sleeves; her arms practically disappeared in them.

Then, although they didn't really go with the gown, she'd donned her thin grey gloves as well, just to be safe.

Gwen hadn't seen the king since their last encounter, and there was no telling what might set him off during dinner. Better safe than sorry.

She was calmer now, she felt. That, or she'd simply cried herself out, and had run completely out of tears.

And she was *famished!* It was such a strange thing, this poisonous curse of hers. On days when she didn't see much of her father, she'd often find herself peckish at best, half tempted to skip meals entirely.

However, on days when she got emotional and upset, by suppertime she often felt like she could eat half a roast boar herself, chestnut stuffing and all. Even if it had been sprinkled with that horrid herb her father made her eat.

Actually, she'd noticed something else odd about that herb. Sure it tasted like chalk mixed with rancid butter, but during really bad days she'd discovered she didn't notice the taste all that much, or didn't seem to mind it. On particularly awful days, she'd find herself practically craving the stuff.

Like she was now.

Gwen speculated as she adjusted her gloves. She wished she could find out more about that strange, blueish herb. What happened to you when you ate it? Could its effects be undone? What was the stuff even named? It was difficult enough for her to research something covertly, but researching something for which she didn't even know the name? It was nearly impossible!

She gave herself a quick inspection in her dull metal mirror, turning to the side to ensure she'd done up the laces in the back properly, took a deep breath and began the long journey to the dining hall.

Once she'd gone down the four flights of stairs and entered the main hallway, Gwen paused for a moment, then opted to take her usual route past the kitchens. Almost immediately she encountered two servants she didn't recognize, and she gave them a quick smile and a nod as she walked by.

One acknowledged her with a wary look, almost fearful. The other didn't acknowledge her in any way, but simply stood there in the hallway, head slightly bowed.

Odd, she thought.

Even stranger was the fact that it wasn't an isolated incident. Every servant or guard she passed by either refused to acknowledge her in any way, or reacted as though they were suddenly afraid to attract her notice. Each encounter left her feeling more and more uneasy, and it soon felt to Gwen as if the cheerful smile she maintained was nothing more than a mask draped over her face. She practically flew down the final two corridors, desperate to end the whole ordeal, wishing for nothing more than to get away from the numerous covert stares, the whispered murmurs spoken just out of earshot.

Another unpleasant surprise awaited her in the dining hall. Leaning against the back wall next to the fireplace, arms crossed and looking supremely relaxed, was Anifail, captain of the king's guard.

He regarded Gwen as she entered, his wavy blond hair partially obscuring his gaunt features. He didn't stand at attention or offer a salute as the other guardsmen might. He never did, not even for her father. Whenever she looked at him she thought of weasels in hen-houses.

"Captain Anifail," she said. "Back from a hard day spent threatening townspeople, I see. Am I to presume you'll be joining my father and me this evening?"

Smirking slightly, he gave her a half-nod of assent.

"Well, I'm sure he'll be here shortly. By the way, you may want to change where you're standing," Gwen said, motioning towards the far corner. "Maybe move a bit to your right, over on the other side of the fireplace."

Frowning, Anifail gave her a puzzled look.

"Well, Father's aim has been a little off lately, and when he tosses bones and scraps behind him they've been landing over there." Gwen gestured at the corner once more. "I mean, I'm assuming that's the reason my father's favourite lapdog would show up to the dining room at this hour."

It was amazing how expressive Anifail's eyes could be. There was a flash of rage, followed by banked anger, which subsided to weary amusement. He hooked his thumbs in his belt and considered her for a moment before speaking.

"Ah, me. Whatever shall I do? The princess is no longer fond of me, and mocks me with cruel words sharper than any sword. I shan't sleep a wink tonight." He smiled. "Still, I suppose it's better to be a lapdog for a king than...a puppy for a princess."

Gwen tried not to react to his words, focusing instead on maintaining eye contact and looking regal. She relaxed her jaw once she realized she'd been clenching it. Anifail simply maintained his calm, relaxed pose, looking smug. He had a smile Gwen wanted to throw rocks at.

"Anifail," Bryn called as he walked through the doorway, idly leafing through a small stack of parchment he held, "do you remember what that fellow's name was, the one we wanted to get to fix the portcullis? I want it done before… wait, never mind. I found it."

Pulling one of the pieces of parchment from the stack, the king walked up to his chair and tossed the remaining atop onto the table to his right. He sat down with a *"Hoomph!"*

"Want me to send for him tonight, Highness?" asked Anifail, who remained leaning against the wall.

"Yes. Tell him to fix it to the point where it works again, but nothing more. I want that thing functional before our visitor arrives." Bryn appeared to notice Gwen, who had been standing behind her own chair. "Daughter," he said, nodding to her.

She briefly considered not bringing up the incident from that morning, but figured it was too risky. Sometimes when she'd done something that made him angry, he'd wait to see if she apologized a second time, and if she didn't he often used it as an excuse to get angry at her all over again.

Of course, sometimes he got angry when she reminded him of what he'd been angry about in the first place, so it was really anybody's guess.

"Highness," she said, giving him a small curtsey. "If I may, I'd like to apologize once more for troubling you this morning. I've thought about what you've said, and have adapted my summer clothing according to your wishes."

He looked at her in puzzlement for a moment, like he had no idea what she was talking about. Then he caught sight of her long sleeves, and gave her the barest trace of a smile.

"Oh, that. Well, no lasting harm done I suppose; it's all worked itself out now, hasn't it? Just need you in long sleeves for the time being — temporary thing. In fact, with any luck, you may be able to wear some proper summer attire before autumn arrives."

Gwen simply stood there, a little bewildered. No scowl, no name-calling or other nastiness, nothing! He simply accepted her apology, just like that.

What was going on?

She studied his face. It took a moment for her to figure it out.

He was happy!

"That's, uh, good news, Highness," Gwen said as she sat down in her chair.

"Indeed. Well, Anifail, I spoke with the cook, and the roast squab will be here shortly. Until then, would you like to go over some of these work orders with me? Get everything organized?" Bryn gestured towards his nearby pile of parchment.

"Of course," said Anifail, pushing himself away from the wall and sauntering over to the king's end of the table. "Soonest begun is soonest done."

"Captain, I had no idea you were a poet," Bryn chuckled.

Gwen's confusion deepened.

Her father no longer seemed the least bit bothered by what had happened that morning, which was unusual in the extreme. He seemed relaxed, and the corners of his mouth even went up from time to time in what she realized was a smile. And, to top it all off, he appeared to have a whopping pile of work to do, based on how high the pile of parchment was stacked, yet he didn't look perturbed in the least.

If it hadn't been for Anifail's puppy comment, Gwen might have believed she'd been transported to a magical land where everything was backwards.

She sat there, paying attention to what was being said, trying to figure it out.

"So, portcullis was the last of the outside work needing to be done, right? And inside the front door there was the bunting, the torch holders… oh, and those tapestries in the front can finally be replaced with the ones in storage." Bryn scratched his chin, looking at the topmost piece of paper. "What else was there?"

"Oiled veneer over the beams, and trim to make the wood look fresher," said Anifail, taking a handful of documents and resting them on the table in front of him.

"Ah yes! Thank you, Captain."

Veneer over the beams? If he was talking about the same beams Gwen thought he was, they needed to be replaced completely, not simply patched up and made to look better.

"Father?" she asked, unable to contain her curiosity. "You're in high spirits this evening." She managed to stop herself from adding, *Have you been drinking?*

The king looked over the table at her, fingers pressed together, smiling faintly. "Yes, I believe I am. An excellent mood, actually!"

"Is there a reason for it?"

"There is. A good reason, in fact, the source of which is so unusual it bears mentioning." Bryn smiled cheerfully at her. "The reason, my dear Daughter, is you."

"Me?" Gwen immediately became more alert.

"See? Didn't I tell you it was unusual? I mean, most of the time you're just a staggeringly dull and ill-behaved disappointment," he laughed.

She felt a small pang of hurt from that. Still, compared to his usual jibes, that one wasn't bad at all.

"Well, Highness, I suppose I'm delighted," she said.

Bryn's eyes lit up a little. "Would you like to know *why* you're the source of my good mood?"

Honestly, she didn't like the look on his face when he'd said that last bit, but it didn't seem like a very good idea to say no. Gwen nodded for him to continue.

"Well, Daughter, it seems word of your beauty has made its way to the ear of a young prince from Bespir, to the north of us, who has sent a courier to tell me he wishes to meet. It seems he may be interested in courting you."

Now she understood. It was a joke, a chance for a cruel laugh at her expense. No wonder he was in a good mood: opportunities like this one must be rare. Gwen took a few slow, deep breaths before speaking.

"Well, I'm glad you get a bit of fun at my expense. Doubtless you'd like to read aloud the letter you've prepared, informing him of my condition, telling him not to bother. Very amusing. I've cried rather a lot today, but who knows? There might be a few tears left."

Both Bryn and Anifail looked momentarily confused by her words. Then, after a few moments, the king was laughing a great, booming laugh, one that echoed off the stone walls.

Anifail didn't laugh, but simply sat there, smirking a little to himself, waiting patiently for Bryn to finish.

"Oh, Daughter," Bryn managed to gasp about a minute later, wiping away a lone tear. "Oh, I forget how truly entertaining you can be. *Send him away,* she says. Oh, that is priceless! I wish there were more people I could share that with."

Gwen studied her father, confused. "You're not turning him away?"

"Gwenwyn, why in the world would I turn him away? Especially after all the effort and money I've spent circulating rumours about your breathtaking beauty?"

Gwen thought she'd understood the joke, but suddenly it was as if the punch line was out of her grasp.

"Why would you do that?" she asked, genuinely bewildered.

"Why, to attract the notice of some dashing young prince, I would imagine." His eyes appeared to twinkle as he spoke, and he was clearly pleased by her confusion. "And 'lo, it's happened! My daughter has a suitor." Bryn leaned back in his chair and sniffed, as though moved to tears.

Anifail covered his mouth with the back of his fist, his shoulders shaking a little.

Gwen still didn't get it. Oh, she still knew this whole setup was just a cruel joke, that much was obvious. She just didn't see what they found amusing about it. What was she missing?

"You're waiting until he's down here to tell him? Oh, you want me to see his reaction, is that it?"

That only caused Bryn's guffaws to intensify. He sat there shaking his head, as though unable to believe what he'd heard.

"Oh, Daughter, you crack me up. Really. I mean, why would I tell him anything at all?"

Gwen stared at him, perplexed. "I'm *poisonous*, Father! He can't so much as touch my arm! Why would you not tell him?"

"Oh, I suspect he's got more in mind than touching your arm," he laughed, tenting his fingers and looking over them at her. "He is, from all accounts, a rather energetic young fellow, with quite a reputation when it comes to young ladies. You've got enough of your mother's looks; I don't think it'll be hard to convince him settling down and getting married isn't the end of the world."

Married?

Gwen didn't know what to think. She simply sat there, staring along the table at him, trying to understand.

"You really don't get it, do you?" Bryn asked finally, shaking his head in mock sorrow. "What do you think I've been doing all this time, hmm? What do you think you were for? Did you think I'd go to the trouble of tracking down the specifics of a thousand-year-old tale, spend hours researching the secret of a mysterious poisonous herb, fork over a small fortune for the bloody stuff, all just so nobody could *touch* you? Did you think I was doing all of this just to make you *sad*? Are you really that thick?" He laughed, sitting back in his chair. "Your touch may be impressive, my daughter, but it's your beauty, and your saliva that I'm after."

"S-saliva?"

"Exactly. I won't tax your limited intellect by trying to explain what a neurotoxin is, but suffice it to say you're positively loaded with the stuff. You're immune, of course, but for anyone else just a drop of your saliva causes euphoria, numbness, convulsions, and eventually death. All it takes is a little bit in the mouth, or brushed on the lips." He smiled in a way she didn't like. "Say, a kiss's worth?"

Gwen went cold. She could feel the blood drain from her face, and her father's words slowly made awful sense.

"You're going to kill him?" she asked disbelievingly.

"How dare you imply such a thing, Daughter! This is a Goddess-fearing household, and the holy teachings regarding sin are quite specific!" The king folded his hands and regarded her smugly. "I spoke with Vicar Rapaul at length about this, just before he was... sent away. Why, it's no sin to ensure your only daughter is married to a proper young gentleman! It's also not a sin to forget to mention your rather unfortunate condition before your betrothal, or even after. No, Daughter, I'm not killing anybody."

Gwen felt sick.

"Why?" she cried. "Why would you do this? Killing a prince from another kingdom? Do you want to start a war?"

"Goodness, how quickly they forget! I just told you, Daughter — *I* won't be killing anybody! My conscience will be clear. I will continue to receive Eirene's blessings, and the crystal I'm holding during our very public weekly devotion to the Goddess will continue to glow, thus proving to the people of the kingdom that I am free of guilt, pure of heart, and can continue to be king. Whether or not Eirene continues to bless *you* is another matter; the vicar couldn't really say one way or another. He personally felt you would lose Her favour, your crystal would darken, and you'd be banished from Calderia." He shrugged. "Or put to death. The Ecclesial Courts take a dim view of queens murdering their husbands. Myself, I figure there's a good chance Eirene would continue to bless you. After all, it's not a sin to be *poisonous*, is it? And then, why, I'd be able to marry you to someone else all over again! Either one works out well enough, I suppose."

"But why would you do this?" Gwen asked. "For what reason?"

"I'm doing it because Calderia is an insignificant, miserable little kingdom. Because we're a land known for farming and animal furs and nothing else. Because the only way this Goddess-forsaken place is ever going to improve is through an affiliation marriage with a neighbouring kingdom."

"An alliance?"

"Alliance," Bryn scoffed. "It's much more than that. An affiliation marriage combines two kingdoms by mutual agreement, becoming a single country through a blessed royal marriage: a princess and a prince, becoming king and queen. New blood from both countries cooperatively ruling the newly unified country in a manner that ensures both of the former countries are well represented. Although," he gave her an oily smile, "if anything should happen to one of them...."

Gwen could hear blood thrumming through her temples, and her head swam. Now it was clear. Power would fall to Gwen. Her father was arranging for her to become the sole ruler of two kingdoms.

"I — I know nothing about being a queen!" Gwen protested.

Bryn smiled at her patiently and looked at her over his tented fingers, and with horrible certainty, she suddenly understood this had been what he'd planned for her all along. She was to be a tool, an assassin's dagger, a silk-rope garrote wrapped around the neck of whoever her father decided to marry her.

If Eirene continued to bless her afterward, she'd be a figurehead, a mere puppet, with her power-hungry father holding the strings and making her dance. And if the Goddess considered what she'd done a sin — if her crystal went dark at the weekly devotion to Eirene — Gwen would be found unfit to rule and banished. Or worse.

And it wasn't exactly hard to guess who would rule both kingdoms in her stead.

Her cheekbones hurt from trying to remain expressionless.

Eventually Bryn and Anifail continued talking to each other about castle business, their conversation barely registering. She hardly noticed when dinner had finally been brought to the dining hall, and couldn't even manage a quick word of thanks to the servant that set her plate in front of her, a reaction that was usually automatic. She simply sat there, staring right through the table, slowly trying to put the pieces of her life back together.

From a fairly young age, Gwen understood she would forever be alone. She'd never know the tenderness of a kiss, never feel the flutter of butterflies in her stomach as a handsome young man leaned forward to press his lips to hers. She'd never feel a loving caress upon her arm, the warmth of another's skin, or any of the hundreds of different ways writers and poets described that one thing most people took for granted: simple, human contact. For years she'd understood this.

She'd just never been able to accept it.

And now she knew what cruelty was. It was taking the only thing she'd ever wished for, the only thing she wanted in the whole world, and perverting it. It was giving her what she'd always dreamed, but at a price that was impossible to live with. It was plucking her from a wind-whipped sea and saving her from certain death, only to toss her upon a fire to be burned alive.

It was every fairy tale in the world being torn in two and pulled apart before her eyes. It was her father handing her a puppy and laughing as it died.

It was the end of hope.

He'd taken her to a place beyond sadness, loneliness and fear. Now there was nothing. Just emptiness.

Gwen found herself staring at the small, untouched piece of roast squab sitting on the plate in front of her. Her eyes focused on the small, pale chunk of meat, covered with small greenish-blue flecks —those loathsome herbs responsible for her pain, her misery.

Through the fog that clouded her thoughts, Gwen realized she was about to become sick.

Her chair squawked lightly in protest as she pushed it away from the table and stood. The motion attracted the notice of her father and Anifail, both of whom ceased their talking and regarded her.

"I need to be excused," she said faintly.

Bryn smiled sardonically at her and shrugged, dismissing her with a wave of his hand.

"Yes, go. Don't want you spoiling my good mood, after all. There's some important matters I need to discuss with Captain Anifail anyways. I'll have your dinner sent up for you."

He turned his attention back to the paper in his hands.

Gwen turned her back to them and headed to the exit nearest the stairs, concentrating on putting one unsteady foot in front of the other. Eating that wretched piece of meat was the last thing she wanted to do right now, but she knew she'd soon find it outside of her door, and she wouldn't be able to ignore it. She'd eat it eventually.

"Oh, and Daughter?" the king called out behind her, the barest trace of laughter in his voice. "Your prince arrives here in six days. I thought you might wish to know."

Six days.

Gwen stepped soundlessly out of the room. She waited until she was safely out of sight before wiping away the moisture now spilling down her cheeks.

She had a few tears left in her after all.

Chapter 4

It wasn't until late afternoon the following day Gwen was able to see Rhosyn and fill her in on what she'd learned. Her friend had been aghast at the news.

"This is what he's been planning all along?" she asked. "To get away with murder and still remain king?"

"And double the size of the kingdom, apparently." Gwen swiped at a nearby tuft of grass with the side of her boot. It seemed whenever the two of them wanted to talk seriously about something, they did it while walking through the pasture. Gwen hoped she wasn't coming to associate the beautiful meadow and the smell of horses with the negative and emotional discussions about castle life.

"I'd never even heard of that before — a marriage of what?"

"Affiliation. Yeah, I hadn't heard of it either. Apparently it's more involved than just an alliance. The two kingdoms become one on the day of the marriage. It's a huge deal. A priest even asks Eirene to bless the ceremony."

Rhosyn turned to Gwen, looking perplexed. "She won't though, will She? How can She possibly give her blessing to something like this?"

"I've checked a little. The wedding couple kneels, each holding their crystal. The priest recites a prayer, and She gives her blessing to the arrangement if there's no malice in either of their hearts. So long as the crystal I'm holding glows, it's a done deal," said Gwen. "Father's already figured out how this is all going to work, and he doesn't seem worried about that part, so I don't think Eirene's going to withhold Her blessing in this case. I don't think I have malice in my heart or whatever, but—"

"We can't let this happen, Gwen."

"I know we can't! I've accidentally burned people before, but nobody's ever *died* from touching me! If someone were actually killed because of what I was, I don't think I'd be able to live with myself. What kind of person could live with something like that? As it is, just thinking about what I ended up doing to Rolf, I—" Gwen's voice wavered, and she swallowed hard. "We've got to find some way to warn this prince, try to save him somehow."

"We're not just talking about saving some stupid prince's life, Gwen. This is your immortal soul we're talking about! You haven't done anything wrong, but if something like this is viewed as a sin by the Goddess and your crystal in the temple goes dark—"

"Damnation, banishment. Possibly even worse things. And I totally agree with you," said Gwen. "We've got to stop this."

"So, what do we do?"

"I have an idea."

"What?"

"Simple, really. We tell people. Tell everyone!"

Rhosyn looked at her skeptically. "About your father's plan?"

"Well, that too. But more importantly, we tell people about my condition." Gwen held her gloved and sleeve-covered arms out to either side for emphasis. "Think about it for a second. The only time I'm seen in public is for official ceremonies where it can't be avoided, and I'm never introduced to anyone. The people don't know me, or anything about me. Father replaced everyone who used to work in the castle, and the new servants aren't supposed to find out about my condition. And you can bet your knickers this prince doesn't know about me. This whole plan hinges on keeping it a secret, right? So, let's make sure everyone finds out about me. Staff, townspeople, everyone!"

"We just go around telling people? That is a pretty simple solution." Rhosyn frowned. "Your father isn't stupid though, so he's probably already thought of that. He'll try to stop you."

"For the next five days he can bully me, threaten me, lock me in my tower, whatever he likes. Maybe he makes it so I'm alone and can't talk to anyone, but that won't matter. Even if I'm locked up, you won't be, right?"

"Will that be enough? I mean, I'm trying to imagine a situation where I just walk up to some strangers and say, *Oh hi, guys! Hey, did you know the daughter of the king is poisonous?* I doubt I'll be able to convince many people. Besides, what if your father locks me up as well?"

"Even if he does, eventually he'll have to parade me in front of this prince who's come all the way down here to meet me, right? What's stopping me from just blurting out the secret right then and there? And if the prince doesn't believe me, I'll provide a convincing demonstration. Father is humiliated, and the prince runs away screaming."

"And your father flies into a rage."

"Maybe he'll beat me to death. That would solve everything."

"Gwen!"

"I don't want to hurt anybody, Rosie! I don't want to be an assassin! If he flies into a rage and kills me, where's the down side? His crystal in the temple goes dark; he's forced to abdicate. He's no longer king! Forcing him off the throne like that might even be considered my duty!"

"Don't get like this on me, Gwen," Rhosyn said, grabbing Gwen's sleeve and turning to face her fully. "Don't even talk like that!"

"How else can we stop it though? What else can I do?"

"We'll find a way, Gwen. Somehow we'll find a way to stop this horrible thing from happening, and—"

Gwen saw her friend's gaze focus on something behind her, and heard the faint clip-clopping of horse hooves. She spun around to see what had caught Rhosyn's attention.

"Well," Gwen said, feeling weary beyond measure, "speaking of horrible things."

About forty yards away, cresting the hill, rode Anifail. Behind him, also on horseback, were two guards. A fourth, riderless horse brought up the rear.

Were she and Rhosyn going to be locked up so quickly?

"Crap. Okay, they're probably here for me, Rosie. If I have to go with them, I want you to start telling people about me tonight." Gwen gave her friend a desperate look. "Right away."

"This is surreal. I can't believe this is even happening!"

They looked on grimly as Anifail, smiling, dismounted and walked up to the two of them. His stride seemed a little more jaunty than usual. He stopped little more than three feet away, and the two large horsemen jangled to a halt several yards behind him.

Anifail regarded the two girls for a moment.

"Oh dear," he said. "I must have intruded on a private conversation of some sort. I feel dreadful. Curse this job! Why must I forever be interrupting the whispered conversations of vapid, empty-headed little girls?"

"Could it be because they don't trust you near boys?" Gwen replied.

Anifail folded his arms, his expression one of amusement.

"The princess tells me I shouldn't be around young men." He gave her a nasty smile. "Pot, may I introduce you to kettle?"

"Captain," Rhosyn said, "is it your job to act like an ass, or is it just one of the perks?"

"Just tailoring my conversation to match the temperament of my audience." He smiled, reaching with his gloved hand into the satchel slung over one shoulder. "I've been ordered to deliver two things on behalf of King Bryn. And as luck would have it," he said, looking from Rhosyn to Gwen and back, "I run into both recipients at the same time."

"Oh, you shouldn't have! For us? How adorable," Gwen said, motioning to the two mounted guards behind Anifail. "What are their names?"

Both guards bristled slightly.

"Oh, they're not for you, Princess." He grinned, pulling out a small, shiny glass bauble about the size of a hen egg and holding it between thumb and forefinger. "No, this is for you."

Gwen eyed what he held cautiously. The bauble didn't look particularly special; it wasn't even reflecting the sun's rays all that well, despite the beautiful day.

"Oh, let me guess," she said after a moment. "Concerned I might not cooperate with his plans, my father now offers me an awkward, clumsy bribe." Gwen laughed. "You know, if the king wanted to send me something cheap, pretty, and useless, he didn't need to buy some stupid gemstone. He could have just curled your hair, stuck you in a dress, and sent you."

She heard Rhosyn stifle a giggle.

Anifail gave Gwen a cold smile.

"You know, Princess, I have a theory. Would you like to hear it?" He smiled, palming the bauble and lowering his hands to his sides. "It's about how stupid and predictable you are."

Gwen tried to come up with a witty retort to that, but Anifail continued before she could think of one.

"See, I believe you were telling your friend Rhosyn here about the king's plan. You've probably decided you aren't going to stand idly by and allow His Highness to do this, and were in the process of cooking up some silly plan to stop him." He smiled again. "Yes?"

Gwen was silent.

"And there was probably some drama as well, now that I think about it. Lots of bonding, a few *We'll think of somethings*, and some anguished wringing of hands, hmm?"

"Our conversations aren't anyone's business, Captain," Rhosyn said.

"I'll consider myself answered," said Anifail, grinning, all teeth, at Rhosyn. "Like I said: stupid and predictable."

Maybe it was his smugness, his self-assurance that got Gwen's hackles up, but she found she just couldn't contain herself. "You want to talk stupid? How stupid are the two of you going to feel when I tell the visiting prince what you have planned for him? Hmm? Who's going to be stupid and predictable *then?*"

Gwen could see Rhosyn giving her a pained *I wish you hadn't said that* sort of look, but she didn't care.

Anifail straightened, looking at Gwen in feigned astonishment.

"Oh dear," he said, the barest trace of mockery in his voice. "You've figured that out, have you?"

"Try and stop me! Father's going to need my cooperation on some level, or this whole thing doesn't happen. He's already ruined my life; I'm not letting him ruin anyone else's. He can threaten me, beat me — I don't care! I'll touch the Prince's arm to make my point, if I'm forced to. Or maybe even plant a nice, big kiss on father's cheek right in front of him. Or kiss yours! Won't that be fun?"

The three of them stood there in silence.

"My goodness. You would conspire against the King of Calderia? You would cause him grievous injury, engage in *treason*, all for the sake of foiling his plan?" Anifail asked mildly.

"In a heartbeat!"

"Well, that's that I suppose. How dreadfully embarrassing." Anifail heaved a dramatic sigh. "All those years of work, foiled because the king didn't realize his excitable daughter would open her big mouth and ruin everything the first chance she got. I fear he'll make an example of me, perhaps force me to resign my post."

His words were relaxed and unconcerned, bitingly ironic. The smug captain of the guard still thought he had the advantage, which made Gwen nervous. Despite her concern, she continued to meet Anifail's gaze in a sure, steady manner.

"Gosh you're clever, both of you," Anifail continued. "Nothing to be done but head back to the castle and start packing my bags, I suppose. After I've discharged my duties, that is." He held up the glass sphere. "If I may though, Princess, I crave a small favour. Before I resign in disgrace, humiliated by a mere seventeen-year-old girl, would you allow me the honour of kissing your hand?"

Any glib response Gwen might have had caught in her throat.

Kiss her hand?

What was he trying to do? Gwen had a feeling not unlike the one she experienced the night before — a sense she was the butt of a joke, but unable to grasp exactly how it was funny.

She stood there, trying to puzzle it out. Anifail simply stood before her, his expression one of mock innocence.

"Do it, Gwen," said Rhosyn suddenly. "Let him! Just take off your glove and give him what he so desperately wants!"

That sounded like a fine idea. Gwen flashed a quick grin at her friend.

"Yes, by all means, Captain!" She smiled, tugging at the fingers of her glove until it was loose enough for her to pull off entirely. She held her bare hand out to him with her wrist bent slightly in invitation, arching her eyebrows and giving him a look that dared him to try.

"Well, first things first," he said, gently tossing her the bauble he held. Gwen snatched it out of the air with her hand before it could hit her, and—

The small sphere was cool, but warmed almost instantly. A small shiver passed through her, though she was not cold in the slightest.

She looked at the gem oddly for a moment. Then she held it out to one side with a look of disdain and let go, allowing it to fall to the grass. She looked for some sort of reaction from him, but got nothing. Anifail was already on one knee before her, holding his arm out as if to take a proffered hand.

Gwen held out her hand, a wry smile on her face as she looked down on him, regally. Whatever his plan, there was no way he'd go through with this. The sight of him hastily backing out of this would be very satisfying.

Anifail smirked up at her, took her hand in his heavy leather glove, and bowed his head as if to kiss the backs of her fingers.

Gwen urgently yanked her hand out of his grasp.

"No, let him! Don't feel bad, Gwen," said Rhosyn. "He deserves it! Don't move your hand; let him burn himself. I want to see what he looks like with lips the size of plums."

Gwen just stood there, looking down at her hand.

She hadn't meant to move it.

"Yes, she's right, Princess," Anifail said, a tiny glimmer of amusement in his eyes. "Let me kiss your hand. I'd feel just awful if I didn't."

Gwen extended her hand to him once more, feeling less regal and more uncertain. Again he took it in his gloved hand, lowering his lips towards the smooth, alabaster skin of her fingers.

Again, she wrested her hand free of his grip, pulling it away.

"Gwen?" Rhosyn asked, sounding a bit concerned. "What are you doing?"

Gwen looked first at her hand, and then at Rhosyn, her eyes wide.

"Yes, what is the problem, Princess?" smiled Anifail. "Is there some reason I shouldn't kiss your hand? Will something horrible happen?"

She opened her mouth and drew enough breath to yell, *You know what will happen, you idiot!*

Nothing came out.

Gwen remained in that position, lungs half-full of air that was practically begging to carry her words out of her half-opened mouth. Her brain said the words, loudly and clearly, sending the message to her throat just as she would any other day. Her voice didn't cooperate.

Again and again she tried.

She made no sound.

"Gwen?" Rhosyn looked very alarmed now.

"Princess Gwenwyn, are you saying I'm in danger?" Anifail asked. "Are you saying I shouldn't touch your bare skin? Is that what you're saying?" Anifail laughed, taking a glove off and reaching out to take her hand.

Unbidden, she found her hand pulling away from his.

Grinning, Anifail reached out to touch her cheek with a bare finger. Her neck seemed to bend of its own volition, and she abruptly turned her face away. She took a half-step back as well, though she hadn't meant to do that, either.

Chuckling, Anifail pulled his hand away. Gwen turned to face him, her eyes wide.

"You've stolen her voice!" Rhosyn cried. "You bastard!"

"What? I've done no such thing," said Anifail. "Princess Gwenwyn, what is the name of the young lady standing over there?"

"Rhosyn!" Gwen answered, a trace of fear in her tone. She sent Anifail a confused look. "But, how—"

"And your name, Princess?"

"It's Gwenwyn! Why—"

"And is your father planning anything a young prince might want to know about?" asked Anifail. "Is there a reason he might not want to touch you? Is there anything unusual or distressing about your childhood you wish to share?"

Gwen suddenly found she could only open her mouth, as if about to speak, every time she tried to answer his questions.

"Is today's weather to your liking, Your Majesty?" he inquired.

"Why, yes!" Gwen babbled excitedly, her mouth practically tripping over the words as they rushed out of her. "Most favourable weather indeed. The past three days have been very warm, hardly a cloud in the sky! The grain farmers will think it a blessing, though they'll need at least two or three days more for their fields to properly dry if they're growing wheat. Less for flax, of course, because the oils—"

Gwen bit off the last of her words and clamped her jaw shut with her hands, forcing herself to stop talking. Her eyes felt as though they were bugging out of her skull.

The words she'd spoken had simply poured out of her mouth, like they weren't even stopping to check with her first. It was all stuff she had known, but she hadn't meant to say any of it!

"Well, that appears to be working perfectly. Outstanding," he said, beaming at the two of them. "Getting back to my theory about how stupid you are, I'm assuming neither of you have ever heard of a geis sphere. Ordinarily they contain a single compulsion, but in this case we had them include two. One compels you to shy away from the touch of any living thing, the other limits all your communication to polite chit-chat, discussions about the weather, idle stories, stuff of that nature. Honestly, I hadn't expected that last one to inconvenience you at all, given how stupid you are, but the king felt it was important. Now, on to the other thing. His Highness has penned a request, Rhosyn, and wished me to give it to you in the presence of these two guards."

Anifail pulled a wax-sealed envelope from somewhere and held it out for Rhosyn to take. She did so, opened it, and scanned its contents quickly. Gwen saw her friend's expression turn to one of dismay.

"Because I'm familiar with the horse trails, I've been ordered to act as escort for these guards, bound for Fort Pike," Rhosyn said in a small voice. "I'm to leave immediately."

Gwen's heart sank. Fort Pike was a four day ride from the castle.

"Well, I've already kept you from attending to the king's business long enough, Lady Rhosyn," he said, saluting her. "Be sure these two heavily armed men remain safe in your care, will you?"

"Well then," Rhosyn said after a moment's thought, "I suppose I shall have to head back home and pack some things right away."

"Oh, there's no need for that. Wouldn't want you running off or leaving a note for someone to find," said Anifail. He snapped his fingers at one of the burly guards, who reached behind his saddle and produced a nearly full travel bag. "No, we've already been to your house, taken the liberty of packing you a few things for the ride. So, see you in about a week?"

Rhosyn's shoulders slumped.

Too much was happening too quickly, and Gwen found she could do little more than stand there, wide-eyed and tongue-tied, as Rhosyn was escorted to the riderless horse and helped into the saddle by the captain. Though his face was somber, Anifail appeared to be enjoying this immensely.

Gwen and Rhosyn looked at each other briefly as the trio rode by on their horses, and Gwen could see her own worry and desperation mirrored in her friend's tight-lipped expression. She could think of nothing to say, nothing at all. With the enchantment in effect, even if Gwen could think of something, she was no longer even positive she'd be able to say it.

The three riders rode down the worn, dirt path without looking back, leaving Gwen alone on the grassy hill standing next to Anifail. Within a minute or so they turned a corner of the winding horse trail and were gone.

She was alone. Her best friend had been taken away from her.

What was she going to do?

"Well, that's all done I suppose," said Anifail, briefly considering the sun as though attempting to gauge the time. "Pity I neglected to bring a horse for you, Princess. You'll have to walk back to the castle, I suppose. If you're going to sulk in this field a while, do try to limit it to a few minutes. I've heard that some of the local fur trappers have spotted dire wolves roaming nearby." He smiled at her briefly. "I'm not certain your new compulsion would be enough to protect you; they can run quite fast. Wouldn't want you giving some poor wolf a bellyache now, would we?"

Hopelessness turned to anger in her chest. Gwen regarded Anifail with as much scorn as she could muster and readied a scathing reply.

"I... don't like wolves," she managed to stammer. "They're... mean."

That wasn't what she'd tried to say at all!

Anifail chuckled at her distressed look before casually turning and walking over to his horse, whistling cheerfully.

Standing alone on the grassy hilltop, she wordlessly watched him depart.

Chapter 5

Gwen wished hiding in her room and crying felt more productive. If tears were ideas for getting out of this situation, she'd have about a million by now.

Presently, she had none.

Maybe it had something to do with suddenly being unable to express herself — that her words had been taken away and replaced with those of a polite but slow-witted child. Thanks to the geis she couldn't even raise her voice, or yell, or say anything that didn't make her seem like a flighty, simple-minded little girl. She'd tried hundreds of little ways to try to get around the compulsion, and when it didn't result in her standing there speechless, it resulted in her saying something completely different from what she intended, using phrases of no real consequence.

Even after only a few days of experimenting with the magical effects of the compulsion Anifail had saddled her with, she realized there was no point. The only sentences she could actually say out loud were polite nothings, or snippets of children's stories.

And the weather, of course. Oh, how she hated hearing herself talk about the bloody weather, or its effects on the local crops! How could she ever hope to prevent what her father had planned if she couldn't even find a way to keep from jabbering on and on about flax, or barley, or wheat? Even just remaining silent was better than having to listen to herself drone on about that mind-numbingly mundane stuff.

She snorted softly to herself. Perhaps she could bore the prince so badly he'd leave.

No, that wouldn't work. If her suitor believed she didn't possess a brain in her head, he might be even more likely to go through with marriage, thinking her easily controlled. The only thing guaranteed to work was the truth, which would send him running as fast as he could back to Bespir, or whatever kingdom he was from.

Instead of talking about the weather, maybe her best bet was to remain completely silent. Perhaps it would leave him with the impression that she wished nothing to do with him, that she was aloof and arrogant.

She may as well play up that angle, she thought bitterly. After all, many of the new staff already believed she was like that anyway, thanks to Anifail.

It explained why all the new servants had seemed so afraid of her as she'd walked down to dinner that one night, or any night since. Anifail had been busy planting rumours about her amongst the cooking staff, the valets, and the rest of the help that had been recently hired to attend to palace duties. Gwen had stumbled upon this information thanks to two chambermaids who had been discussing her in the kitchen late last night. She overheard a bit of their conversation as she'd been sneaking downstairs to fill her water pitcher, and what she heard had prompted her to hide around the corner and listen a while.

"—carrying on and breaking things like that. A spoiled brat, that's all she is."

"Yes, but it's that smile of hers that bugs me most, like she's better than the rest of us. She'll pass by me in the hall without a word, crooked little smile in place, not even sparing me a glance. *Look at me; I'm a princess and you're not,* is what she's thinking, I'd wager. And then she'll edge away from me as I walk by, like she's afraid she might touch me and get dirty! Disgraceful, even for a princess!"

"Oh, you don't want to touch her, Liv. I heard something from Captain Anifail the other day. You remember Heidi?"

"Aye, what of her?"

"We never knew what she was sent away for, right? Well, as I hear it, little miss Gwenwyn was throwing some sort of hissy-fit in the library, and Heidi tried to calm her down, touched her arm. Well, the princess, she calls for some guards, has her locked up! For daring to put a hand to her!"

"No!"

"It gets worse. Not happy with that, she ordered a guard to grab Heidi's hand, and she had him hold her whole arm over a heating lamp!"

"What?"

"It's true! Burns like you never saw before! I seen 'em! Guard didn't want to, but Princess Gwenwyn threatened to have him beheaded if he refused."

"Surely not!"

"It's the truth! Captain's own words, my hand to the sky."

"Goddess! I had no idea! And I thought what I heard was bad! Why, just the other day, she—"

Gwen departed quietly rather than listen to any more of what the two women had to say. It made her ill to know these sorts of things were being said about her, but it also made an awful kind of sense. Hiring new staff and spreading these lies about her, sending Rhosyn away like they had: her father and Anifail wanted to make certain there was nobody at all she could turn to in this, her hour of need.

It worked, too. She was friendless, idealess, utterly helpless, and—

Gwen realized she was working herself into another crying fit.

She shook her head as though clearing it, took a deep breath and sighed, smoothing her dress over her legs as she sat there on the bed. She chastised herself for slipping into this frame of mind. Crying wasn't what she needed to do right now; she'd already done quite enough of that. What she needed to do was think, and quickly, because she was almost out of time.

The prince from Bespir had already arrived, and word had it he was somewhere in the castle.

From her small window, she'd been able to watch the standard-bearing honour guard as they'd rode up that morning to the newly decorated and freshly oiled gates of the castle. It had already been about four hours since the prince had arrived, and though her father hadn't yet sent anyone to fetch her, she knew it would only be a matter of time.

And so Gwen had been thinking furiously, trying to force her brain to come up with some new ideas. Though it had already been several hours, all too soon there came a tapping on her door.

"Princess Gwenwyn?" a cautious female voice asked through the door. A moment later the brass handle turned, and the massive door was slowly pushed open, revealing a frightened-looking young girl Gwen had never seen before.

Gwen stood up from her bed. Her motion attracted the notice of the servant, who abruptly halted the door's progress, and somehow managed to look even more frightened.

"P-princess? It's… your father wishes to, uh…. That is, he wants you to come downstairs to the rose garden. To meet your guest."

The girl was quite obviously terrified of her, which was almost enough to make Gwen burst into tears again. Instead, she held her emotions in check, nodded slowly and gave the young maiden as reassuring a smile as she could manage, softening her expression and trying to put the girl at ease. Never in her whole life had the expression on Gwen's face been so at odds with how she was feeling inside.

Without even a smile of recognition or nod of acknowledgment the girl quickly turned and disappeared into the shadows beyond the half-opened door. After a mere second or two, the urgent whisper of the girl's slippers retreating down the stone steps faded into silence. Gwen herself would've probably had trouble running down those stairs so fast.

Sighing once more, she walked over to her hazy metal mirror to make some last minute adjustments to the dress she was wearing. She'd been instructed to wear this specific dress today, and though Gwen had been tempted to wear something completely different, she'd eventually thought better of the idea. Anifail and her father always seemed to be one step ahead of her, and she had no desire to see what sort of punishment they'd mete out in response to some token defiance. Best not to find out.

And the dress was beautiful. It was so beautiful Gwen hated it.

Long and flowing, it was made from silk the colour of corn flowers. It had matching elbow-length gloves, as well as thin straps crossing behind her neck that left her shoulders and back completely bare. The lack of fabric on her shoulders did make her feel the slightest bit naked, though the rather daring neckline might also have had something to do with that feeling as well. It fell wonderfully on her, and although it probably couldn't hold a candle to what a princess from a more prosperous kingdom would wear, it was nicer than any article of clothing she owned. Looking in the mirror, Gwen found herself torn between admiring how she looked in this dress, and despising it for what it represented.

It was bait, plain and simple. And she was the trap.

If only she knew how she could stop this!

Sighing, Gwen closed her eyes and murmured a small prayer to Eirene, begging Her for the wisdom needed to foil her father's plan. That done, she gave the mirror one last look, adjusted her gloves, and then walked out of her bedroom.

If anything, wearing the dress made her feel even more awkward and isolated than previous trips down the castle hallways had. People she encountered still regarded her fearfully, or edged closer to the wall as she passed by. Rather than acknowledge these encounters, Gwen chose to focus her attention on some of the improvements and fixes her father had ordered done in the now slightly unfamiliar hallways.

Threadbare tapestries and other familiar items had been taken down and replaced with ones she'd never seen, or with nothing at all. Various walls had been whitewashed, painted over, or even rebuilt in some cases. In fact, she was surprised to find that the entrance to one particularly dingy hallway had been walled over completely, as though attempting to prevent passers-by from witnessing any evidence of neglect or disrepair.

After some reflection, Gwen realized she felt a kind of kinship with the castle itself. She wasn't the only thing being dressed up and made to look like something else entirely.

Eventually she navigated her way to the rose garden, where she found a uniformed Anifail standing, relaxed, his hands clasped behind his back as he watched two figures walking some distance away. Soon Gwen was standing next to him.

"Princess," he murmured, giving her a sidelong inspection. "You look lovely today."

Rather than try to say anything, Gwen chose to look away.

"Indeed. Quite lovely, actually. Surprising. Very princess-like. Who knew such a thing was even possible?" he added, quiet laughter in his voice. "I owe your father a silver."

Gwen's cheeks burned, and she attempted a small scowl. When the geis prevented that, she decided she'd simply stand and say nothing.

"Are you looking forward to meeting your new husband, Princess?" he asked. "Heart all a-flutter? He's very interested in girls, you know, especially the brainless variety. The two of you should get along like a house on fire."

Lips pressed together, she continued staring off into the distance.

Then, suddenly, Gwen caught a hint of motion to her left. The world twisted sideways for a moment, and she managed to catch herself before she stumbled. Confused, she turned to Anifail, who was already pulling his hand away from her cheek.

"So sorry, Princess. Just wanted to make sure everything was still working as it should." He gave her a thin smile.

Gwen tried sending him a withering glare in return, and unclenched her jaw enough to remark, "It's rather sunny today, Captain Anifail. Very bright."

Again, nothing at all like what she'd meant to say, and even her facial expressions were refusing to cooperate with her. Anifail chuckled softly as Gwen turned away and looked at the ground.

Was this what a puppet felt like? If it was, she'd burn every single puppet in the kingdom, for death by fire would be a mercy compared to this torturous compulsion. She could never recall having been so frustrated in all of her life!

She'd find a way to stop this. Somehow, she'd find a way.

Within minutes the king and his companion appeared from behind a large rose bush, the two of them unhurriedly walking down the cobbled path in Gwen's general direction. Anifail stood a little straighter, his arms falling to his side as they approached. When they were a dozen or so feet away, he gave the two figures an uncharacteristically crisp salute.

"Highness. Highness," he said, nodding to both of them in turn. He then faced Gwen and gave her a small bow, something she'd never received from him before. "May I present Princess Gwenwyn, heir to the throne of Calderia. Princess?" He gestured to the attractive young man beside her father. "His Highness Tremaine Caine, Prince of Bespir."

His name was Tremaine Caine? Seriously?

Lowering her eyes, she gave the prince a slow and deliberate curtsey and said nothing. Almost immediately she regretted her decision. Should she have looked him in the eye? Would that have given him the impression she was willful, or arrogant? Or is that how princesses usually acted? She was hardly ever introduced to anyone, so teaching her the protocol for meeting a prince had probably been a low priority for her father. Still, Gwen wished she knew what he expected, if only so she could do the exact opposite.

Prince Tremaine responded to her curtsey with a bow from the waist that was so low to the ground its only practical function had to be for showing off how flexible he was. After holding it for a few seconds he returned to an upright position, extending towards her a single pink rose in his left hand.

Gwen reached out to take the proffered rose.

Before she had a chance to react, he snatched her gloved hand in his and tossed the rose aside. Then he kneeled before her, and gave the back of her glove a long, lingering kiss.

Startled by this unexpected gesture and not knowing how to react, she found herself looking down her arm at him, his bright hazel eyes staring intently into hers as he completed his kiss. Then he straightened up and took a half-step to close the distance between them.

"Oh, Princess Gwenwyn," he said, smiling ruefully as he shook his head sadly, "you've put me in such a difficult spot. I find I'm torn between leaving here this very minute and staying here forever."

Leave? He wanted to leave? What was he talking about?

A little puzzled, Gwen decided to furrow her eyebrows at him. At least she could still control some of her expressions.

"Well, you see," he continued, squeezing her hand gently, "when I'd received word about how stunningly beautiful you were, I had several serfs imprisoned for daring to exaggerate to their prince. I see now I should rush back and give each of them both their freedom and a heartfelt apology, for I can scarcely remember the last time I beheld anything quite so beautiful in all of my life."

And then he smiled at her.

It was a remarkable smile, different than any smile she'd ever been given before, confident and charming. Gwen felt the fluttering of butterflies in her stomach. She could feel herself blushing, and for a brief instant she—

Wait... butterflies? Why were there butterflies? What was going on?

It was the moment, she realized. It was just like that moment she was always reading about in fairy tales, where the boy met the girl, and the girl met the boy, and they stared into each other's eyes and knew—

The Prince's charming smile transformed itself into an amused grin, and laughter danced in his eyes.

"Liked that, did you? One of my better ones," he murmured through his cheerful, cocksure smile. "I debated all the way up here which line I was going to use, spent a little bit of time cleaning that one up. I had a backup line ready — a very tactful one, of course — just in case you turned out to be a total dog. After all, my sources have been wrong in the past." He stood at arm's length and looked her up and down appraisingly. "They certainly weren't wrong this time."

Her blush deepened, and her reaction caused his smile to become even wider, and even more amused.

"Oh, you're going to be fun! I'd heard you mostly kept to yourself, and your father has been telling me you weren't very worldly, but I wasn't expecting *this*," he laughed, his tone delighted. Then, turning his head, he focused his attention to her father. "And she's how old?"

"Seventeen, Highness," Bryn replied, quietly.

"Marvellous! A full five years my junior! Younger wives are very much in fashion at the moment. And I'm nothing if not fashionable." He gave her a sly look. "Still, there are other things to consider. If it's alright with you, Highness, I think I should like to spend some time getting to know your daughter."

"Of course! She sent her lady-in-waiting away a few days ago, unfortunately, but—"

"Oh, did she?" he asked, his smile getting a tad bigger, his gaze still locked on her.

"Yes, but I'm certain we could find a member of your personal escort or some other chaperone for—"

"We won't be needing one of those," Tremaine interrupted airily.

"But, Prince Tremaine, such things aren't—"

"Oh come now, Bryn!" he sighed in mock disappointment, his smile never losing its arrogantly amused quality. "And we were getting along so well, too. Look, this is a big step up for your kingdom, and the last thing you'd want to do is jeopardize our budding friendship by starting off on the wrong foot, right? I mean, if my future father-in-law doesn't even trust me to be a gentleman while alone with his daughter, how could he possibly trust me with the responsibility of running our new, unified kingdom?"

"No, no, you're quite right," agreed Bryn hurriedly, his tone so apologetic and subservient that Gwenwyn knew it was an act.

As if to confirm her suspicions, she caught a glimpse of her father's half-hidden, knowing smirk out of the corner of her eye. Contrite, accommodating, eager to please... everything he was doing suggested he was a weak king, easily dominated. If this young prince was used to getting his own way, the idea of having a pushover for a father-in-law would be an attractive one.

It wasn't as if her father had to worry about her chastity, after all. Not with the enchantment that had been put on her.

"Indeed," said the smiling prince. "You'll find I'm right about most things, actually. Plus, there are the feelings of this lovely young woman to consider. Arranged marriages are hardly romantic, after all." He gave her another smile that sent another unexpected collection of butterflies fluttering around her stomach. "Handsome I may be, but it's not fair to expect a girl to fall in love with me at first sight, is it? Why, that sort of thing takes at least an afternoon!"

Bryn laughed dutifully at that, and Anifail gave the prince a patiently amused smile.

"Right then. That's settled," Tremaine said, turning the full force of his confident grin upon Gwenwyn, and then bowing from the neck. "Let's go for a walk, shall we? We can escape the company of these dreadfully boring old folk, and you can show me some of this lovely kingdom of yours."

He held out his arm for her to take.

She briefly stared at it, anxious and uncertain, feeling like a trapped animal. Everything was happening too quickly, and she didn't seem able to stop any of it!

Not knowing what else to do, and to avoid awkwardness, Gwenwyn took the proffered arm. The two of them then began walking down the garden path, leaving the company of Anifail and her father. She couldn't see behind her, but she could almost feel her father's smile upon her back.

This prince already seemed convinced he'd be marrying her... and even seemed to be looking forward to the prospect. She couldn't tell him what she was, nor could she show him! Yet if she did nothing and allowed herself to be married to this young prince, it would be the same as murdering him!

What was she going to do?

Chapter 6

"You don't exactly talk much, do you?" Tremaine said. "A little on the meek side? Perhaps not the sharpest sword in the rack?" Gwen watched speculation settle over his face, and noticed him study her as they walked. "Ah well, no matter; you're certainly a genius in other ways."

What an unbearable, odious toad, she thought.

The two of them had been walking for nearly half an hour, making their way to where the apple orchard met the horse pasture, and the butterflies had fled Gwen's stomach long ago.

What little superficial charm and tact he'd displayed for the benefit of her father had all but evaporated once they'd made their way down the garden path to the edge of the field. His small talk was smugly self-assured, and full of barely concealed innuendo and lewd suggestions that made her wish she could curl her lip in disgust from time to time.

He also kept *accidentally* allowing his hand to brush up against the fabric covering her leg, sometimes even going so far as to pat her behind! Her geis would force her to twist away involuntarily any time he attempted to touch her skin, of course, but every time she did he simply laughed and accused her of being coy. Nothing seemed to blunt his enthusiasm.

And there was the way his gaze crawled all over her. She could almost picture him licking his chops as he was doing it, like a dog eying a steak.

There was, however, a much bigger problem. Much to her dismay, she discovered she was enjoying everything Prince Tremaine did. Really, *really* enjoying it.

She'd never been afforded this kind of attention! Even as she realized how much she loathed this arrogant princeling, she'd feel an unexpected little thrill at some of those hungry looks of his. A couple of times she actually caught herself about to smile.

Could she be this desperate for human contact? Was she so deprived of attention that she was reduced to welcoming the advances of this ill-mannered pig of a prince? How sad was that?

Worst of all, none of these unexpected feelings were helping her come up with a way to stop what was happening.

"Come on, you've got to say *something*, Princess," Tremaine laughed. "How will I be able to tell you've fallen madly in love with me unless you talk to me? Come, I've spoken too much already. Tell me more about this kingdom of yours. Or your father — tell me about him. How did he ever become king? The poor fellow seems scared of his own shadow."

Gwen took a breath, and wondered what sort of drivel would end up coming out of her mouth this time.

"We've all manner of trade, Sir. Hides, furs and agriculture mostly, but there are some devilishly clever leatherworkers in town as well, with an excellent reputation far and wide."

Well, at least she wasn't talking about the weather.

"Simple, simple girl," Tremaine chuckled sadly, looking up into the sky. "All farming and skinning and little else. Still, nothing wrong with that, is there? Much better than knowing a couple of things and being full of yourself all the time. Might even be considered ideal, in some ways." He looked her up and down. "An empty vessel, just waiting to be filled. With knowledge, I mean."

Gwen felt herself blush at that, though she found herself unable to actually sneer at his condescension. His comment did bring up a good point, however; if she was going to make any progress at all here, she'd have to find some way to gain control of the words coming out of her mouth. All of these nothings and pleasantries she spouted weren't going to dissuade him in the slightest. But how could she say anything else? If the geis kept replacing her actual words with meaningless small talk—

What if she tried to saying something that was already meaningless small talk? Could she take control of what she was saying then?

Gwen took a breath.

"I... have never been... to Bespir," she managed, her words coming out as though her mouth were filled with marbles. But it worked! She'd meant to say every one of those words, and not a single one had been replaced. It wasn't much, but it was a start.

"You haven't? Well, to be perfectly honest, the best thing about Bespir," said Tremaine, favouring her with a wide, toothy grin, "is me. Frightfully dull place when I'm not around. No parties, no banquets...just a gaggle of miners and merchants, servants and shopkeepers. That's not to say you won't like it better there, of course." He sniffed, glancing briefly over their surroundings as they walked down the lush, green horse trail. "It's certainly an improvement over this place."

Okay, she'd managed to get one whole sentence out. If she kept the conversation limited to small talk, she could control what she was saying. How did this help exactly?

What if her small talk wasn't really small talk at all? Could her geis identify the difference? What if she could find a way to bury some sort of hidden meaning into what she said?

Like dropping hints about what her father was really like? Or maybe arousing the prince's suspicions a little?

"Yes," she said, giving him as significant a look as she could manage. "I'm very much looking forward to leaving this place. Very much."

"Oh, believe me, I understand completely. Tell me, does this entire kingdom smell like horse? I've been unable to smell anything else since arriving."

"Getting away from… things… would be wonderful."

"Yes, you said that already."

Argh. Of course he wouldn't delve into what she was saying, or ask what she meant. He didn't really care in the first place! She had to come up with something else, something that would show him her true nature, warn him off.

She couldn't just tell him, obviously, so that was out. The only thing that might grab his attention was to show him, provide a demonstration. How could she do that, though, if the geis prevented her from touching any living thing?

Mid-step, Gwen had a revelation that was so surprising she almost tripped.

Living things, Anifail had said! She couldn't touch anything that was alive!

What about things that used to be alive? Or were very recently alive? A technicality at best. Still, would the effects of the geis sphere stop her from touching things like that?

It was worth a shot.

"I… loved that rose you had, earlier." Gwen sighed, wistfully looking around the meadow. "I love flowers. So lovely and romantic."

The prince picked up on the heavy-handed hint in practically no time.

"Flowers? Why, say no more, Princess," he said, walking a handful of steps off the path and bending over to pick some daisies.

As Prince Tremaine did this, she took the opportunity to peel off the long, silk gloves she wore. She hurriedly tossed them aside and stood there on the path, waiting.

Tremaine had only picked about five or six flowers before turning and heading back to her. His gaze wandered over her now-bared arms, and his cocksure smile got even wider, as though her gesture meant something. Then, as if remembering he had them, he held out the meagre collection of flowers to her.

She reached out to take them, hoping for the best. Her fingers wrapped around the stems and leaves, and she pulled them close to her, feeling relief wash over her. She'd done it!

Making certain the prince watched, she held up the handful of flowers and, slowly and deliberately, she stroked one of the daisy petals with her bared index finger. It immediately changed colour from white to beige, and then to a withered brown. The faintest plume of smoke appeared briefly, and the air smelled of burning leaves and perfume.

Exultant, she turned to Tremaine to see his reaction. His eyes were narrowed in thought, and he appeared mildly puzzled.

"Well, that's certainly odd," he said, frowning. "Are all of the flowers around here so delicate? Or is it something special about this particular kind?"

Gwen could only stare at him incredulously as he took a flower from her, peered at it, and then ran his own finger over one of the petals, as though he expected to see the same result. His frown deepened, and he looked back to Gwen with a *how did you do that?* sort of expression.

She felt like screaming.

Well, at least she'd gotten his attention. Still, if she couldn't explain why her touch did what it did, her efforts might be for naught. He'd simply ask her father about it, and the king would find a way to smooth things over, convince the prince it was nothing — a parlour trick, or some prank she enjoyed playing on guests. The marriage would go on, and Prince Tremaine would be just as dead. She needed to convince him to leave, and in a hurry, without talking to her father first.

The technicality was key; her geis made it so she couldn't touch things that were alive, but she could touch flowers once they'd been pulled from the ground because they technically were no longer alive. What about her ability to talk? Could she find a technicality in that?

Anifail had told her she was limited to polite chit-chat, discussions about the weather, and—

Idle stories!

She couldn't talk about herself at all, of course, but what if she wasn't talking specifically about herself? What if she were telling him about herself as though it were a story? Would that get around it?

Gwen took another breath.

"I like stories, too," she said, running her finger over the petal of another flower, causing it to darken and smoulder. "There's this one story I know quite well; it's about a princess. Her touch was poisonous — everything she touched withered and died."

She did it! She'd found a way out of this mess!

The prince cocked his head, looking confused. He regarded her, and then the flower she held, and his eyes got the tiniest bit wider.

"You see," she continued, touching more petals, one after another, "back when she was a baby, her father did something to make her that way, because he planned to kill a certain prince and take over his kingdom. And so, once she was old enough, he arranged a marriage between the two, and he cast a spell on his daughter so she couldn't tell this prince anything about herself."

Tremaine's eyes went even wider as he watched each petal she touched smoulder and burn. He paled slightly.

"But the princess didn't want to hurt anyone, and so she found a way around her father's spell and even managed to warn the prince right before they were married. The prince, fearing what other things the princess' father might do, saddled the nearest horse and galloped back to the safety of his kingdom without telling anyone in his entourage he was even leaving." Another idea came to Gwen, and she added, "Once he was safe, he warned all of the other neighbouring kingdoms about this princess and what she could do, so no other prince would fall victim to her father's wicked plan."

Prince Tremaine stood completely still now, staring at nothing and looking shocked beyond words.

She'd gotten through! Gwen was so relieved, she actually felt the tiniest bit dizzy.

They stood in silence on the meadow path, neither saying a word.

"Is that... do you mean to tell me that—" Tremaine ran his fingers through his hair, his distress now quite plain. "Are you seriously implying that you're... that if I touch you, I'd—" He looked at the remaining flowers she still held, all of which were wilting. The stems were beginning to give off a faint hissing sound.

Gwen tried to say *yes*, but found herself unable. She tried to nod, but her neck wouldn't cooperate. So, instead, she smiled prettily at him and said, "Would you like to visit our royal stables? We have lovely stables, filled with lots of lovely fast horses."

Swallowing nervously, and looking as though he'd just stepped in a nest of vipers, the prince gave Gwen a terse nod of his head.

"They're this way. I love horses. Sometimes I feed them apples," she said, turning back the way they'd come and motioning for him to do likewise.

Gwen was giddy with relief. She'd foiled her father's plan to use her to kill the prince! And, if Prince Tremaine did as she hoped and spread the word about her condition, her father wouldn't be able to spring this particular trap on any other unsuspecting princes, either!

She looked behind her occasionally as she walked to see how he fared. He still looked thoroughly shaken, and whenever she turned to look at him he'd straighten his posture, and regard her cautiously. Once, a sudden move she made caused him to panic, and he stumbled a little.

Gwen stifled a giggle. In mere minutes she'd transformed this arrogant princeling from a smugly confident lout to a wide-eyed nervous wreck. Gone were the accidental touches through her dress, the pats on her behind. His eyes no longer prowled hungrily over her, but were instead filled with a fearful wariness, the sort of look with which Gwen was all too familiar.

She sighed.

Even though she'd found a way to do what she'd set out to do, a part of her was still the tiniest bit sad, and was already missing some of the looks she'd been getting from Tremaine this past half-hour. For a few brief, fleeting moments she'd felt like an attractive, desirable young woman.

Now, given the new looks the prince gave her, she felt more like a monster.

Chapter 7

Gwen was once again sitting on her bed, in the familiar confines of her bedroom. She'd been strangely calm these last few hours. Calm, and the tiniest bit elated. She wasn't sure if this heady feeling of pride was because she'd successfully saved the Prince's life, because she'd saved her soul, or because she'd thwarted her father. Probably a little bit of all three, now that she'd had time to think about it.

"Gwenwyn!" her father bellowed from somewhere below. The furious thumps of Bryn's boots against the stone steps of her tower were quicker than usual.

Her massive door exploded all the way open, smashing against the stone wall so hard that one of the brass hinge-pins popped off and tinkled musically against the stone floor. The king stormed in shortly after, hair mussed and crown slightly askew. He looked at Gwen, his face a mask of fury.

"What did you do?" he roared, moving forward threateningly. "Where is Prince Tremaine?"

Gwen cocked her head at him, somehow managing to retain most of her previous calm. Then, she stood up from the bed and gave him a small curtsey.

"Your Highness," she said in a cheerful, upbeat voice. "Lovely weather we're having today."

He stood there staring at her a moment, looking like he was about to explode. Then he began patting himself down, hunting through his pockets. Within moments, he pulled out a dull marble-like object that Gwen recognized as the geis sphere.

Holding it up briefly, he turned and threw the sphere against the stone wall nearest him. There was a loud *pop*, and the thing exploded into a small shower of luminescent dust. At precisely the same time, Gwen felt a sensation like pins and needles wash over her, though it disappeared so quickly she didn't even have a chance to cry out in surprise.

"Where is he?" Bryn snarled, taking another stride closer to Gwen. "Where is Prince Tremaine? Nobody's seen him; everyone thought he was with you!"

"Oh, that obnoxious prince I met? He left, all sudden-like." She gave her father a half-smirk, and then sighed dramatically, as if heartbroken. "I guess he just didn't care for me. What can I say? The man has no taste."

"He was perfect! He thought you were ideal! It had all been arranged, right down to the date!" Bryn took off his crown and frustratedly ran a hand through his thinning curls. "We need those mines up north! Without the mines, the whole trade plan is dead in the water!" His eyes narrowed. "Where did he run off to? Tell me, now! There might still be time to salvage this, despite your—"

"He's gone, Father! Even if you find him again, you're never going to talk him into marriage now; he doesn't have a death wish!"

Bryn's eyes grew wider, and his nostrils flared. His already ruddy complexion got a shade darker.

"What did you do to him? You couldn't have told him about yourself... and you couldn't have shown him, so how—"

"A flower!" she laughed. "Can you believe it? All of your planning, your scheming, your efforts to turn me into a killer and damn my soul, all undone by a couple of freshly picked flowers. Oh, and I don't think you'll be able to try this little trick of yours again. I took care of that as well. I couldn't actually tell him anything about me, but I did manage to share this one fairy tale I know. It's all about a king who tried to use his only daughter to kill a prince and take his land. Pretty soon everyone will know about me, about you, and all about what you were hoping to accomplish!"

He stared at her, taking slow, deep breaths. Beads of perspiration appeared on his now-scarlet brow. She stared back at him confidently, and with just a hint of smugness, feeling more calm than she'd ever been during any of their previous confrontations.

"You stupid, useless child!" Bryn growled finally, slowly raising a trembling hand as though he were about to strike her.

"No glove today?" asked Gwen, giving him an extra-large smile.

Bryn bared his clenched teeth, snarling some unintelligible curses through them. Then, gaze still locked on hers, he slowly and deliberately unfastened the brass buckle of his heavy leather belt.

Perhaps it was everything she'd been through up to that point: standing up to her father, thwarting his plans. Perhaps it was knowing her father didn't care about her, had never cared, in fact. Still, whatever the reason, the familiar sight of Bryn undoing his heavy leather belt resulted in Gwen having a very unfamiliar thought.

No. She wasn't going to let him use that belt on her. Not today.

Gwen steeled herself, hands to her side and clenched into fists.

"Are you sure that's a good idea, Father? Haven't you heard?" She gave him a quick, tight smile. "I'm a very dangerous young lady. I touch people, and they blister and burn. Touch them long enough and they'll die. My tears can melt skin like it wasn't even there. And... what else was there? Saliva! You know, it occurs to me I've never seen what my saliva can do. Let's find out!"

And with that, though it was not at all ladylike, Gwen took a step toward her belt-brandishing father, and she spit in his face.

There was only a tiny amount of spittle that actually managed to land on the king. It was perhaps the size of a head of a pin, hardly anything at all.

His reaction to that tiny little bit of saliva, however, was tremendous.

Dropping his belt, Bryn turned white as a sheet and reeled backwards as though struck, and a look of profound panic now replaced his mask of rage. He let out an urgent cry, sounding like a wounded bear trying to imitate a crow, and fell tumbling onto his back, pawing at his face with his hands.

Gwen retreated a step as she watched him roll over into a kneeling crouch and grab fistfuls of the fur-lined purple robe he wore, shoving the material into his face and rubbing vigourously. As he wiped his face, he spoke several muffled words she couldn't make out.

After several moments, Bryn's face emerged from the folds of his robe. His complexion seemed blotchy and red, though Gwen couldn't tell if her saliva had caused it, or if it was due to the frenzied rubbing of his face. A tight ball of tension knotted in her stomach.

The king got to his feet. His eyes were wide as he stared at her, and his fingers trembled.

"You crazy little wench!" he shouted in a voice laced with both anger and disbelief. "Do you know what you almost did? I'll tan your miserable, skinny hide! I'll beat you like a two-copper mule-skin, you—"

Gwen took a threatening step forward and cleared her throat noisily, pursing her lips as though preparing to spit at him again.

Blanching slightly, he hastily backed away from her. Then, almost tripping over his loose, half-draped robes, he stumbled backwards to the open doorway and quickly fled her chambers, throwing her one last hateful glare before disappearing into the dark recesses of the stairway.

There had been a touch of fear in that glare too, Gwen realized.

Trembling but exhilarated, she walked over to the heavy door and heaved on it until it slammed shut with a resounding thud. Then she sat down upon her bed and focused on breathing. Her heart thumped madly, and her ears roared. Everything took on an unreal sort of feeling.

She'd done it. She really, really had. There was no way for her father to use her like he'd originally intended.

And she'd stood up to him, even forced him to back down! Just the thought of it was enough to cause Gwen's breath to catch in her chest.

She sat there for a long time, considering what was likely going to happen next. Her father considered her nothing more than a tool, that much was obvious. She was probably in danger now that she'd thwarted him, which was equally obvious.

Still, her aggressive move had caught her father completely off guard. It was as though he hadn't ever considered her a threat before, or he hadn't really thought of her as dangerous, despite having intentionally made her this way.

Well, he certainly thought she was dangerous now. Maybe she wasn't in too bad shape after all.

The real question was what would he do now? His plans were in tatters, and there was no way he'd be able to marry her off to anyone once word of Prince Tremaine's experiences started circulating. Maybe this marked the end of her father's scheming.

After a couple of hours spent pondering the ramifications of her actions, she heard a muffled noise by her bedroom door, like something being slid onto the topmost step. Her dinner, probably brought up to her. Just as well; there was no way she'd risk a trip down to the dining hall tonight.

Gwen briefly considered just leaving it outside her door, but realized she wouldn't be able to for long. She was famished, and found herself craving that blue-green herb she knew had been sprinkled on whatever they'd brought her. Well, she'd had a very emotional day, and that sort of thing always played havoc with her appetite.

Sliding off her bed, she went over to the door and opened it, slowly.

Atop the step in front of her door was a medium-sized wooden box and blanket. Sitting inside of it was a small, floppy-eared brown puppy.

It seemed to perk up the instant it saw her, and its pink tongue lolled to one side as it panted up at her, an expression of eager curiosity lighting up its face. It regarded her with big, brown eyes and *wurfed* at her.

Gwen closed her eyes before her tears had a chance to turn everything blurry.

She carefully closed her bedroom door, doing her level best to ignore the faint whine she heard beyond it as she clicked it shut. That done, she focused on breathing deeply so she wouldn't start sobbing. She knew that if she started, she wouldn't be able to stop.

Her father's message was plain as day.

This wasn't over.

Chapter 8

Gwen spent the next couple of days laying low, and not drawing any attention to herself. In fact, she barely came out of her chambers at all, and spent most of her time in her tower, looking out the window nearest the meadow, waiting.

Late afternoon on the second day, she finally caught a glimpse of what she'd been waiting for.

She quickly stripped out of her dressing gown and threw on her riding clothes, slipped into her boots, tossed a grey cloak over her shoulders and ran out of her room and down the stairwell. Once at the bottom, Gwen flew down the second-floor hallway, down the stairs leading to the kitchen, and out the servant's entrance. Most of the castle staff who encountered her looked surprised or confused, but all of them hastily got out of her way.

Soon she was running down the path leading to the royal stables, her own pent-up anxiousness propelling her forward. When she was fifty yards or so away from the barn, she spied a familiar figure unsaddling a horse, and she nearly wept with relief.

"Rosie!" she cried, running even faster toward her friend.

Rhosyn's head turned and, upon seeing Gwen, she dropped the saddle she'd been holding and ran to meet Gwen, rushing over the uneven pasture nearly as quick as Gwen herself. When at last they met, they barely slowed down enough to prevent serious injury, hugging one another fiercely.

"Oh, Goddess! I… oh, shoot! Hold on a second," Gwen sniffed, pushing Rhosyn away from her long enough to wipe away her caustic tears with a sleeve. Then she wrapped her arms around Rhosyn and hugged her even more tightly than before. "Oh, how I've missed you, Rosie!"

"Hey, girl," Rhosyn said, her tone soft and sad. She extracted herself from the embrace of her friend and considered Gwen at arm's length. "Are you okay? I just got back; what's happened? Did anyone—"

"I did it, Rosie!" Gwen said with a hint of laughter that managed to cut through her tears. "I really did it! I figured a way around the enchantment, and sent the prince high-tailing it out of the kingdom!" She realized something and frowned. "I had to send him away on Juniper though, and we'll probably never get him back. I'm really sorry, but he's just one horse, and I couldn't risk letting Prince Tremaine anywhere near the castle after—"

"Whoa, whoa, hold on a sec," Rhosyn said, her eyes widening. "You *stopped* it? You got rid of the geis? Wait, of course you did, or you wouldn't even be able to talk about it! Well, what happened? Tell me everything!"

Gwen told Rhosyn as many details as she could remember, hurriedly bringing her friend up to speed. Rhosyn's jaw practically hit the ground during Gwen's retelling of her confrontation with the king.

"You spat at him?" she asked, amazement in her voice. "You spat at your father? Wow, look at you go! That's just… wow! And he hasn't come to see you since?"

"No, I haven't run into him at all. He hasn't come up to my chambers, and I've hardly left the tower these past few days. Things have definitely changed, now. Although," Gwen sent her friend a troubled look, "I'm not entirely sure what's going to happen next."

"Well, I'm sure that goes double for your father right about now. He's probably trying to figure out how he can salvage this whole situation as we speak," Rhosyn said, nodding thoughtfully. "You know, you might be in real danger, Gwen."

"I've been sort of thinking the same thing. But really, what can he do? I'm his only heir. And at the end of the day, no matter how angry or upset he gets, I'm still his daughter."

"Gwen, let's look at the facts. We both know he doesn't care about you. Just look what he was willing to put you through! He's the most despicable, evil man I know of, and that's just based on the things we know about! Imagine what sort of stuff he's done we don't know! I can't imagine the fact you're his daughter is going to make a lick of difference. If he can't try marrying you off to someone again, he'll try something else, find some way to use you as a weapon or otherwise ruin your life. Someone like him isn't simply going to let things lie."

"Yeah," said Gwen with a heavy sigh. "You're probably right. But if we don't even know what he's planning, how can we do anything to prevent it?"

Rhosyn's eyes seemed to light up, and a smile tugged at the corners of her mouth. "I brought you a present from Fort Pike."

"Hmm?"

"Uh-huh! I even wrapped it," she said, grinning hugely. "You're not going to believe it, either! C'mon, I'll show you!"

And with that, Rhosyn turned and bolted back in the direction of the stables. Gwen ran after her, feeling a little confused. They both came to a stop near the saddle Rhosyn had dropped in her haste to greet her friend.

"You know, you didn't need to get me anything, Rosie," Gwen said, watching as her friend hurriedly opened one of the saddlebags and dumped its contents onto the ground.

Rhosyn rooted through a few of the items that had tumbled out, then proceeded to dump the contents of her second saddlebag onto the grass as well. She appeared to locate the object she was looking for right away, grabbed it off of the pile, and then stood and held it out for Gwen to take.

The bundle was rectangular, and had been wrapped in a green and white scarf. Gwen looked a question at her friend as she accepted it.

"What is it?"

"Open it and find out, silly," Rhosyn laughed.

It only took a few seconds for Gwen to unwrap the scarf, revealing an ancient-looking and cracked leather journal. Its pages weren't trimmed particularly neatly, and some of the pages looked as though they might fall out. About a dozen coloured pieces of twine served as bookmarks here and there.

"Uhm, thanks?" Gwen said, inspecting the journal. "It certainly looks, well...old."

Rhosyn's smile got even bigger. "Two-hundred years old from what I've been able to gather. That stuff your father feeds you?" She nodded to indicate the book Gwen held. "It's a plant called *chi'darro*. There's even a drawing of it inside, information on how to find it, where it grows."

Gwen stared at her friend disbelievingly, then stared at what she held. She realized her mouth was hanging open.

"I think that book is where your dad got all his information. You won't believe how I came across it!" Rhosyn chuckled. "While the soldiers were getting settled at Fort Pike, I did some snooping around. It was just sitting there in the captain's room, in a small dust-covered bookshelf, right in the open! Your dad probably figured it would be safe there; Fort Pike doesn't even have a captain any more, and nobody goes in that room. Nothing there but a desk, a bookshelf, and some cobwebs. I'm guessing Calderia's fighting men aren't really big on reading. By sending me away, your father practically handed it to us!"

"Why would he do that though? Why send you to the same place he buried this information?"

She grinned. "Maybe your father doesn't remember allowing me to keep you company during your reading lessons, and figured

I can't read. Maybe he forgot it was even there. Or maybe he figured everything had already been arranged, so it wouldn't matter. Whatever the reason, I'm not going to object to the Goddess smiling upon us for once, are you?"

"Not at all! Oh, Rosie, thank you! This is huge! Now that we know what the herb's called—"

"We know a lot more than that, Gwen," Rhosyn said, her expression darkening. She indicated the journal with a quick nod. "I read as much as I could on horseback. Check the page bookmarked with the yellow string."

Gwen looked a question at her, then did as she was asked, thumbing through the pages until she found the page in question. The handwritten notes were in an ancient and foreign-looking cursive style, and appeared to continue on from the previous page.

—shovld be introdvced very gradvally to the system dvring early development, adding no more than a single speck of chi'darro, no greater than the size of a pinhead, for each pint of mare milk boiled. Regvlar application shovld commence at no earlier than two months, bvt before the age of six months for maximvm enzyme prodvction, and to ensvre no avtoimmvne complications. (see svbject 'Tsarina', page seven)

Furrowing her brow, Gwen looked up from the book. "Instructions? It sounds like they were testing on people. This must be what my father did to me as a baby!"

"They were creating a very special type of assassin, from what I've gathered. There's more, though," said Rhosyn, looking grim. "Read the next part."

Gwen did so, and within moments was staring down at the words in shock and disbelief.

"There was a 'better than half' chance I could have died?" Gwen turned to her friend, eyes wide. "He knew it could have killed me as a baby, and he did it anyway?"

"That is how little he cares about you, Gwen," Rhosyn said, angrily. "That's how badly he wanted this plan of his to work —the chance he was willing to take with your life, all so he could expand his kingdom. To him, you're nothing more than a tool." Her expression softened slightly. "I'm really worried, Gwen. I think you're in danger, like I said. A king who could do something like that to his own daughter might be capable of anything!"

Too stunned to reply, Gwen nodded mutely.

The two girls stood there in silence for a while.

"It's not all bad, though," Rhosyn said eventually. "The details were hard to find, but there were several spots in the book that mentioned a possible way to undo what was done to you."

"What? I can get rid of this curse? How? Tell me!"

"Okay, whoever wrote this journal used the words *in theory* whenever they talked about it, but it says eliminating the herb from your diet would stop these enzymes, whatever they are. So basically, if you stop eating the *chi'darro* regularly, your body will take care of the rest. They figured it would take about five days or so."

"You're kidding? That's all I've needed to do this whole time? I just stop eating that horrible-tasting stuff? For five days?"

"It's not quite that easy, Gwen." Rhosyn gestured to the open book again. "There was a whole section where they tried doing just that. It mentions that several girls volunteered to stop eating the herb so they could document what happened. They all went through withdrawal, and it sounded pretty awful from the descriptions. I guess it's sort of like when that one farrier your dad hired tried giving up fortified wine, except this sounds way worse." She frowned at Gwen. "All of the girls eventually decided to start eating their *chi'darro* again, and none of them lasted the full five days. Most of them didn't make three." Rhosyn looked troubled. "One of them actually died."

"I'll make it," Gwen said, setting her jaw. "I know I will. Goddess, five days from now! Oh, Rosie! Do you know how happy you've made me? This is the best present I could possibly imagine!"

"And I'll bet you didn't even get me anything!" Rhosyn teased, laughing. After a few moments she appeared confused, and looked a question at Gwen that was soon answered by the appearance of fresh tears. "Hey, don't you get like that on me, Gwen. Come on, this is fantastic news!"

"Oh, I know!" Gwen smiled, brushing away tears. "These are happy tears, believe me. Oh, Rosie, you're the greatest friend in the whole world!"

"Yeah, I am pretty terrific," Rhosyn said with a grin.

"Okay, so no more eating that stuff. Ever," said Gwen with a note of finality. "I've already had breakfast, but I skipped lunch today, so in theory I've already started. I've got service to attend at the chapel late this afternoon, but I'll spend the rest of the day going through this book, seeing if I can find out anything more."

"Just make sure you have a good hiding spot for it. I'm pretty sure if your father discovers you have that book, you lose your advantage, and things fall apart."

"I'll only need to keep it hidden for five days, Rosie," Gwen said solemnly. Then she gave Rhosyn a smile. "After that, I'll be throwing this bloody journal right in his face!"

Chapter 9

Gwen barely paid any attention at all to the vicar's soft-spoken words during service. She'd simply stood there the whole time, holding her fist-sized crystal, her mind racing through the details of Rhosyn's discovery.

A few familiar words caught Gwen's attention.

"—cherish life in every one of its forms, and do no harm to Her creations," the vicar proclaimed.

"Do no harm," she intoned dutifully, along with the dozens of other people who were attending service with her.

The crystal she held continued to glow brightly.

She noticed some of the newer staff watched her covertly as she handled her crystal, looking the slightest bit confused. Doubtless, if they believed the lies Anifail had been spreading about her, they wondered why her crystal glowed just as brightly as anyone else's, why she should still be considered worthy of receiving Eirene's divine blessing after all of the horrible things she'd allegedly done.

People believed what they wanted to, Gwen supposed.

It seemed so unfair that everyone appeared so willing to believe these things that were being said about her, despite the fact that she'd clearly been given the blessing of the Goddess, here in front of everyone. Rather than dwell upon the injustice of it all, Gwen simply stared straight ahead, recited the words that were required of her at the proper times, and focused on the reassuring glow of the crystal she held.

Once service was over, she placed her crystal in its usual spot on the altar and breathed a whispered prayer to Eirene, asking the Goddess for the strength and wisdom to make it through the next five days. That finished, she fled the chapel and headed towards the south castle entrance, intent on retreating to the privacy of her room as quickly as she possibly could.

Anifail was waiting for her at the bottom of her tower, looking smug and relaxed as usual.

"Oh, there's the young would-be assassin," he said, unfolding his crossed arms and regarding her with his familiarly half-lidded and unconcerned gaze. "So, our princess believes herself to be a spitting cobra now, does she? Goodness, such a clever little girl. And to think, it only took you seventeen years to figure that one out. You should feel proud. That's rather quick learning for someone of your limited abilities."

Gwen looked up at him, her expression defiant. She briefly toyed with the idea of making as if to touch his face, or perhaps clearing her throat as if to spit at him, but she quickly dismissed both notions. Anifail's whole manner suggested that he wanted her to try something, so no doubt he was prepared for just about anything she might do.

So, rather than do anything that might make her situation worse, she decided to ignore him entirely, moving to step around him and continue on up to her chambers.

Anifail's arm appeared before her, blocking her way to the stairwell.

"His Highness, your father, would like a few words with you over some supper," he murmured in a sleepy yet dangerous tone. "Sort of now-ish, in fact."

"Really? Well, how special," Gwen replied, witheringly. "Tell him I'll be with him shortly."

"Oh, I shan't have time to tell him anything of the sort, Princess, since you'll be turning yourself right around and heading straight for the dining hall this very minute."

She studied him. "And why would I do that, Captain? Because my father's special little errand-boy told me to?"

"Why, no," Anifail said, smiling at her. "I imagine you'll do it because of all the wonderfully delightful things I've been authorized to do in the event you refuse. I'd tell you all about them, but quite frankly I don't wish to spoil the surprise. Quite honestly, I'm rather hoping you decide to throw a hissy-fit, tell me off, and march upstairs to your bedroom. Is there any chance of that happening, Princess? Any chance at all?"

Gwen drew herself up and held his gaze as confidently as she could for about a five-count. Then she turned slowly around and walked unhurriedly in the direction of the dining hall. The sound of Anifail's quiet chuckling infuriated her, but she resolved not to outwardly react. She wouldn't give him the satisfaction.

Her walk to the dining hall was uneventful, though she did encounter several of the castle staff along the way. They still gave her wide-eyed, fearful looks and stayed well out of her way, most of them nodding deferentially to her as she walked by. Gwen had stopped trying to smile at them to put them at ease; no amount of smiling seemed to help. Instead, she just focused on keeping her face as impassive as possible, staring straight ahead as she navigated the castle halls.

She slowed down slightly as the dining hall entrance came into view, realizing that her shoulders were beginning to bunch up with anxiety and concern. This would be the first time her father had been in the same room as her since their encounter in her chambers, and he'd had lots of time to prepare. Gwen had no real clue what she could be walking into.

Taking a moment to adjust her gloves, she took a couple of slow, deep breaths, then pushed the doors open and stepped inside.

Bryn sat at his usual place at the head of the table, a veritable feast placed before him. There were all kinds of delicacies piled high around the king's chair, some which she'd never seen before, not even at the largest of the royal banquets she'd attended. It was easily more food than even her father would have been able to eat in an entire day.

Gwen noticed something else unusual, too: two armoured guards, both covered from head to toe, both wearing sinister-looking hoods that completely obscured their faces in shadow. They stood on either side of her father, gauntlets clutching shiny pikes that looked to be quite sharp and functional.

Here for his protection, she thought.

"There she is!" Bryn called out good-naturedly from his seat, arms held up and out as if to greet her. "There's my lovely daughter! Come, come, sit down and give me a hand with all this." He waved at the collection of prepared dishes, a few of which smelled so delicious they were making Gwen's mouth water. "After all, I shouldn't get all the fun, should I?"

She saw a place had been prepared for her halfway down the table. A silver-trimmed platter she'd never seen before, utensils, and a crystal goblet were located a good fifteen feet away from both the king and his feast.

Gwen frowned, trying to piece together what cruel jape he'd planned so she could prepare for it to some degree. Perhaps he would force her to eat a plate of gruel or something while he dined on these exotic dishes right in front of her. It had certainly been a while since he'd pulled that one.

Not really knowing what else to do, Gwen slowly walked over to the place that had been set for her, pulled the chair out a bit, and sat down daintily. Though she did her best to ignore it, she was very conscious of the odd smile her father gave her.

She regarded the shallow silver-trimmed plate before her. It seemed ill-suited to hold something runny like gruel.

"Now, which would you like first, Daughter? You've dozens of mouth-watering, savoury dishes from which to pick!" He laughed, waving a gesture over the expanse of food before him. "Why, there's so many I haven't even sampled them all yet, and I'm practically stuffed already!"

Gwen tried not to look perplexed. Her father seemed genuinely happy about something, which was certainly enough to rouse her suspicions. It might be best to sit and say nothing, let him talk. He'd never been a particularly patient man, and she knew he would eventually share the details of whatever new torture he'd devised for her.

Rather than answer her father Gwen simply sat there, hands folded in her lap.

"Oh come now," Bryn said, his chair squawking noisily as he stood up and away from the table, that unsettling smile still fixed firmly upon his face. "You must be starving! Surely there's something on this table that... wait, I know!" He pointed at a large copper stewing pot. "Honey-roasted boar with curried pineapple. That's your favourite, isn't it? Here, let me get a helping of that for my wonderful, wonderful daughter!"

And with that, the king himself side-stepped around the table until he was near enough to the stewing pot to ladle two servings of piping hot stew into two serving bowls. Carrying both awkwardly, he came around to her side of the table and placed one of the bowls gently in front of her. Then he gave her a deferential nod, chuckled good-naturedly, and headed back to his seat with his own bowl. His step looked jauntier than usual.

This was weird.

Curried pineapple was indeed her favourite, and although the aromas from it and the stewed boar were already causing her hunger pains to intensify, she made no move to even touch it. The fact he knew it was her favourite — that he actually remembered she loved this particular dish — seemed extremely suspicious.

That the king had actually served her, a smile on his face, made it doubly so.

Gwen was about to lift a spoonful of stew from her bowl when she realized she couldn't actually eat any of this. She'd very nearly forgotten she had already promised herself not to eat any more of that herb! Her favourite meal, served maybe once a year at best, and she wasn't going to be able to eat a single bite!

The timing of it just seemed so unfair. She stared down glumly at the bowl of stew in front of her. Then, she furrowed her brow and looked closer.

Not a single blue fleck of *chi'darro* anywhere.

Bright yellow pineapple chunks in a familiar, thick yellow cream sauce, with tantalizing hints of dark orange and pink, suggesting a generous amount of boar meat throughout. She poked through the contents of her bowl with a spoon, but failed to uncover a single trace of the herb her father usually sprinkled on every morsel of food she was served.

It had to be some sort of trick. Something wrong with this dish, perhaps.

Then again, Bryn himself had served it to her. If he'd poisoned her food and she died as a result, his crystal would go dark at the temple, and he'd be forced to abdicate the throne. Plus, he'd served himself a bowl of the same stew, with the same ladle, and it hadn't appeared he'd been keeping track of which bowl was which. She sent her father a confused look.

"Oh, come now. Try some!" Bryn said around a mouthful of the stew, looking both relaxed and amused.

After a few moments hesitation, she tasted a spoonful.

It was pure bliss. It seemed especially delicious to her just then, possibly because she hadn't eaten since breakfast. Of course, maybe it just tasted better when it didn't have that foul herb sprinkled all over it.

And why didn't it, exactly?

"Father? Why doesn't mine have any *ch*— uh, any of that blue stuff in it?"

Gwen breathed a silent prayer of thanks she'd stopped herself before referring to the herb by its actual name. That would have been a rather difficult thing to explain away.

Bryn put his spoon down and smiled at her. "Because it affects the taste, Daughter! We're sampling these dishes to figure out which ones are the tastiest. Oh, don't you worry, we can sprinkle on some seasoning for you later, once we've settled on which of these dishes we wish to serve our guests." He looked at a nearby plate and smiled an even bigger smile. "Ooh, a raspberry pistache! Want one of those? It may spoil your appetite, and there's so much more to try, but—"

"Guests?" Gwen looked at her father, and then the extravagant banquet before them, confused. "We're having guests tonight?"

"Oh, don't be silly, Gwenwyn!" Bryn leaned back in his chair and gave her a familiar, contemptuous look. "No, these are all just for us. I just thought you should sample some of these delicacies as well, to see if any meet with your approval. I'm sparing no expense! After all," he said, a triumphant glint appearing in his eyes, "this is your wedding feast we're talking about."

What?

Too stunned by his words to form any of her own, Gwen sat straight-backed in her chair, staring at the king with wide eyes.

Her reaction caused Bryn to chuckle. The chuckles soon became guffaws, and eventually transformed themselves into a hearty, booming laugh. Gwen couldn't recall ever seeing her father laugh this hard, not even the time when that elderly tinker had tried bowing to him and accidentally fallen into the castle moat.

"I know, isn't it wonderful?" he asked between laughs, slowly getting the better of his mirth. "My only daughter's getting married. And it couldn't have happened any more perfectly, either. I couldn't have planned it better!"

"Prince Tremaine?" Gwen asked, mystified. "But, why? Why would he come back? I showed him—"

"Oh, I'll admit, Daughter, you had me plenty upset when you found a way to warn that first prince," Bryn said, his hard tone suddenly at odds with the amused, jovial expression on his face. "I'd really had my hopes set on Bespir, and those iron mines. But no, I'm not talking about your sweetheart, Prince Tremaine."

"But then—"

"I did, however, receive a rather special visitor the day after Prince Tremaine left; a very out-of-breath messenger from Rhegar, who rode a full day and night on horseback just so he could deliver his message to me in time. You see, Gwenwyn, when word arrived in Rhegar that my own dearest daughter had been promised to wed the Prince of Bespir, King Alwyn of Rhegar sent me this note, written by his own hand," said Bryn, reaching to his left for what appeared to be an official-looking letter. He held it aloft for her to see, smiling at her. "He begged — *begged* — that I consider his proposal for an Affiliation Marriage with Rhegar instead!"

"What?" Gwen's stomach tightened. "But Tremaine was supposed to tell—"

"Oh, I'm sorry. You hoped your prince would carry word of your condition far and wide?" Brin snorted contemptuously. "Even if the first thing Prince Tremaine did upon his return was to hire messengers and send them to each of our neighbouring kingdoms, it would take weeks for the messages to arrive! And that's assuming they're able to get past the men I've hired to watch the roads for the next little while. Oh, I promise you, it will be quite some time before news of your encounter with him reaches the other kingdoms, more than enough time for what I have in mind."

Gwen could think of nothing to say to that. She sat there, staring at her father, feeling lost.

"And it's an even better fit than Bespir ever was! I'd been hoping for Rhegar. Bespir was my third choice!" he crowed. "But now, thanks to my dear, sweet daughter, we'll soon be united with Rhegar, instead of the dreary mining kingdom of Bespir! Calderia will have a coast!" Bryn's eyes got a faraway look. "A coast, and two bustling port cities. I can't even recall the last time I saw the ocean…."

"No!" Gwen whispered, only half-aware she'd actually spoken aloud.

"Oh, yes," Bryn said, smiling at her in a self-satisfied manner.

"And honestly, it's going to be so much easier now as well." He held up the letter again, like it was some sort of trophy. "King Alwyn wishes for the marriage between you and Prince Gavin to happen as soon as possible. I've already sent a missive agreeing to the date he's proposed, and I've been informed the prince will arrive mere days before the wedding. Much less time needed to maintain the subterfuge, and convince your suitor you're nothing more than a normal, sweet, innocent young girl. He doesn't even need to meet you first; I was assured in the letter Prince Gavin will do exactly as his father, the king, wishes in this regard." His smile widened. "He'll be marrying you sight-unseen. Which means there'll be even less of a chance for you to interfere with my plans this time around."

Gwen said nothing, and merely stared down at her rapidly cooling bowl of curried pineapple, wondering where her appetite had gone.

"Oh, and there's one last thing, Gwenwyn. I'd especially like to thank you, Daughter," Bryn said, somehow making his self-assured grin even wider as he regarded her. He folded his hands over his stomach and leaned back in his chair, the very picture of relaxed contentment. "Thank you so much for telling me about those little tricks you managed to figure out, those loopholes in the geis you discovered. Touching flowers, reciting fairy tales, all of it. Very informative. I thought I'd covered all the possible ways you could get around the compulsion, but obviously there were a couple I hadn't considered. I'll be making sure the next geis sphere I arrange for you doesn't allow for any of those possibilities."

He wanted to upset her, she realized, to intimidate her. That was the whole reason for this visit. He was re-asserting his control. That's why the guards with the hoods were here, to intervene should she become upset enough to spit at him again, or attempt to touch him. He wanted to show her he still held all the cards, and perhaps break what remained of her spirit.

Gwen just sat there, staring off at nothing.

But he hadn't won. There was still one thin strand of hope Gwen was desperately clinging to. She knew about *chi'darro* now, knew how its effects might be undone. Five days without it, and she might no longer be this way, no longer a deadly weapon wielded by her father. In five days time, she could be watching all his plans unravel like a poorly woven blanket.

She'd save this Prince Gavin from her father. Then, perhaps, the prince might be able to save her.

For now, though, she had to let him believe he'd won.

Raising her head slightly, she gave Bryn a cold, impassive stare from where she sat. Then, after a few moments of that, she moved to rise from her chair.

The two guards instantly moved forward, placing themselves between Gwen and where the smiling king sat.

Gwen picked up her bowl. Glaring first at the two guards, and then her father, she walked slowly and deliberately down the length of the table, stopping once she was within reach of the stewing pot. Her hand trembled slightly as she lifted the ladle and spooned two additional helpings of boar with curried pineapple into her bowl, all under the watchful eyes of the two armoured guards.

Then, stopping only to pluck a silver spoon from her place-setting, she walked away from the dining table and headed towards the hallway doors.

"Well then," Bryn called loudly from his seat, laughter in his voice, "that's it, is it? You don't find any of these other dishes to your liking? Well, no matter. I'll pick out the rest of the feast myself. I'll be sure to inform the cook he's to prepare a generous amount of curried pineapple, of course."

His tone was mocking, and she could picture the triumphant look on his face. A part of her desperately wanted to spin around and hurl curses at him, but she held herself in check. Whenever she spoke to him in anger, she always ended up giving away information she didn't intend, and she had no wish for him to learn of her most recent discovery. Not yet.

Five days from now, however....

Gwen kept walking, her father's voice following behind her.

"Yes, you may be excused, I suppose. Obviously you'll soon be busy getting fitted for dresses, picking out decorations with your lady-in-waiting, all of that exciting stuff." She heard him laugh. "I'll have some seasoned food sent up to you once I've finished sampling all of these wonderful, wonderful dishes."

Gwen pushed the door open and walked into the hallway, leaving the king and his escort behind. She drew a couple of deep breaths, forced herself to relax, and then headed down the hallway in the direction of her bedchamber.

It would be important to keep up appearances these next several days. In a way, it was a lucky thing her father had wanted her upset, because it gave her an excuse to hole up in her tower, away from him and anyone who might report to him. Her meals would be brought to her chamber, she knew, which meant all she needed to do was get rid of the food and leave empty plates. With a little luck, she could stay up in her room for the whole five day ordeal, and no-one would be the wiser.

She had to do this right. Five days without eating the herb, and she couldn't let anyone figure out what she was doing.

Clutching her bowl of stew close to her chest, she picked up her pace a bit as she walked down the hall, suddenly very eager to reach her quarters.

Chapter 10

Getting through the whole night without eating any *chi'darro* was a hell unlike anything Gwen had ever known.

Gwen found herself shaking for no good reason. Her thoughts kept returning to the plate of lamb that had been brought up for her a few hours after she'd left her father in the dining hall. Figuring to hide it somewhere until she could safely dispose of it later that evening, she'd brought it into her room, dumped the food into an old, empty jewelry box in her closet, then left the empty plate on the stone steps just outside of her bedroom door.

Then, for the next hour, it seemed as though she couldn't think of anything but that cold chunk of lamb meat and serving of roasted potatoes, just sitting there in the bottom of her closet. No matter how she tried to distract herself, she'd find her thoughts wandering to the herb-covered food just waiting for her, less than four short strides from her bed.

Finally, able to stand it no longer, she'd gone to her closet, fetched her jewelry-box, and thrown it out of her bedroom window.

She watched the wooden case fall just shy of the moat, hitting the hard-packed ground heavily enough to break open slightly. Squinting, Gwen thought she could make out one of the potatoes.

Shortly after disposing of it, she'd stared down at the small, broken box longingly for nearly ten minutes before realizing that's what she was doing.

Chiding herself for an idiot, Gwen returned to her bed, took a deep breath... and began thinking about the tiny flecks of blue-green herb still clinging to the surface of the empty plate that lay just outside her door.

It took all of her will to keep herself from even opening her bedroom door to check the plate. Sometimes, she'd tried convincing herself she was just going to take a peek, so she could make sure it had been taken away by the castle staff. Deep down, however, she knew the real reason why she was tempted to open the door. It was those tiny flecks of herb, just sitting there.

And so she'd forced herself to lie there on her bed, staring at the ceiling, trying like mad to think of *anything* besides how badly she wanted to kick her bedroom door open, pick up her plate and lick it clean.

When she finally heard one of the servants creep upstairs and quietly take her plate away, she'd wept, but only partially from relief.

Though exhausted, it seemed she could sleep no more than five minutes at a time, because every time she dozed off she would have such intense, nausea-inducing nightmares that she'd be jolted awake, her heart racing. Grotesque, misshapen monsters would appear from the shadowy recesses of her mind and chase her, calling her by name, laughing. Some would transform into a wolfish likeness of Anifail, snarling and bristling. Others would simply collapse before her and start smoking and bubbling, crying out in pain. Sometimes they turned into people she'd accidentally hurt during her childhood. Other times, they became enormous, whimpering dogs, looking at her with desperate, pleading brown eyes as they smoldered and burned.

That had been Gwen's first whole night without *chi'darro*, and it had been hell.

The following morning was even worse.

Bleary-eyed, Gwen staggered out of bed, feeling so weak and dizzy that she began to wonder if she'd caught some sort of cold the day before. She realized she'd lost track of time and had forgotten to wash herself last night, which was when she had originally planned to discretely dispose of the food that had been brought for her. Then again, impulsively tossing her food out the window had eliminated the need for that trip, she supposed.

In addition to feeling terrible, she noticed her neck was swollen slightly, and that she'd developed a strangely patterned rash high up on her arms, near the shoulders.

It took nearly an hour for her to get dressed. At first she suspected something had been done to her clothing, because whenever she tried something on, it seemed to hurt. She even found her finely woven silk blouse scratchy and bothersome against her bare skin.

Eventually she descended the stairs of her bedchamber tower, slowly and carefully, her legs trembling almost as badly as a newborn colt's. Once she was safely down the stairs, Gwen made her way to the kitchen and informed the cook in an unsteady voice that she would like her breakfast sent up to her, due to the fact she was feeling sick.

The expression on the cook's face made it clear he required no convincing of this fact. He practically shooed her out of the kitchen with a half-loaf of rye bread and a cup of warm cream and honey, which he assured her would calm her stomach if it was giving her problems.

Grateful for the fact that the cook had neglected to sprinkle either item with any herb, she accepted the proffered food, thanked him wearily, and began the impossibly long journey back to her bedchamber.

Her legs cramped several times as she ascended the stairs to her room, forcing her to stop periodically. By the time she reached her bedroom door, she found herself out of breath and fighting to stay awake. Every part of her just wanted to lie down and rest.

Gwen stumbled inside her room, almost spilling the contents of her cup while attempting to perch it and the rye loaf on a nearby stool. Then, bread and honey-cream forgotten, she fell into her bed. This time, unlike the previous evening, she was asleep the moment her head touched the pillow.

And then her nightmares began anew, though stronger and more vivid than the ones from before. Each new dreamscape that popped into her head provided her with fresh horrors dredged from her imagination, impossible to ignore.

Huge spiders with crowns atop their brow chittered at her from the darkness of a dungeon cell, their mandibles salivating, their legs twitching with eager anticipation. Dire wolves with hollow, bleeding eyes rushed at her from a copse of trees near the apple yard, snarling, and yelping, and frothing black tar from their mouths. Half-remembered toys and comfort dolls from her childhood playroom fell apart or began bleeding at her touch, shrieking for her to stop. Sad, mournful folk regarded her in the labyrinthine hallways of a dark, sinister castle, each of them holding up a mirror that Gwen found herself unable to look into for too long. Her reflections were always corpse-like, or snake-like, or some other foul horror to behold.

In one mirror, she appeared as a likeness of her father.

Her troubled sleep was deep as well, and when the sights and sounds of her night terrors were finally enough to jolt her out of her slumber, it seemed a comparative mercy. She lay there in bed for a long time after, trembling uncontrollably and gasping for breath.

After a while Gwen slowly rose from her bed, her every muscle taut and sore, and she went to the window to try and gauge the time. According to the sun, it was still only mid-morning.

One full day down, four to go.

When she opened her bedroom door, Gwen discovered that a more substantial plate of breakfast had been left outside of it. There were poached eggs, a thick slice of ham, and a small wedge of yellow cheese, each of which had been dutifully covered with a small sprinkling of a familiar blue-green herb.

She stood at her open door for a long, long time staring at the plate and its contents. Just the thought of being that close to the stuff stirred feelings of anxiety and dread. It felt to her as though getting too near her plate would result in her being unable to control herself.

It was nearly five full minutes before she mustered up the courage to kick the plate and its contents over, sending them tumbling down into the darkness of the stairwell. Almost immediately she regretted her decision, since word of what she'd done might get back to her father, and she didn't wish him to become suspicious during her ordeal.

Kicking her food down the stairwell might be brushed off as a childish tantrum or something of that sort, which her father would likely interpret as sulking, so she'd probably be okay. Still, she resolved to make sure her *next* meal was disposed of properly. Like she'd planned.

Closing her bedroom door, Gwen spied the food the cook had provided her with earlier, sitting there on a nearby stool. Realizing she was ravenous, she devoured the honey-cream and rye with wolfish abandon, though it seemed to taste far more bland and stale than it aught to have, especially with her being so hungry. Regardless, she finished it quicker than she'd thought possible, and prayed it would settle her roiling stomach as the cook had suggested it might.

An hour later, she was practically hanging out of her bedroom window, retching noisily, clutching either side of the stone window frame for balance.

She was there for a good fifteen minutes or so, alternating between being sick and taking huge gulps of air. When the intense nausea finally did pass, Gwen stumbled back to her bed and sat down, staring at nothing. The room was spinning a little, and dark spots appeared around the edges of her vision from time to time.

Hunger no longer troubled her stomach, but her abdomen felt tight and cramped. Her throat burned, and she was parched.

Her water jug was very nearly empty, she noticed. That was odd. She'd filled it last night, and couldn't remember drinking from it recently.

Gwen picked up the jug and, walking with slow, careful steps, she opened her bedroom door and headed back down to the kitchen.

Somehow, this trip took even longer than it had earlier that morning. Though her legs were still shaky, she managed to haul the now-full jug, another loaf of bread, and a wedge of hard cheese up the stairs and back up to her room. While the very notion of eating was repugnant to her right now, gathering untreated provisions for later seemed like a good idea.

Once she'd wrapped the food in a blanket and hidden it in her closet, she hobbled back over to her bed and sat down, smoothed her dress against her legs, sighed lightly… and then burst into tears.

She didn't even know why she was crying exactly, but she couldn't seem to stop. It just felt like her entire world had suddenly transformed itself into an empty void — a vast expanse of bleakness and despair. She cried harder than she could remember ever crying before, and by the time she managed to stop she discovered her throat was once again parched, and the inside of her mouth had gone bone dry.

Gwen drank almost half of the jug of water she'd brought upstairs with her. Then she decided to lay down on her bed and attempt to relax, perhaps stare up at the ceiling a while and just focus on breathing and calming herself. She inhaled a deep breath of air through her nose, and then another….

And suddenly, it was late evening. Her entire room was dark.

Perplexed, Gwen sat up in her bed, or tried to. Her arms felt shaky, and didn't appear to be up to the task of propping her up. Groaning, she rolled herself to one side of her bed and lowered her feet to the floor, doing her best to ignore the cramps that had taken up residence in her calves and thighs, as well as the terrible itching sensation she felt around her shoulders and upper arms.

She hadn't slept, had she? It certainly didn't *feel* like she'd slept, that was for sure. Her eyes felt dry and scratchy.

After a few moments spent trying to steady herself and remain upright, she lit a lamp atop her dresser and then shuffled over to her door, feeling about a hundred years old. When she opened the door, she spied a bowl of stew and a small, buttered dinner bun sitting on the top stair. The stew had gone cold long ago, and looked slightly greasy.

The smell of *chi'darro* and stew hit her without warning, and her stomach lurched unpleasantly. Gwen couldn't tell if the smell was making her hungry or ill, but regardless, she covered her mouth and nose with her hand and hastily retreated away from the door.

About a minute later, she found herself retching out of her window once more. Thankfully, it appeared there was nothing left for her stomach to get rid of this time.

When Gwen came away from the window, her abdominal muscles were hurting quite a lot, especially when she tried to stand up straight. Hunched over, she walked back over to her open door and silently considered the bowl of stew, still half-covering her mouth and nose. A short while later she was rooting through her closet for some dress or other outfit she'd grown out of — one that might not be missed. When she found one, she brought it to the doorway, threw it over the bowl, gathered everything up into a bundle, and then dashed over to the windowsill and shoved the whole thing, dress, stew and all, out into the night air.

She couldn't see what happened to the clay bowl, but she could hear it crack and break apart as it careened off of the stone of the castle wall and fell to the ground below. That one *definitely* came short of the moat, she realized, and it was too dark to see where it ended up. Still, not many people walked the area between the wall and the moat, so it probably wouldn't be noticed.

A missing bowl might be noticed, however.

Gwen cursed quietly under her breath. Why had she done it like that? She wasn't being very smart about this at all! At the time it seemed like the most important thing was to get the food out of her room as quickly as possible, and she'd panicked. Why was the mere *thought* of that herb making her so anxious all of a sudden?

Well, she should probably try to relax, possibly even try to sleep some more. It certainly felt like she needed it.

Despite once again being exhausted, most of her evening was spent tossing and turning. She couldn't get comfortable, and the itch that had started high on her shoulders was now bothering her lower back and legs. Any time she felt like she was about to drift off, she'd suddenly feel like she couldn't breathe, and would sit up in her bed, gasping for air.

At some point in the pre-dawn hours, Gwen was possessed by a feeling of terror and dread that practically suffocated her, and the strangest thought forced itself into her head.

She needed honey. Or black-current jam. Now. Or bad things would happen.

Heedless of how her limbs felt, Gwen got out of bed, threw open her door and raced down the stairs, taking them two at a time. Her heart was pounding in her chest, and she felt mere inches away from death.

Halfway down the stairs, she realized she'd suddenly forgotten her reason for leaving her bedroom in the first place. The urgent feeling had disappeared just as quickly as it had arrived.

Confused, and more than a little afraid of what was happening to her, she climbed back up the stairs with agonizing slowness and returned to her room.

Her brief sprint and sudden anxiousness made her even more tired than she already was, and she found herself unable to make it all the way to her bed, collapsing to the floor beside the door instead. Her heart, though racing mere moments ago, now felt as though it were barely beating at all.

She was deep asleep before she'd even finished moving.

If possible, the nightmares were even stronger this time around, with everything appearing bigger, moving faster, scenes rapidly shifting from place to place, disorienting her. For hours and hours she was eaten alive, cut into pieces, burned to cinders, and drowned. Eyes stared at her, and snarling lips pulled themselves back to reveal far too many rows of sharp, gleaming teeth. A pair of bright yellow vipers had somehow found a way inside her chest, and were desperately throwing themselves in every possible direction, trying to get out.

A loud knocking noise at her door jolted Gwen awake, and she could hear a young girl's fearful voice calling to her. She noticed it was morning.

She also noticed a dragon made entirely of shadows lurking by her dresser, and spiders the size of her hand roamed the stone walls of her bedroom.

Her nightmares had followed her into the real world.

The knock at her door came again, more insistently this time, and Gwen could make out the words 'feeling okay?'

Ignoring the shadow-dragon, which was now hissing at her and bleeding liquid fire out of both eyes, Gwen opened her mouth and tried to yell the words 'I'm fine, thank you.' A hoarse, apologetic wheeze was all that came out. She coughed several times before trying again, and heard herself half-scream the word 'fine!' at the door, her voice sounding more like a raven's than a young girl's.

She had to keep control, she realized. This was all just part of what was happening to her — just momentary torment she'd have to endure for a couple of days more. Rising slowly to her hands and knees from her spot on the cold floor, perspiration beading her brow and upper lip, Gwen forced herself to ignore the nightmarish apparitions in her bedroom and focus her thoughts.

It was morning, she figured, so the girl at the door had probably been bringing her breakfast. If that was the case, she needed to get rid of it.

Gwen half-crawled over to the door and reached up, gritting her teeth and doing her level best to ignore the fact that her ornate door handle was now a mass of writhing snakes. She grabbed it, twisted her wrist, and slowly pulled the door open.

A bowl of porridge sat there, roaches and other armoured bugs crawling all over it, chittering noisily. Beside it was a glass of bubbling blood.

That wasn't real, Gwen told herself. She'd been brought her breakfast, that was all. It wasn't a glass of blood, and those weren't bugs.

She steeled herself and reached out to take the shallow bowl in both hands, but when she did it felt like she couldn't close her hands all the way, like her fingers had fallen asleep. Still on her knees, she tried several times to pick up the bowl, doing her best to keep from getting upset or frustrated at how impossible that simple task seemed to her all of a sudden.

Eventually she opted to slide the bowl along the floor and into her bedroom. She made it almost five feet inside before the bottom of the bowl caught a groove in a rough bit of stone and sloshed half its contents onto the floor. Dozens of shiny black newts erupted from the slopped porridge and quickly scurried in all directions.

Gwen was too tired to be upset. She could deal with the mess later. Right now she was seeing things from her nightmares, so attempting to clean things up was kind of pointless anyway. The porridge was no longer outside her bedroom door, and she hadn't eaten any. That's what was important.

With agonizing slowness she crawled over to her bedside, pulling the sheets right off of her mattress so she might have something to wrap herself in. She did so, collapsed to the floor, and instantly began to shiver.

Her bedroom door was still open, she noticed, but she was suddenly too tired to care.

It didn't much matter if she kept her eyes opened or closed, the nightmarish things danced around before her regardless. She lay there, musing quietly that being exhausted actually seemed to be reasonable protection against things like nightmares. It was hard to become anxious about snakes and wolves and dragons if you were too tired to be properly scared of them.

Hours passed this way, her passively watching the horrific, macabre sights that were being offered up by her imagination. After a while, she realized she could hear some of the apparitions as well. One of them made a sound exactly like a girl's scream.

Eventually, she thought she could make out a gruff, angry voice spitting curses. She caught the word 'porridge', and another word that sounded like 'mess'.

Rough leather talons gripped her skin through the blanket and rolled her over, and Gwen tried to cry out. Now on her back, she opened her eyes halfway and blearily looked around her room.

It was dark. A marmot the size of a large dog was by the door, trembling. Standing above her was a sinister-looking black lion, with curls of fur poking out at odd angles, a tarnished crown perched crookedly on its brow.

Her father, she realized.

Gwen quickly tried to smile and say she was just feeling a little ill, but her voice didn't want to cooperate.

Eyes widening, the black lion turned into a growling bear, who then reached down and pulled away a corner of her toasty warm blanket. Immediately, a horde of spiders made up of ice and snow skittered over the stone floor and began biting her arm, the icy chill of their venom making her cry out in fear.

"Goddess! Her arms!" she heard her father's voice gasp. "*You!* Fetch Captain Anifail, at once!"

The marmot bowed and scurried away.

Cursing and muttering under its breath, the black bear wrapped the rest of the blanket around her and picked her up with its gloved paws, depositing her roughly atop her bed. It looked at the porridge on the floor, and then back to her.

"What in the name of the seven hells did you think you were doing?" her father's voice roared.

Gwen protested weakly, and tried to say she was fine… but she couldn't tell how successful her attempts were. Really, she just wanted to sleep… that's all she wanted to do right now. Sleep and rest.

She felt a hard slap across her face.

"No you *don't!*" Her father's voice snarled. "*Anifail!*"

"Highness?"

"The brat hasn't been eating — she's got that rash on her arms again! My study, desk drawer, bottom-left side! A leather pouch with red string around the top. Run!"

Gwen tried to shake her head, and managed a small whimper of objection. Then, she realized she was being shaken, and an angry voice was screaming at her to stay awake.

Before she knew it, rough hands were forcing Gwen's jaw open, and gloved fingers hooked into the corner of her mouth and pulled it to one side. A familiarly bitter, chalky taste flooded her senses, and she suddenly realized what it was they were putting in her cheek.

Urgently, she began thrashing around, biting at fingers, attempting to spit as much of the *chi'darro* out as she could. She heard a short hiss of surprise, and then a short time later, she heard the sound of a man screaming through violently clenched teeth. It sounded a lot like Anifail.

"Hold her still! We've got to get her to eat some of it!" her father shouted.

Cool water was poured onto her lips and face, and she suddenly found herself choking and gasping for breath, involuntarily swallowing some of the liquid that had been poured inside her cheek. Within moments there was a warmth in her stomach that began spreading up to her shoulders, and then slowly out to the rest of her.

The nightmarish visions slowly began to recede.

She'd failed.

"Okay. That should be enough," her father muttered. Then he turned his attention on her, looming over her as she lay on her bed, his face a mask of fury. "What in the name of all the gods did you think you were *doing*, Gwenwyn? You could have died, you *stupid, stupid girl!*"

A soft, agony-filled hissing through clenched teeth could be heard coming from her doorway. Bryn looked off to one side, and his brow furrowed.

"Right. Captain, let's go have a look at that hand. I've got something in my study that'll take the edge off, speed up the healing. You! Guards! Nobody in or out of here until I give the order. Got it?"

Without even sparing her a glance, the king left her bedside and exited the room.

The warm feeling she felt in her chest was growing stronger, and a euphoric bliss seemed to envelope her, promising happiness and warmth and safety.

Despite this pervasive sense of well-being, Gwen turned over onto her side and began weeping softly into her pillow.

Chapter 11

"You look awful, Gwen!" said Rhosyn in a hushed voice as the two of them walked down the meadow path. "Was it really that bad?"

"Worse," Gwen croaked. She'd started feeling a lot better these past few days, but her voice was still rather awful-sounding, and her throat burned and itched. "You should have seen what I looked like just two days ago."

Rhosyn considered her friend carefully, then glanced down the trail behind them to ensure the two hooded guards weren't within earshot. Then she gave her head a tilt and leaned in closer.

"So, you're escorted everywhere now?" she asked, her voice a mere whisper.

"Anytime I want to leave the castle, yeah. It was that, or I wasn't even going to be able to come out here and visit you."

"Can you try again?" she asked. "You know, giving up eating that stuff?"

"No," Gwen sighed. "My meals are supervised now, and the kitchen staff have all been warned that I'll get sick again without my 'medicine'. And honestly, I'm not even sure I could do it again. Even if I had lots of help and support, I don't know if I could put myself through that a second time. It was pretty awful. I felt like I was dying."

"I wish I hadn't found that book," Rhosyn said, scowling slightly. "It wasn't fair to raise your hopes like that."

"Nonsense, Rosie. You were looking for a cure, the same as me. Not your fault that this one didn't work. Besides, finding that journal is still a blessing." Gwen glanced at the two guards, and then spoke to Rhosyn in a hushed whisper. "I've been thinking a lot these past few days. We know what this herb looks like, right? From the drawings in that book?"

"Right," Rhosyn agreed.

"And more importantly, we now know where it grows, too. I've checked some of these notes, and looked up some of the places on the big map in the library. Nearest is less than a week away, by horseback. They're far, but not too far."

"Not too far for what, exactly?"

"I could run away!" she said in an excited whisper. "If I do need to continue eating that stuff, I could just pack some things and sneak off to where it grows!"

"You mean 'we', don't you?"

"What? Rosie, I can't ask you to give up your life here," said Gwen, shaking her head. "You've got the horses! You have a *boyfriend*, and I just couldn't stand it if-"

"You mean Darin?" Rhosyn's eyes went hard. "I don't think I'd exactly call him my 'boyfriend' at the moment."

"What do you mean?"

"I think he's trying to gather information from me," she said, her tone becoming cold. "The night I got back, shortly after I gave you the journal, he showed up at my place. He brought dinner with him in a picnic basket, asked me how my trip was."

Gwen gave her friend an odd look. "But why would that make you think-"

"Gwen, Anifail didn't give me a chance to tell anyone I'd left. At first I thought that maybe you'd told Darin so he wouldn't worry, but you've never actually met him! And even if you had, how would you have been able to tell him while under the effect of the geis sphere?"

"Hey, and how did he know precisely when you had returned from your trip?" Gwen asked, frowning. "That does sound kind of odd, now that you mention it."

"Exactly. So I asked him how he'd found out I was gone to begin with. He just sorta shrugged it off, said that some friend must have told him. After that, I started paying attention to some of the things he was asking me. He wanted me to elaborate on my duties as your lady-in-waiting, and tried to get me to talk about our friendship."

"But why?"

"Gwen, I'm the only friend you have. Do you seriously think a certain *someone* wouldn't try to take advantage of that?"

"You think he's trying to find out stuff for my father?" Gwen asked, heart sinking.

"I'm positive. I followed him for a while when he left that night. He headed towards town at first, but when he figured he was far enough from my place, he headed straight for the castle." Rhosyn twirled a stray lock of hair unhappily. "So yeah, there isn't exactly anything keeping me here. 'We' could run away from this place. You go, I go."

"Oh Rosie, I'm so sorry! I know how much you liked him." Gwen pursed her lips and considered. "If you want, we can come up with a list of things to call him when you're breaking up with him. Actually, I should see if I could get him locked up or something! That might be fun."

"Break up with him? Gwen, why would I do something like that?" Rhosyn asked with a smirk.

"Because he's *using* you, Rosie! That's a horrible thing to do!"

"So? Let's use him right back! If he reports to the king, we can feed him any sort of lies we want! If I simply got rid of him, your father will probably just look for some other way to find out what's going on. A way we may *not* know about."

"Ooo, that's a good idea! If my dad thinks everything's okay, we'll have an easier time slipping away when it's time to leave!"

"Exactly," smiled Rhosyn, though her expression was the slightest bit wistful and sad.

Gwen didn't really know what to say to her friend, or how to ease her obvious pain. She knew how excited Rhosyn had been when she'd first met Darin — finding out something like this had to be killing her.

They walked in silence, the only sounds coming from the clunky armour of the two hooded guards dutifully following a dozen or so paces behind them. Eventually, Rhosyn cleared her throat, looking a bit troubled.

"There's only one problem I can see with this 'running away' plan. It's a pretty big one though." She gave Gwen a significant look. "You told me yourself that you started hallucinating and getting sick after missing only a couple of days of eating that herb. There's no way you'd make it through a week of horseback riding without the stuff, is there? And if your father's the only one who has it, then how exactly... uh—"

Rhosyn stopped talking entirely, and considered the smile Gwen was giving her.

"Royal study, bottom left drawer of his desk. A leather pouch tied with red cord. That's where he keeps it." Gwen gave her friend a sidelong grin. "That's the one good thing that came from everything that happened. Dad saw me, figured out what I was doing, called for Anifail, and got him to fetch a whole bag of the stuff. Mentioned exactly where he could find it, right in front of me. I don't know if it's his whole supply, but even a small pouch should be enough until I can locate some more."

"He just mentioned it in front of you? Well then, he's probably moved it somewhere else by now."

"I don't think so. He probably thinks I was too out of it to have heard him say it. Mind you, he probably wasn't that far off the mark — I was seeing spiders on the walls at that point, and could barely stay awake. And even if he suspects I heard him, he's way more worried that I'm trying to *avoid* eating that stuff right now. I doubt he's too concerned I might go and steal a bunch of it for myself."

"Hmm. True," Rhosyn agreed.

"Plus, he's got a lot on his mind. The wedding is happening in just a couple weeks time, and he's been working hard to get everything ready, so he's got to be juggling a lot of torches right now. A stash of herbs he's got hidden in his study is probably the furthest thing from his thoughts."

"So if it's in the study, how are you going to get it?"

"I'm trying to figure that out myself, but the important thing is that we've got to be ready to go once I've found a way to grab it. I can't just grab it now, because he'd notice it's missing. We'll need supplies readied first. Money, clothes, tack, things like that. I should be able to get my hands on some silver, as well as a few other things we can bring along and sell later. However, if I were seen carrying saddlebags or provisions or anything suspicious like that, word would definitely get back to the king."

"I'll come up with a list, and start gathering some things," Rhosyn said, nodding slowly. "You've never been on a trek like this before, but I just spent a whole week on horseback, and know just about everything we're going to need for a trip like this. In fact, I'm still mostly packed from that last trip."

"Okay, so you be sure to let me know if there's stuff you need that you don't have, or can't get access to. In a pinch, I should be able to find a way to smuggle what we need out of the castle. Out my window might work, depending on how fragile it is, though we'd probably have to coordinate a time or—"

"Ah, *there* you are!" a familiar, cocky voice announced from somewhere behind them.

Both of the girls stopped walking and turned to face Anifail, who was now standing directly between their two armoured escorts, not twenty feet away. The expression on his face was as self-satisfied as his tone had been.

"You know, I wasn't entirely sure I'd find you out here, Princess," he said with a smile. "I mean, after all, you have so *many* friends and acquaintances that when it came time to look for you, I scarcely knew where to begin! Stroke of luck, finding you in the very first place I thought to try. I could have been wandering for days, knocking on doors, asking all your *other* friends if they'd seen you, or if—"

"How's the hand, Captain?" Gwen inquired sweetly.

Anifail's calm, easygoing smile fell away at that, and though he tried to keep his expression neutral, he wasn't entirely able to keep his lip from pulling into a sneer. The muscles in his jaw clenched slightly, and Gwen noticed his right hand come up and touch the heavy bandage wrapped around his other hand.

The burn she'd given him was probably still very painful. Gwen briefly wondered if enjoying that fact made her a bad person.

"Lunch is being served, Princess. Supervised, of course, to ensure you don't cause any more careless accidents of this nature," he said, motioning with his bandaged hand. "I do appreciate your concern. It was quite painful, actually, and the pain has lingered for the past couple days. But then I spoke with your father about what would be happening these next few weeks, and some of the things we ended up discussing, well...." He gave her a wolfish grin. "I find it hurts much, much less now."

Gwen was unsure exactly what it was he was talking about, but it sounded fairly ominous.

"Well, if you find it's still bothering you, I'm sure she'd be more than happy to kiss it better, Captain," Rhosyn said in almost the exact same, sweet voice Gwen had used.

Anifail smiled patiently at that, and then turned and waved a gesture behind him, indicating the path leading back to the castle. "If you would please come along with me, Princess? I suspect your lunch is getting cold."

Gwen gave Anifail a flat stare, then turned to Rhosyn. The girls embraced one another, briefly.

"We start getting ready tonight," whispered Gwen. "Right away."

"Your window, every midnight. Drop a note, or whatever you need smuggled out," Rhosyn whispered back.

"I will. Be careful."

"You too."

And with that, Gwen turned away from her friend and began walking towards Anifail and her two watchdogs. She barely even acknowledged the three men as she walked past them, heading for the castle.

It'd probably only take a couple of days to gather the necessary things, she mused, at which point they could be off and rid of her father for good. That meant hatching a plan for how she was going to get into his study, and fast. Everything hinged on her getting access to that pouch. Once that was done, they could pretty much leave right away. She'd be free, and her father's plans would be in ruins.

Out of the corner of her eye, she noticed something in Anifail's expression, a kind of cheerful malice that was different than usual.

It made Gwen suddenly wonder if it was already too late.

Chapter 12

That first night, at midnight, Gwen hadn't been able to drop anything but a hastily scrawled note out her window for Rhosyn.

"Well," Gwen murmured quietly to herself, looking over the collection of things spread over her bedsheet, "I'm certainly making up for it tonight."

It had been harder than she'd thought, preparing for a one-way journey like this one. The first time she'd tried, she had ended up with a veritable mountain of things she'd wanted to bring with her. She'd included everything from riding outfits she had yet to grow into, all the way to a small collection of ceramic dolls that had once belonged to her mother, or so she'd been told.

When she had looked at the first pile of stuff, she soon realized that bringing everything she wanted would not be practical at all. She'd have to leave a great deal of things behind, things that were precious to her. It had taken several long hours for her to completely understand and accept what that meant.

Now, her collection of items consisted of three changes of plain, sturdy clothing, a cloak, two standard-issue daggers she'd 'borrowed' from the guard barracks, a large travel satchel, a small flint box, two waterskins, two heavy blankets, and a small wooden chest containing every necklace, bracelet, or potentially valuable piece of jewelry she'd ever been given. When properly rolled up and packed, everything fit snugly inside the travel satchel, and the whole thing looked as though it'd fit through her bedroom window without issue.

Gwen looked around her bedroom at all the items that hadn't ended up on the blanket. She knew it would be difficult saying goodbye to the rest of her things, some of which she'd never even dreamed she'd be parting with.

And things were about to get even more difficult.

She drew a deep, relaxing breath, glancing at her bedroom door apprehensively.

Tonight, she had to see how hard it would be to steal the herbs from her father's desk, and that meant sneaking down to her father's study and rooting around for them. Of course, what made this difficult was the fact that she was expressly forbidden from entering Bryn's study, and had been for years.

If she got caught, she might not get into too much trouble. She wouldn't be taking anything tonight, just verifying that there was indeed a leather pouch with a red cord sitting in her father's study desk. However, if she was seen snooping around the king's study, it would definitely rouse suspicion and make things harder for her later on.

Gwen just had to confirm she'd have access to the pouch, so she'd know she could fetch it when the time was right. And, if all went well tonight, that time might be as soon as tomorrow evening.

It all depended on her being able to get down to the study, verify everything she needed to know, get back up to her room, write a quick note, and then toss her bag of stuff outside the window, all of which had to be done by midnight if she was going to catch Rhosyn in time.

Which meant she only had about an hour left.

Gwen sighed. She'd stalled long enough.

She gave her bedroom door another nervous glance, gathered up her courage, and took a deep breath. Then she pulled her door open and ventured through it.

There was scant light illuminating the stairway, but Gwen found the darkness a little comforting. She'd prefer not to be seen at all, of course, but she knew it would be unavoidable once she got to the bottom of the stairs and into the main hallway. The castle staff she encountered might not think twice about seeing her roaming the hallways at this comparatively late hour though, since most of them hadn't been working there for more than a couple of months anyways. Still, a stray piece of servant gossip making its way to Anifail might be enough to undo her whole plan, so the fewer people she ran in to, the better.

Once at the bottom of the stairs, she peeked left and right down the hallway before proceeding into it, dark grey shawl wrapped to cover most of her light brown dressing gown. She had opted to go barefoot so she'd make less noise, and the cool stone of the floor made her want to shiver, despite the fact that the rest of her seemed unreasonably warm. Her stomach was a tight ball of worry, and her lungs felt like they weren't getting enough air.

Instead of heading straight to her father's study by way of the library hallway, Gwen opted for a less-traveled route near the inner courtyard garden, a trip that took her no more than a couple of minutes. Once there, she slipped through the courtyard door and into the blessedly dark, night air. Grass poked between her toes as she tip-toed across the lawn, heading for a similar entrance located clear on the other side.

Gwen arrived at the arched doorway, and suddenly became aware of voices coming from the hallway on the other side of it. She side-stepped into a shadow cast by a nearby bush and froze in place, heart pounding in her chest.

Two men, kitchen servants from the sound of it, walked the length of the hallway, discussing various tasks they'd be performing on the morrow. Gwen listened to them intently, tracking their progress down the hallway, past the courtyard door and beyond, alert for any sign they were aware of her.

Once she could no longer hear them, she waited for another minute or so, and then carefully opened the door in front of her and poked her head beyond it, looking from side to side.

Nobody there. So far, so good.

She quickly entered the hallway and hurried down it, heading towards the study entrance. Her bare feet made light 'pit-pat' noises against the floor, despite how quiet she was trying to be. There was nobody else in sight however, so perhaps speed was more important than stealth at this point.

Once in front of the study door, she took a few moments to gather herself and looked around for anyone who might have spotted her. Her heart was beating rather fast — half from the short run down the hall, and half from the risky nature of what she was in the middle of doing.

Satisfied there was nobody else around, she gripped the door handle with a tentative hand and twisted the knob slowly. Once she could no longer turn it, she pressed her other palm against the side of the door and began to push with agonizing slowness.

The well-oiled hinges didn't make a sound as the door opened. Gwen crept in, her eyes wide and alert, taking in as many details as she could.

His study had changed quite a lot since she'd last been in it. On her left there were now rows upon rows of animal heads and stuffed hawks mounted high up on the wall, as well as various different bows and spears mounted beneath them, each angled in a way that made their relationship with each animal fairly obvious. Far off to her right was a crackling fireplace, two high-backed chairs, a large throw-rug, a couple of end-tables, and a few landscape paintings dotting the walls here and there. Her father's desk was directly opposite her, along the far wall, sitting beside a bookshelf and a few other strange pieces of furniture she didn't recognize at first glance.

Gwen very carefully eased the door shut behind her, stopping it just before it completely closed. Then she breathed a quiet sigh of relief, which caused her to realize she'd been holding her breath.

Forcing herself to relax, she slowly walked across the rug-covered floor to her father's desk and crouched down beside his chair, directly in front of the drawer he'd described to Anifail that day in her room. Her hand reached out to wrap around the tarnished brass handle.

"Wave Dancer," she heard her father's voice announce in a loud, clear voice, as if having arrived at a decision.

Gwen froze, heart in her throat, her hand mere inches from the drawer handle.

"Seriously?" Anifail's voice replied, giving a good-natured snort of derision. "If you like that one, why not *Queen of the Sea*? Or even *Floating Cliché?*"

"Come on, it's not that bad a name for a boat," her father laughed, slurring his words the tiniest bit.

Within moments Gwen understood, and it was like forgetting how to breathe.

They were both in the study. With her.

Anifail and her father were both sitting not fifteen feet away from her in their high-backed chairs, facing the fireplace.

She'd never considered they might be in the study this late, and hadn't even thought to check.

Panicking, Gwen scrambled past the chair and underneath the desk, hoping the shadowy recess would hide her well enough not to be discovered. After a moment's thought, she also grabbed the desk chair by its legs and carefully pulled it towards her for extra cover. Then she curled herself into as tight a ball as she could and huddled into her corner, trying to stay as quiet as possible.

There were no sounds at all for several minutes, save for the gentle popping of burning wood from the fireplace. Each passing second seemed to multiply Gwen's anxiousness.

"Where did I go wrong, Anifail?" Bryn asked in a quiet, wistful voice.

"Sorry?"

"With Gwenwyn, I mean. What should I have done differently?

Could I have done anything differently? She's so willful, and with everything else I'm trying to arrange, having to deal with *her* all the time is...it's frustrating."

There was a lengthy pause. A bit mystified, Gwen tilted her head slightly so she might hear better.

"Honestly, I don't think you could have done anything differently. You were consistent, and you were firm. Disciplining her yourself was dangerous, and yet you managed to bring her to heel often enough, willful or no. I've known fathers who aren't a tenth of the man you are, and yet they can make their own children quake in fear with nothing more than a look, or a gesture. I suspect the fault lies with her." Gwen heard Anifail exhale through his nose and take a long drink of something. "I share your pain, though; it's frustrating for me as well. Every day, I get the same old cheek, like she thinks it's some sort of game. It's as if she's always just sort of assumed she could talk to me like I was some sort of servant. Nobody talks to me like she does, nobody."

"I know, I know. She's got too much of her mother in her, unfortunately, and I'm sure you remember what she was like," said Bryn, pausing long enough to take a drink of his own. "You'll have your chance to level things out on that score eventually, never you fear."

Gwen didn't like the sound of that one bit.

Anifail snorted. "It can't happen soon enough. Still, it's only a couple of weeks away. It seems like it's taken us forever to get here."

"Aye," said Bryn. "It's been a long road, but we're almost there, Captain."

"To Prince Gavin of Rhegar," said Anifail.

"To my future son-in-law. May he rest in peace," agreed Bryn.

Gwen heard the soft clink of two glasses touching.

For the next five minutes or so there was no conversation from either of them, no sound at all except for the occasional crackle from the fire. Still huddled under the desk, Gwen realized a few things about her predicament.

She'd left the study door open a crack, which meant she'd have to leave while both Anifail and her father were still in the room. If they moved to leave and discovered a partially opened door, their suspicions would surely be roused.

There was also a time limit — she needed to get out of the study and back to her room in time to drop her travel gear, along with a note. And she couldn't very well do that without first checking the drawer for that bag of *chi'darro*, which was the whole reason why she'd come down here in the first place.

She sat there, curled up in a tight little ball under the desk, waiting, becoming more anxious with every passing moment. Eventually she realized that regardless of how frightening the prospect was, she needed to do something.

Well, there was the drawer. Gwen was still mostly hidden from view where she was huddled, but she could probably get the bottom drawer open without making too much noise. She'd open it, check for the leather pouch her father mentioned, and then close it, all as slowly and carefully as possible.

Gwen reached out from her shadowy alcove and laid a few tentative fingers atop the edge of the drawer. Then, just as she was about to slide the drawer open, she realized it might be a better idea to wait until Anifail or her father was talking, so that their conversation would mask any noise she might accidentally make.

Hand poised and ready, resting along the side of the drawer, she waited for her moment.

Minutes passed.

"Say, did you ever hear from that fellow about the bunting for the inside balconies? Weren't we—"

Gwen pushed the drawer open, quietly, only half-listening to the words her father was saying. Once she'd opened it a hands-breadth, she leaned forward to peek inside.

A dark brown leather pouch tied off with red cord was sitting inside, atop some papers and old inkwells. It was about the size of her fist and looked to be fairly full, which meant it was probably more than enough to sustain her during her trip.

Her father was still talking, she noticed, so she slid the drawer shut, an action that produced the barest whisper of wood sliding against wood. As soon as it was done, she pulled her hand back.

The sound of her father's voice cut off the precise moment she did so.

Had he seen her hand just now, or heard the drawer close? It sort of sounded like her father finished his last sentence, but Gwen hadn't really been listening to what he was saying.

She sat there amid the painful silence, anxiously waiting for the next words to be spoken.

"Oh, do you mean the fellow with that green and yellow fabric? Or are you talking about the one from out of town?" Anifail asked. Gwen heard him move in his chair, and could also make out the shuffling of papers. "I think we might be further ahead to go with the local fellow, for obvious reasons."

She allowed herself a quiet breath, relieved.

"True, we can always tax him later, which is almost like getting a discount," Bryn agreed. "However, I'm not sure I liked the pattern as much. What if we—"

Gwen didn't even stop to think; she knew this was her moment. As her father spoke, she pushed the chair away from her with agonizing slowness, and then scooted around it on all fours, alert for any sort of sound she might be making as she did. Then she slowly got to her feet and tiptoed out from under the desk, making her way over to the study door, her eyes locked on the two high-backed chairs next to the fireplace. She could make out her father's hand resting on a chair arm, idly swirling the pink-amber contents of a brandy snifter as he spoke.

She was two feet from the door by the time he'd stopped talking, and the sudden absence of noise caused her to freeze in her tracks, mid-tiptoe.

Her eyes were still focused on the two chairs by the fireplace.

Though both men were hidden from view, she saw her father's hand still atop his armrest, swirling the drink it held in an idle, unconcerned manner.

"I suppose that would work," Anifail eventually replied. There was the sound of more papers being shuffled. "Really though, I'd prefer—"

Gwen took another two steps, grabbed the handle in front of her, and gently swung the door open about a foot or so. Then, holding her breath, she slipped out into the hallway and quietly closed the door behind her in one careful, fluid motion.

There was a soft 'click' as the door fully closed.

She quickly glanced up and down the hallway, and, seeing nobody at all, breathed a thankful sigh. She then tore down the hallway and back out to the garden, her pulse racing, an excited smile on her face. Cool evening air greeted her, and soon she was running in darkness, blades of grass once more poking between her toes, feeling positively giddy with both excitement and relief.

She'd done it! She'd sneaked into the study, and with her father and Anifail still in it no less! If she had the nerve required to pull something like that off, actually stealing the pouch and making off with it when they weren't there might be a piece of cake!

Tomorrow. She'd do it tomorrow night, perhaps an hour after midnight.

That meant getting back to her room and smuggling her stuff out the window tonight, so Rhosyn could get everything ready. She'd write a quick note as well, so Rhosyn would know precisely when, and had enough time to prepare the horses. Once she stole the pouch and made her way outside she was pretty sure she'd want to put as much distance between herself and this place as she could, and as quickly as possible.

Once Gwen had crossed the courtyard garden and made her way back to more familiar surroundings, she opted to locate an empty water jug and fill it. That way, she reasoned, if she was seen returning to her room now, she might have something to explain why she was out of bed at that hour. Come to think of it, the water jug might help with tomorrow night's activities as well, allowing her to claim she'd become thirsty in the middle of the night and had come down for a drink. She could come downstairs from her bedroom with the jug, and then she'd simply never return.

The very thought of it made her so happy, she was near tears.

Water jug in hand, Gwen practically flew up her tower stairs, burst through her bedroom door, closed it behind her, and did a spontaneous dance of happiness. Her heart was still pounding from the excitement of everything, and it felt like the smile on her face would never be leaving.

Her eyes fell upon the bundle on her bed. What time was it, anyway? It had to be pretty close to midnight by now. Maybe a little past, actually. She'd completely lost track of time, hiding under the desk like she had been.

Gwen hurried over to her desk and got out her box of inks and quills. She tore a page out of the book she practiced her writing in, dipped a quill in the ink, and scrawled a hasty note.

Everything's set. Tomorrow night, an hour past midnight. Meet you at the stables. —G

She quickly dabbed the excess ink away with a blotter and then blew on the parchment, willing it to dry. Once she'd figured her writing wouldn't smudge, she folded the paper in half, went to her bed, and tucked it into her travel satchel on top of all the other things she'd already stuffed in there.

Bundle in hand, she went to her window and leaned forward, looking for some sign of Rhosyn. The moon was out, and she could see reflected bits of moonlight dancing off of the rippling water of the moat, but the grassy area directly below her was too dark to see anything.

Was Rhosyn even down there?

Gwen considered for a few moments, then hoisted her bundle up to the window and pushed it out. Once that was done, she leaned back outside to see if she could catch a glimpse of it as it fell.

The pack was a light beige colour, which made it a little easier to spot, thanks to the moonlight. She watched it silently tumble away from her and into the darkness below. A moment later, she heard the faint 'whump' of something soft hitting the grassy ground next to the moat.

Gwen didn't have to peer into the darkness for very long before spotting some activity, for it wasn't long before she could make out a figure in a familiar light cloak pulling away from a nearby section of wall and hurrying over to where her bundle lay. Within moments both the cloaked figure and her travel satchel were gone, nowhere to be seen.

Tomorrow, then. It was really, really going to happen!

She practically sprinted over to her bed and dove in, hastily blew out her night lamp, closed her eyes tightly and covered herself with her sheets. All of a sudden, Gwen couldn't think of anything in the world she wanted more than for tomorrow to hurry up and arrive.

For Gwen, the hardest part of the following day was hiding her smile. She had to force a frown onto her face periodically, occasionally remembering to scowl and look morose. What made it especially difficult was the fact that her father was too busy taking care of wedding arrangements to supervise her meals personally, and Anifail had reportedly left the castle and was not expected back until later that evening. Life was usually a lot more cheerful when she didn't have to interact with the two of them.

Of course, as the day progressed it became much easier to keep from smiling, because her anxiousness and uncertainty increased the closer evening got. Though she tried to nap in the afternoon, she found she was too excited, and instead spent a few hours staring up at her ceiling and worrying over details. By bedtime, she was a nervous wreck, and by the time midnight arrived she was more terrified than she could ever remember.

It wasn't going to stop her though. Starting a brand new life was probably *supposed* to be terrifying.

Gwen waited until well after midnight before changing into her riding clothes and donning her cloak. Then, after a few deep breaths, she grabbed her empty water jug, opened her bedroom door, and quietly walked down the stairs.

Everything seemed much darker than the previous night, which wasn't exactly a bad thing. Less light meant less chance of being noticed if she stuck to the shadows and kept to the same route as before. Her cloak was much darker than the one she'd been wearing then, which probably made her more difficult to see. She was wearing her boots this time, however, and had to walk much more slowly than before just to keep quiet.

She arrived at the bottom of her tower steps in short order, and quickly peeked left and right down the hallways. There was nobody roaming the halls that she could see, most people having gone to bed long ago.

Gwen followed the same route as she had before, heading to the courtyard garden and making her way to her father's study in a roundabout way rather than proceeding directly there. As before, she stuck to the shadows and cut through the courtyard garden, stopping just outside the hallway entrance. She could hear no servants chatting in the hallway this time, but Gwen remained outside the entrance for a few moments regardless, readying herself for what she needed to do.

"You can do this," she reminded herself in a whisper, putting her empty water jug down on the grassy lawn. "You did it last night, and they were in the *room* with you then!"

Well, if her father was in the study tonight, he'd either be reclining in the same chair as the previous night, facing the fire, or he'd be sitting at his desk, and in both cases he'd be facing away from the door. Either way, she'd have a good chance of spotting him before he spotted her.

Breathing a few deep, relaxing breaths, Gwen grit her teeth and slowly pulled open the door in front of her. When she peered through the entrance and into the hallway, she saw nobody.

Walking into the hallway, she made her way towards the study, though much slower than she had the previous night. If there was anyone nearby, the last thing she wanted to do was to let the 'clip-clop' of her boots on the stone floor alert them to her presence.

Even walking as slowly and carefully as possible, her boots would occasionally make a noise loud enough to cause her breath to catch in her chest.

When she finally arrived at the study door, she pressed her ear against it and listened carefully. The only sound she could make out was the furious thumping of her own heartbeat.

Carefully, slowly, Gwen opened the door and slipped inside.

The fire had burned down to embers, casting a dull red glow over one half of the room while shrouding the other half in darkness. The shadowy stuffed animal heads lining the wall nearest her looked extra spooky in that light, and unnerved her.

Crouching, she looked across the room at the two chairs sitting next to each other in front of the fireplace. Neither looked to have anybody seated in them. Same with the chair by the desk.

The study was empty.

Breathlessly, Gwen hurried over to the desk and opened the drawer, snatched the small leather pouch and tucked it into her pocket. Then she practically flew back to the hallway, quietly closed the door shut behind her, and then quickly made her way back to the courtyard garden.

In the dark, she almost tripped over her empty water jug. Once she caught herself, she felt bubbles of nervous laughter rising up from her chest, and she clamped a hand over her mouth to keep from letting them out as she picked the jug up with the other.

It was done, and it had taken her less than a minute. The most difficult part was already over.

Her journey to the kitchen area was mercifully devoid of any sort of company as well. It began to feel to Gwen as though she were the only one who was even awake at this hour, which was even better than she'd hoped. Everything was going perfectly.

And then, once she'd arrived at the servant's entrance near the kitchen, the doors she usually took when she wanted to go outside, she realized who would still be up this late.

Castle guards.

Most of the entrances were gated up after a certain hour, the two exceptions being the front entrance, which stayed open and was always guarded, and the servant's entrance, where kitchen supplies were often delivered. It too was guarded.

Gwen felt a flutter of panic. She'd occasionally gone out late at night to meet with Rhosyn, but that had been before the new staff, and it hadn't happened very often. She had no doubt she could play willful princess and get by them without too much trouble, but if she did that they'd certainly remember her. If she left the castle at this hour and didn't come back, it would arouse suspicion, perhaps cause them to notify her father.

Why oh why hadn't she remembered the guards sooner?

There really wasn't any other way out of the castle available to her. How could she get out without drawing attention to herself? Her mind raced through some of the possibilities.

An idea came to her.

Pulling her cloak hood over her head enough to cover most of her face, she clutched her empty jug firmly and marched purposefully through the servant entrance doors, directly between the two guards standing on either side of it.

"Oi! You!" a harsh-sounding voice rasped. "Where you goin'?"

Gwen half-turned towards the two guards, most of her face still hidden, and did her best to sound as tired and annoyed as possible.

"Water for the kitchen. From the brook," she said, holding up her jug for emphasis.

"What's wrong with the well water?" the second, younger guard asked in a voice that was much less gravelly.

"Dead pigeons," she shrugged, already turning back and continuing on her way. "Drowned. Chef found 'em when he was making tomorrow's bread."

The first guard groaned tiredly.

"It's like I keep telling 'em, put a lid over the damn thing! It's bad enough catching a chill while on night watch, I don't need to be eating poison and puking my guts out once my shift's over."

"That sort of thing happen often?" the younger guard asked.

"Aye, every now and again. Milkmaids want to bring in cats, to keep the stray pigeons and rats away, but Chef says he'll have none of it. Of course, a few wooden planks'd take care of the whole problem, but I'm just a guard, so what do I know? I swear, make like you know anything about bread, or cookin', or even common sense, and that guy—"

Gwen left the two guardsmen to their newest topic of conversation, slowly making her way out into the night, trying to act like she thought a kitchen servant might just in case they were still keeping an eye on her. After a moment's thought, she began swinging the empty jug back and forth as she walked, as though she were bored enough to try to amuse herself. Before long, she was far enough away that she could no longer hear them talking.

She stole a glance behind her, and after judging that they could no longer see her in the darkness, she dropped her water jug, changed course and began walking hurriedly towards the stables. Her legs seemed filled with a nervous sort of energy, the kind you felt when you were running down a flight of stairs as fast as you could, barely in control of them at all.

Aside from the crunching of dry grass and twigs under her boots, the only sounds that could be heard were crickets and frogs sounding off in the nearby grasses. Despite barely being able to see where she was going, and though she had only made trips out to the stables once or twice in the dark, Gwen wasn't at all worried. In fact, she was so familiar with the paths leading to it that she could probably have walked there with her eyes shut tight.

After about five minutes or so of trekking she could make out the dark silhouettes of several horses, and the stable as well. The outside torches weren't lit, but there was a faint light coming from the window that spoke of a candle or lamp burning somewhere inside, likely from the small room that served as Rhosyn's quarters.

Gwen crept over to the front door and opened it, tip-toeing into the dimly lit stable area shortly after. She didn't know why she was creeping exactly, but now that all of the difficult stuff was behind her...well, sneaking around in the dark was just kind of fun. She couldn't ever remember being this excited before.

Once inside, she looked around briefly. There were two packs, one of which was hers, sitting against the wall just inside the entrance, and Gwen could see two heavily laden saddle-bags draped over a nearby table. A small lamp burned on a dresser by Rhosyn's bed, providing just enough illumination for Gwen to see the huddled bundle of blankets in the bed next to it.

"Rosie!" Gwen called in a hushed voice. "I'm here! Time to go."

The bundle moved and shifted a little. Gwen rolled her eyes impatiently.

"Come on, sleepyhead! It's not *my* fault if you didn't think to nap this afternoon!" she admonished, picking up her travel pack. "Did you manage to get everything we needed?"

Suddenly, the blanket covering the bundle was thrown to one side, and Gwen let out a short, sharp exclamation of surprise. Her travel pack slipped from her fingers, forgotten.

"Well," said Anifail, his voice dangerously quiet, "I was wondering when you were finally going to show up."

Chapter 14

"W-what are you doing here?" was all Gwen could think to ask. Her legs scarcely felt up to the task of holding her upright all of a sudden.

"Me? Doing? Why, I'm resting," Anifail said, still reclining lazily on Rhosyn's bed. "Relaxing a bit. Being a captain is hard work. I honestly didn't intend to lie down when I first got here, but this bed looked so comfortable that I just had to give it a try." He pressed a hand against the bedding, as though demonstrating how pliant it was. "Bundled cotton — who knew peasant stuffing could be so agreeable to sleep on? Why, I have half a mind to swap my down-filled bedding with—"

"What have you done with Rhosyn?" Gwen half-screamed. *"Where is she?"*

"Oh, relax, Princess. I haven't done anything to her… she's perfectly safe." Anifail flashed her a quick grin. "Or at least, she was perfectly safe the last time I saw her."

Gwen quickly converted as much of her fear into anger as she could, and focused it. She gave a significant look at Anifail's bandaged hand, and then regarded him coolly.

"I'll give you a choice, Captain. You can tell me where she is, right now, or—" Gwen took off one of her riding gloves and gave Anifail as deadly and serious a look as she could manage, "I can listen to you desperately trying to tell me between screams of agony."

Anifail chuckled sadly at her, shaking his head.

"My, such a dangerous little minx all of a sudden. So fierce, so *terrifying! Ooooooh!*" He shook his outstretched hands at her in faux terror. "Why, if it weren't for my years and years of training, I fear I might wet myself right here and now."

"Make all the jokes you want, but if you don't tell me where she is, you won't be walking out of here! I promise you that!"

"Oh, you *promise?* Dear gracious me." Anifail creased his brow, as though in thought. "But what about your crystal in the temple? What would the Goddess think of you after doing something as awful as what I fear you might be suggesting?"

"I think the Goddess would make an exception," Gwen spat. "We don't lose her favour by killing roaches or other vermin, after all."

"How clever. Well then, how about this instead? I'm not going to tell you where Rhosyn is, but allow me tell you a little bit about her situation, using small, easy to understand words. And once I've done that, if you still want to torture or kill me, you'll have my blessing."

"I *will* do it, Captain. Don't for a second think I won't."

"Hmm? Well, that must explain why I'm so dreadfully nervous," said Anifail, sounding supremely unconcerned. He gave her a patiently amused smile. "For starters, as I've said before, Rhosyn is safe. She's probably better off than she deserves, considering what my sources tell me she was planning. I mean, kidnapping a princess? I'm no expert, but that certainly seems like the sort of thing one might call 'treason'. By rights, she should be in the castle dungeon, waiting for some hooded fellow to come along and chop her head off!

"Now, despite how *serious* an offense this is, I did take into account just how much you care for her, and decided to spare her the indignities of confinement in the dungeon. Wouldn't want a delicate thing like her stuck all alone in a nasty place like that, would we? Of course not."

Anifail began inspecting his fingernails, whistling tunelessly.

"Where?" Gwen demanded through clenched teeth, taking a step towards him and raising her arm threateningly. "Tell me where she is! Now!"

"She's hidden away in a very special place, Princess. It's a place where nothing can get in or out, save for breathable air. And myself, of course." Anifail's smile got bigger. "Nobody else knows where she is... not even your father. Just me. And I'm afraid that's all I'm going to be telling you, Princess Gwenwyn." He looked at her in mock disappointment. "I suppose that means you'll be killing me. Well, I do hope it's a quick death, and not a long, drawn-out affair like your lady-in-waiting has ahead of her."

"She... *what?*" Gwen's eyes widened. "You said she was safe!"

"Oh, she *is*, Princess. As safe as can be. Her continued safety, however, does rather unfortunately depend on me visiting her every day. You know, bringing her food, water... trifling things like that. Poor girl." He feigned sudden comprehension. "Oh, hang on, *now* I see the dilemma! If you *kill* me, I'll no longer be able to provide her with those things, and she'll die. How dreadful!"

"Maybe I *don't* kill you, Captain," she said, trying as best she could to sound confident. "Maybe I keep you alive, and torture the information out of you, or—"

"I think, perhaps, you don't appreciate how extraordinarily meaningless your threats are, Princess. Now, despite knowing how difficult it must be for you, I'd suggest you stop and actually think for a moment. You are addressing the one person in the world who knows where your friend is tucked away right now. There is *nothing* you can threaten me with."

"Like hell there isn't! You'll let her go, or I'll—"

"Oh dear. I'm starting to suspect you'll need some sort of

demonstration of your impotence," Anifail said, swinging his legs around and standing up from the bed. He considered Gwen a moment, then cleared his throat. "Alright then *little girl,* here it is. Threaten me again, and sweet little Rhosyn won't have a visitor tomorrow. Or the next day… or possibly even the day after. Take a second to think about what that means. No food, no water… just her sitting there, alone, in the dark, wondering what'll happen next, or if anyone will ever come for her. Now then." He gestured for her to continue. "You were saying?"

Gwen was so tantalizingly close to freedom she felt like crying. The travel packs at the door, the saddlebags on the table, the pouch of *chi'darro,* the horses grazing nearby… all of the ingredients necessary for her to leave this place forever. Anifail wouldn't dare to try to physically stop her; she could simply walk out of here. And yet she couldn't.

She had everything she needed except for her best friend. There was no way Gwen could leave Rhosyn like this.

And Anifail knew it.

"Alright," she whispered after several long moments. "I understand. I won't try to threaten you."

"Oh, I'm sorry, but did you think that was the end of the demonstration, Princess?" Anifail reached into a vest pocket with his gloved hand. "No, I'm positive a girl as dense as you requires much, much more convincing than that. Now, here's a bit of fun. Let's see if you recognize what this is."

Anifail drew something from his pocket and held it up so that she might see. Gwen gasped, and instinctively backed away.

It was a geis sphere.

Anifail chuckled.

"Ah, so you *do* know what it is. Yes, I suspected that after your experience with the first one, even someone as bafflingly stupid as you would learn to recognize them. This one was much cheaper than the last one. This time, instead of spouting off meaningless nothings, you'll be utterly silent. Nothing but sweet, blissful silence from our princess until it's destroyed." He smiled wistfully. "That, or until you plant a kiss on the lips of a certain Prince Gavin, whichever comes first."

"Don't touch me with that!" Gwen said, edging away from him.

Anifail pretended to look confused a moment, and he regarded the dull, glassy orb he held.

"Why, it would hardly be an effective demonstration if I simply tricked you into touching it, or forced it upon you, would it?" Anifail chuckled, as though greatly amused. "No, I wouldn't dream of settling for something like that. Instead, you're going to *ask* me to give it to you."

"What?"

"You are going to ask me, very nicely, if I might allow you the esteemed privilege of putting this new compulsion upon yourself. And then, once that's done, you're going to reach out with your bare hand and touch this bauble."

The sick feeling in Gwen's stomach intensified as she realized the full extent of her helplessness.

What could she do? If she did anything Anifail didn't like, Rhosyn would be the one who would end up paying for it.

"If you let Rhosyn go, I'll take the sphere," she offered.

"Oh, no no no... that wasn't what I asked for at all! How about you take a moment, think about your friend, and try once more."

Once again, it appeared Anifail and her father were one step ahead of her, and there seemed nothing she could do. They were now holding Rhosyn hostage, and would use her to ensure she followed their plan to the letter.

She was trapped.

Gwen slumped her shoulders, defeated.

"I'll take it," she said, meekly.

"Oh come now. A princess has better manners than that," Anifail chided. "Again!"

"Please give it to me," she whispered, hating the words as they left her mouth.

"Not *nearly* good enough," he said, a little bit louder this time, flashing her a smile of grotesque glee. "These will be the last words of yours I hear for quite some time, and I wish to savour them. Beg, Princess."

Gwen felt the beginnings of tears forming.

"Please, Captain. I… please, let me take that from you. I'll do as you've said."

Anifail shook his head. "Well, obviously you're not that accustomed to begging. And you understand, don't you, what'll happen if you find some clever way to warn your future husband of your condition? If you do anything but *exactly* what I or your father tell you do? Tell me, what will happen then?"

"You'll let Rhosyn die," Gwen whispered.

"That, or I visit her and do something so, *so* much worse. Now, knowing how utterly helpless you are, I want you to convince me you understand everything I've just told you." He strode forward and leaned in close enough to whisper into her ear. "*Beg. For. It.*"

"Please, I—" said Gwen, her voice catching slightly. "I'll do whatever you and father say. I promise I will. Just please…please don't hurt Rhosyn!"

Anifail smiled at her.

"Well, because you asked me so nicely, I suppose it's not too much to ask. Here," he said, holding the hated sphere out towards her. "You merely have to touch it."

Shoulders shaking from suppressed sobbing, Gwen reached out with a trembling hand and touched the top of the sphere with her fingertips. It felt cool, then warm, and a small, familiar shiver passed through her.

"There, now was that so bad?" Anifail asked, pocketing the orb. "I'll make sure this ends up somewhere safe. Now, we're absolutely clear? Your cooperation with every aspect of the king's plan. Your *full* cooperation. That's the only thing that will keep your lady-in-waiting alive. If you alert anyone to what you are — the prince, the castle staff, *anyone at all* — I will be forgetting all about that poor, sweet young girl you're so fond of. Am I understood?"

Gwen tried saying 'yes'. When nothing came out, she merely nodded in agreement. A tear trickled down the side of her face, leaving a trail of wetness along her jaw.

"Well, good. Now, kindly return to the castle, *with* your travel pack, and go to bed. Be sure to return anything that doesn't belong to you as well. That includes whatever you lifted from your father's study. The next time you go snooping around there, perhaps you'll remember to wear shoes, so as not to leave footprints of dead grass throughout the garden lawn. Oh, and Princess?" He gave her a particularly nasty grin. "When I see you again, I'll expect you to be looking very, *very* contrite. Head bowed, eyes lowered, treating me with respectful deference, that sort of thing. I believe it's safe to say your friend Rhosyn *sincerely* hopes you do a particularly terrific job of it."

He sat back down on the bed, sighed contentedly to himself, and then gave her a wave of dismissal, as though he was shooing away a pet.

Picking up her pack, Gwen hurried out of the room and fled into the night, sobbing noiselessly.

Chapter 15

Gwen somehow managed to spend even more time sitting in her room, staring out her window in despair as the days slowly turned into weeks. She hardly slept, and when she did she'd end up having nightmares featuring her struggling helplessly, trapped in some inescapable, terrifying scenario or another.

She spent a good deal of time taking care of the horses, since Rhosyn couldn't perform the daily chores that needed doing. It wasn't the horses' fault that their keeper wasn't around to attend them, and it hardly seemed fair to Gwen that they suffer as a consequence. Servants and staff around the castle likely thought it was strange, a princess doing stable work herself, but she really didn't care. Tending horses was actually one of the only sources of real pleasure she had these days.

Her only real contact with anybody occurred when she was summoned to the dining hall for her daily meals, which were still being supervised.

Occasionally she'd find Bryn and Anifail there as well, eating a quick meal while taking care of whatever scrap of castle business had occupied their attention. Half the time they didn't pay her any mind at all, practically ignoring her as she sat there and ate. There were moments, however, where she'd catch one of them regarding her with a smirk, or chuckling over some whispered comment the other had made.

Gwen would do her level best to ignore them both, eating her food in silence, and then quickly retreating to the isolation and comparative solace of her bedroom.

Once there, she would just stare out the window, considering her situation, wondering about her best friend, and generally just thinking in circles.

She'd come up with some idea or clever plan, and her thoughts would immediately return to Rhosyn's predicament, how she was being held hostage for her cooperation. Often, Gwen thought about trying to follow Anifail to find out where he'd imprisoned Rhosyn, but every time she considered doing it she began to think of what would happen if she was caught. If she showed even the slightest amount of resistance at this stage, or if it was discovered she was planning anything at all, it would probably go very badly for Rhosyn.

It didn't stop her from staring out the window, thinking of things she might do and then immediately dismissing them, wishing things were somehow different. She'd thought she'd felt trapped before, when Prince Tremaine had been her unlucky suitor, but that was nothing compared to this. It was like a spiritual noose sitting around her neck, with her helpless to do anything about it.

When the day finally came that she caught glimpse of a royal procession approaching the castle gates, Rhegar's colours flying merrily in the wind, it was as though she could feel that noose tightening, making it difficult for her to breathe.

Gwen knew it was just a matter of time before she was told to come downstairs and meet her newest suitor, and she dreaded the summons. She was once again wearing that long, flowing dress she'd worn upon Prince Tremaine's arrival, the one she simultaneously loved and hated. Just as before, she had no idea what she could do to avoid what seemed inevitable at this point.

Really, what could she do? Her only hope was that she might find a way to prevent this marriage without it appearing to have anything to do with her, and how exactly was she supposed to do that? If something went wrong and the wedding was called off, her father and Anifail would naturally assume she had something to do with it.

The sound of slippers on her bedroom stairs came much sooner than she'd anticipated, a mere half-hour after she'd first spied the Rhegarian convoy in the distance. When it sounded like her visitor had arrived at the top of the stairs there was a few seconds of anxious silence, followed by a tentative knock at her door.

"Princess?" an older woman's voice called from beyond the door. "Your father sends for you. Your presence is required in the rose garden."

Gwen walked over to the door so that she might open it and give the speaker, whoever it was, a quick smile of thanks. However, in the few seconds it took for her to get there, she could already hear the woman hastily retreating back down the tower stairs.

The rumours had been getting worse and worse. Most of the staff avoided her entirely now, throwing her fearful, worried looks from time to time. On the rare occasion when she did walk into a room and encounter servants or other castle staff talking to one another, they would often stop their conversation mid-sentence and regard her warily, as though they'd just been talking about her, or were suddenly afraid she'd order them hanged. In fact, a few days ago, she'd overheard a conversation where a chambermaid professed to hate 'that spoiled brat of a princess' who no longer even deigned it necessary to speak to lowly servants such as them.

Though it seemed incredibly unfair, she resolved not to think about all the rumours or other things that were being said about her, because it wasn't helpful. Gwen already knew she was entirely alone in this, and dwelling on that fact or getting upset wouldn't do her any good at this stage. She needed to keep her head clear, and her eyes open for opportunity. After all, things had looked impossible before, when Prince Tremaine had come, and she'd still managed to find a way out then, hadn't she?

She could find a way out of this mess yet. She just had to pay attention, wait for her opportunity, and be ready for it when it came.

Gwen didn't bother to adjust her dress or inspect herself in the mirror. She merely walked out her door and headed down to the garden, just as she'd been asked to do. She'd been instructed to wear this dress today, but nobody had specifically told her to do her hair, put on jewelry, or spend any time at all on how she otherwise looked. Though it was little more than token rebellion, she resolved to ignore the spirit of what she was asked to do whenever possible and do the absolute bare minimum whenever she was ordered to do something.

The long journey down the various halls and stairwells seemed to take forever. When she finally got to the garden, she almost didn't recognize it.

There were gaily decorated poles and bunting everywhere, as well as some lawn furniture and parasols Gwen had never seen before. The area was also abuzz with activity — dozens of servants scurried about, making small adjustments to this or that, smoothing out whatever imperfections they were able to find. Elegant flower pots and tree planters lined the edges of the garden, arranged in an artful and considered fashion. She was also surprised to see three large peacocks wandering about, idly inspecting their unfamiliar surroundings.

A white gazebo now sat in the very middle of the widest part of the main garden path, looking as though it had always belonged there. Standing within it, appearing to be in the middle of a discussion, were Bryn and Anifail.

This whole setup seemed rather odd to Gwen. Most times foreign ministers and royal dignitaries were greeted by the king in the throne room, not in the rose garden. What reason could they have to meet outside?

Gwen headed for the gazebo. She arrived just in time to catch the tail end of what her father was saying.

"—control his hounds. If he had, maybe we'd still have *four* peacocks, and not three!"

"He is being whipped as we speak, Highness," Anifail said, in about as apologetic a tone as he ever used.

"Hmph. Well, good," Bryn sniffed, turning his attention to Gwen and furrowing his brow at her. "Gwenwyn, we'll be meeting Prince Gavin and the rest of his escort from Rhegar. You are to stand behind me, at this spot." He pointed to a section of the gazebo floor. "Do nothing except curtsey when mentioned or addressed. Oh, and do something about your hair, would you?"

Gwen gave a small curtsey of acquiescence, her eyes lowered and her head bowed. She made her way over to the spot where her father had pointed, doing her best to ignore the amused expression on Anifail's face as she did so. Once there, she stood as straight-backed as she could, staring off into the distance.

A few seconds later, Anifail sauntered over and stood beside her.

"Hair," he breathed quietly. "Now. Or someone goes hungry tonight."

Gwen gritted her teeth, and ran her fingers through her hair a few times, brushing it back over her shoulders and away from her face. Anifail grunted quietly, and then went to stand on the other side of the king.

They stood there in the shade of the gazebo for nearly fifteen minutes, leaving Gwen with little to do aside from watching the peacocks wander bemusedly around the garden. She quickly became so bored from just standing there that she began to fidget, and when the first signs of a flag-bearing procession could be seen she was actually the tiniest bit relieved, despite her anxiety.

The procession itself was impressive — a dozen riders and about fifty or so uniformed men on foot forming two columns, several of them bearing standards or strange, ribbon-like flags that trailed in the wind like horse tails. The horses were amazing to behold. Any one of them could have easily shamed anything Calderia's meagre stables had ever produced. Directly between the two columns, near the back, were six horsemen riding a few lengths ahead of a very posh and tastefully decorated two-horse carriage.

The sound of the approaching assemblage caused the three

peacocks that wandered the garden to hastily retreat from view, their presence rendered meaningless now that they could no longer be seen. How much effort had her father expended just to bring them here, only to have them run and hide from the very people they were meant to impress? The thought amused her somewhat.

Gwen watched, feeling both nervous and slightly awe-struck, as the columns of standard-bearers and soldiers advanced towards them. When the lead foot soldiers were ten feet or so from the gazebo, Gwen heard a faraway voice bark unintelligible orders, and both columns came to an abrupt halt, turned to either side, and marched outward with crisp, military-like precision. It became obvious the two columns were making room for the horsemen and coach in the rear, both of which were slowly bearing down on the gazebo.

It was equally obvious that the soldiers and horsemen before her had practiced doing this sort of thing. A lot.

She became aware that she could sense a bit of nervousness coming from her father, whose eyes had widened slightly at the display. Even Anifail looked a little tense and uncomfortable suddenly, and Gwen allowed herself a tiny smirk. Calderia was nowhere near the size of some of the other nearby kingdoms, after all. Perhaps the two most important men in the kingdom were questioning just how important they really were, comparatively speaking.

Gwen kept her eyes lowered as the coach and riders got closer, doing her best to remain small and insignificant. Given the circumstances, it wasn't difficult.

The majestic carriage and lead horsemen advanced on the occupants of the gazebo, and Gwen noticed that somehow the gait of the horses were synchronized — that each horse's step was coming down upon the grassy earth at precisely the same time, almost like soldiers at a military parade. Everything about the procession seemed designed to leave the viewer gaping in wonder, and impressed beyond measure.

She had a sudden flash of insight; *this* was royalty. Real royalty, and not the make-believe, self-important dressing up that Bryn and Anifail played at. Her father was a mere chieftain compared to what she was seeing here.

The thought should have made Gwen more afraid, and yet she wasn't. She was elated, in fact. Prior to this moment, she hadn't even considered that there was someone in the world her father didn't outrank. Seeing all this, she knew there were people out there — rulers of other kingdoms — who were *considerably* more powerful than her father.

The Prince of Rhegar might just be one of those people.

There wasn't much for her to do aside from standing there on the gazebo, watching things unfold before her. The unnaturally well coordinated horses trotted forward, two by two, the resplendent carriage trailing not far behind them. Gwen watched the horses with an appreciative eye, and then let her eyes wander upwards to inspect the riders of those horses.

The sight of one rider three lengths behind the lead horse on the left caused her breath to catch, and her heart to skip a beat.

He was, quite simply, the most perfect man Gwen could imagine.

His hair was dark, and fairly long, with just enough curl to make it bounce every time his horse took a step. He sat in his saddle like someone born to it. The cleft in his chin was barely enough to cast a shadow, but it squared his otherwise pointed features perfectly. Even were he not several inches taller than his immaculately dressed companions, he would have stood out.

He wore peasant gear — a deep red tunic and brown leather vest, well-worn riding gloves, thick brown leather trousers, and sensible riding boots unadorned by decoration or spur. If Gwen had happened upon him in the woods, she would have assumed he were an ostler, or farm hand, or something of that nature.

And he was beautiful. She's never even considered that a man could be beautiful before this particular moment, but it was simply what he was. Watching him ride towards them, Gwen suddenly felt like she understood some of the love poetry that had eluded her for years. Just watching him — his expressions, how he moved — was unlike anything she'd felt before.

Gwen barely even registered the elegantly-dressed fellows riding with him, or anything else that was going on. All of her attention was focused on this dark-haired rider, who crowded out anything else she might have noticed.

He glanced over at her briefly at one point, their eyes locking for just a moment. He gave her an indecipherable look before hastily lowering his gaze, shifting slightly in his saddle.

The two lead horses carried their riders forward until they were about twenty feet away from the gazebo staircase, at which point they came to a sudden and abrupt halt. As they did so, it seemed that every other horse behind them came to a complete stop as well.

The instant the horses had halted their advance, the peasant boy leaned forward and slid off his horse with practiced ease. As he did so, the finely dressed boy beside him widened his eyes.

"Majesty!" the fellow said, sounding alarmed, practically falling off his own horse in an effort to reach the ground quickly. "Please, *I'm* supposed to get down before—"

"Trevor? Who's prince?" the peasant boy asked tiredly, eyebrow raised.

"Yes, of course," said the elegantly dressed boy, stepping backward and bowing respectfully.

Gwen's eyes widened, and her heart gave an extra loud 'thump'.

This plainly dressed fellow garbed in earth tones, wearing a plain outfit and sensible riding kit befitting a stable-hand or ordinary horseman, *he* was Prince Gavin?

Silly though it was, she suddenly found herself regretting not having spent more time on her hair.

Almost immediately after this revelation of hers, there was a sudden commotion originating from somewhere near the carriage.

"—quite enough of that! Can't you see this is making them nervous? Help me off of this accursed thing, you— … no, not like that! Give me your hand! There! Now, help me out of this. Ready, and—"

A well-dressed man with an impressive white beard groaned mightily as he emerged from the side of the carriage, accompanied by several pages, each of whom was offering their assistance as he made his way out of the horse-drawn vehicle and into view. He spent a few moments straightening himself and brushing out his sleeves. When he finally turned to face Bryn, a beatific smile lit up his face, and he raised his arms to either side, as though he were the one who was welcoming them.

"*There* they are… at long last! Our newest family. Oh, just the sight of you all fills my heart with joy," he said, striding forward around the horses and toward the gazebo, looking as though he was coming to give them all a tremendous, grandfatherly hug. Gwen could sense consternation coming from her father, like this whole thing wasn't going exactly as he'd expected.

"It…yes, welcome! Mine too! And—" Bryn furrowed his brow, managing to look even more confused. "Sorry, ambassador is it? I'm afraid I was only expecting the arrival of Prince Gavin, and haven't made any—"

"*Ambassador?* Ha!" the boisterous old man laughed, seemingly oblivious to the fact he'd cut off her father mid-sentence. "No sir! Why, I may be older than dirt, but I dare say my age wasn't about to stop me from lugging these old bones here and attending my only son's wedding!"

"*Son?* Then you're—"

"King Alwyn Vargasmedt of Rhegar," he said, giving them a bow suggesting that his bones weren't quite as old as he'd deprecatingly claimed. "And I'm honoured to finally meet you, King Bryn. You're a man after my own heart, I can tell already."

"It… King? You're—" stammered Bryn, looking like a man who was completely out of his depth. Doubtless he'd prepared a courtly speech to be recited for Prince Gavin alone, but was completely at a loss with how to respond to this newest development.

"Yes, I know it's unfair, me showing up like this without mentioning anything about it in my letter, but I simply had to come!" The white-haired king quickly made his way up the gazebo steps and stood before Bryn, regarding him with a smile before opening his arms and enveloping him in a hug, as though they were old friends. Bryn's perplexed expression deepened, though he did eventually manage to return the embrace.

Gwen decided she liked this wizened old king. Anyone who could interrupt her father and cause him this much consternation was okay in her book.

King Alwyn stepped back after a few moments, still beaming delightedly at her father, and then swiveled his head to look in Gwen's direction. If anything, his smile got even wider.

"And *you!* You must be Princess Gwenwyn! Oh, the rumours were indeed true." He gave her a playfully wry look. "I fear you may be about to create an unintended economic crisis, marrying my son. When they start stamping your likeness on our new kingdom's coins, why, they'll be so beautiful that surely *nobody* will wish to part with a single one!"

Yes, Gwen definitely liked this old man.

Smiling her first genuine smile in a long, long time, she gave him a curtsey while bobbing her head respectfully.

"You honour us too greatly, Highness," Bryn said through a tight-lipped smile. "I'm sure Princess Gwenwyn appreciates your kind words, though she cannot actually say so at the moment, I'm afraid."

"Oh?"

"Yes, a Calderian wedding custom — the bride-to-be takes a vow of silence once her hand has been promised in marriage, so that the very next person to hear her speak is her husband, once they've been joined." Bryn increased the intensity of his smile. "My daughter takes tradition very seriously, and is nothing if not dutiful."

"Really?" King Alwyn looked a little perplexed by that, but then gave a light shrug. "Well, it takes all sorts, I suppose."

"Indeed," Bryn agreed, smiling. "I also wished to apologize for this highly irregular greeting spot, but I'm afraid that with the wedding mere days away, the throne room and the main hall are a bit of a mess. We have craftsmen working in there day and night to make sure everything looks perfect for the big day."

Well, that explained why they were all meeting here in the garden, at any rate.

"Oh, there's no need to apologize! This whole thing probably came as a bit of a surprise for you, what with Rhegar proposing this marriage out of the blue and all. Quite understandable that you'd need a bit of time to prepare. I'm sure everything will be quite satisfactory, and all will go as planned. Which reminds me." Alwyn looked behind him. "Gavin! Come along, boy. There's a certain young lady up here who has been waiting quite patiently to meet you."

The plainly-dressed prince had been attending his horse, but upon hearing his name stood up a little straighter and turned to regard them. Then, he came over to the gazebo entrance and slowly walked up the steps, eyes lowered and head slightly bowed. Once he'd arrived beside his father, the king, he straightened his back and simply stood there, stiffly.

He was also studiously ignoring Gwen.

"Highness, Princess, if I may introduce—" Alwyn began, turning towards his son. It was at that point he seemed to notice what the prince was wearing, and his entire posture changed slightly. He regarded Gavin with a flat, disappointed look. "Really?"

"Do you wish me to change, Highness?" Gavin asked quietly.

King Alwyn gave a light sigh, shaking his head and turning back to Gwen and her father. "If I may introduce my son, Prince Gavin. Gavin, if I may introduce you to King Bryn, and your betrothed, Princess Gwenwyn of Calderia."

Prince Gavin said nothing, but simply bowed to each of them in turn, not even looking at them as he did so. When he was finished he turned his head slightly to one side and stared off into the distance, as though inspecting some feature of the garden.

The grey-haired king gave his son a look of consternation, then walked up to him and whispered something angrily in his ear. Gavin's posture became even straighter, and his eyes went hard. He turned and considered Gwen, his grey eyes reminding her of smooth river rocks lying in the sun for some inexplicable reason.

Gwen tried not to focus on the uncomfortable pitter-pat of her heart.

Gavin continued staring at her a few seconds, and eventually his expression softened into a look of resignation. He took a step forward,

"Oh, Princess Gwenwyn," he said quietly, his voice a monotone, "your presence humbles me. My night of starless skies has become a sunny dawn upon glimpsing your beauty."

That said, he took her gloved hand in his and bowed his head, pantomiming a kiss upon the back of her knuckles.

It was quite obvious to Gwen that he hadn't meant a single word.

Prince Gavin finished his bow and returned to his stiff-backed stance, his hand still holding hers awkwardly.

"I can see now that this place is paradise," he continued glumly, averting his gaze, "for I've heard it said that paradise is where love dwells, and I now consider myself the most blessed man in all the world to have been chosen as the one you shall soon call-your-husband-may-I-please-be-excused-now-Father?"

Nobody did or said anything for a good, long while. Gwen felt as though she'd been splashed with ice water, and could sense her cheeks were beginning to redden.

Eventually, King Alwyn managed a scowl.

"Yes, fine," he muttered angrily, waving a dismissive gesture at his son. "Go. Attend to your horse, or something useful."

The prince gave them all a slight bow of his head before turning around and stomping his way down the gazebo steps, his shoulders hunched and his hands bunched into fists. The four of them watched in silence as he stalked back to his horse and led it away.

King Alwyn coughed apologetically and smiled wanly at the three of them.

"Ah, my most humble apologies for that undeserved behaviour. It's entirely my fault, I'm afraid." The grey-haired monarch sighed heavily, shaking his head. "Despite spending all these years attempting to impress upon him the seriousness of his duties and the art of statecraft, outright telling him what would be expected of him, I'm afraid the prospect of this marriage has dashed some rather unfortunate romantic hopes he'd had." He smiled sadly at Bryn. "A girl back home, one he kept secret from me. Forbidden love, all that. I only just found out about the whole thing myself fairly recently."

"Is that going to be a problem?" Bryn asked, sounding a bit rattled.

"What? Oh, no-no-no," Alwyn said, shaking his head vigourously. "No, he's a good boy, and he'll do what he's told. Just a smallish tantrum meant to embarrass me, I expect. Kids, hey?" His gaze wandered over to Gwen, and his expression became even more apologetic. "And you certainly didn't deserve that, Princess Gwenwyn. Why, you're even lovelier than I'd expected, and I'd heard a great many things about how lovely you are. My son's a lucky boy." He gave Bryn a crooked grin. "Must have had to beat suitors off with a stick as she got older, hey?"

"Yes, quite." Bryn smirked. "In fact, you wouldn't believe the lengths I had to go to just to keep her virtue intact."

Alwyn laughed good-naturedly at that, clapping Bryn on the shoulder. "Well, come, let's discuss some of the preparations, if you're not too busy. If you like, I could even order my staff to assist with some of the decoration, if you have need of them."

"That would be very much appreciated," smiled Bryn. "We've hanged most of the bunting already, but there's still—"

Gwen stopped listening at this point, as she realized something. Prince Gavin's reaction to seeing her had been unexpected, it was true, but eventually she'd understood something more important, and her thoughts now raced as she considered it.

A girlfriend.

That was it — the thing she was looking for. A tiny sliver of hope.

If Gwen were to reveal herself and cause Prince Gavin to flee, she'd be blamed, and Rhosyn would suffer the consequences. However, she'd just learned this prince had a reason not to want to marry her. If Prince Gavin, smitten as he was with this other girl, just happened to flee in order to return to her, Gwen wouldn't be the one held responsible.

If she could find a way to covertly encourage him to sneak away, to race back to his kingdom on horseback and marry his sweetheart, well, he couldn't very well marry her, could he? She just had to find some way to convince him to follow his heart.

Gwen didn't know how she could do that yet, but then, she'd only just thought of the possibility. She'd have to give the notion serious consideration later.

The best thing about it was this wasn't something her father or Anifail had planned for. Bryn hadn't expected this complication at all. His reaction to the prince, and even the surprise appearance of King Alwyn, made that perfectly obvious. He might recognize the danger something like this posed to his plans and take steps to prevent anything from happening, but then again he might be too busy with his preparations to give the matter his full attention.

Gwen wouldn't let anything go wrong this time. She'd be as smart and as careful as possible. She could do this.

The beginnings of a tentative happiness bubbled through her, and Gwen felt her arms and shoulders relax marginally as she let go of some of the stress she hadn't even realized she'd been holding there. Only half-listening to her father and King Alwyn talk, she took a deep, careful breath and let out a quiet sigh. She suddenly felt more relaxed than she had in days, perhaps weeks.

Her sigh also contained the tiniest bit of regret.

Gwen realized she had privately looked forward to receiving a few appreciative, hungry looks, much like the ones Prince Tremaine had given her. Crazy though it seemed, a small part of her couldn't help but feel the tiniest bit disappointed that, in Prince Gavin's eyes, she didn't measure up to the girlfriend he'd been forced to leave behind.

Chapter 16

Two days after meeting King Alwyn and Prince Gavin, elation slowly gave way to panic. None of the ideas she'd come up with had been as clever as she'd hoped, and the only ones that held any promise were hugely risky, or had little chance of succeeding. Or both.

And the wedding was tomorrow.

Gwen's first thought had been to send Gavin a message, describing her condition to him via written note. Or, if her new geis prevented that, perhaps just a simple note encouraging him to ditch the wedding and return to his girlfriend in Rhegar.

The problem with that whole approach was the evidence it would leave behind. With Rhosyn gone, there was nobody she could trust. All of the servants were brand new, hired by either Anifail or her father, which meant there was no way she'd simply hand one of them a note penned by her own hand. Besides, most of the castle staff didn't know how to read, so how would she even communicate what to do with the note in the first place? Hand gestures?

At one point she'd considered writing a note and keeping it with her, waiting until she was alone with Prince Gavin so she could give it to him directly. However, the prospect of walking around with that kind of incriminating evidence terrified her. What if Anifail ordered her searched, and found the note on her? What if her father caught her attempting to meet with the prince with a secret note, or even just a blank piece of paper, some ink, and a quill? He'd know what she was up to, certainly.

In the end she'd come up with an idea that seemed a safe bet. Gwen had found an old folding paper fan in one of the castle storage rooms, and had taken to carrying it with her wherever she went. She'd also located a small piece of pressed charcoal used for sketching, and after wrapping it in a shred of cloth, had found a way to tuck it into one of the folds of the fan. The paper of the fan was a pale yellow, but it was light enough to write a message on if she flattened it out. All she needed to do was meet with the prince face-to-face, hurriedly scrawl a message on the paper of her fan, show it to him, and then dispose of it after. That would be the easy bit, since every room in the castle had torches, or lamps, or a fireplace.

Of course, that would only work if she could get anywhere near Prince Gavin.

It was as if he knew when she was around, and was intentionally avoiding her. Gwen would overhear a scullery maid or other servant mention seeing him in the kitchen, or the inner courtyard, or the main garden, and she'd run down to wherever he'd been sighted, hoping to find him. She was always disappointed, though she was often left with the impression she'd missed him by mere moments.

In addition to overhearing snippets about where the prince was or what he was doing, Gwen also tried to listen in on some kitchen gossip and other rumours, hoping to find out more information about Prince Gavin's girlfriend, like her name. However, most of the whisperings were centered around this dashing heartthrob of a young prince who had swept into Calderia and set every local maiden's heart aflame. Gwen had heard Gavin's charming grin described more times than she could conveniently count, although she herself hadn't seen him as much as smile yet.

They marvelled at how polite he was, at his memory for servant's names, and his friendly, outgoing manner. They went on and on about how fit he appeared, how perfectly proportioned his shoulders were to his chest, and what a talented horseman he was. He even took care of his horse himself, they said, and reportedly waved away offers of help, preferring to do everything himself no matter how big or small the task. As far as the castle staff was concerned he was perfect in every single way, save for the fact that he was marrying *that haughty, spoiled brat of a princess, Gwenwyn.*

That, and hunting. Gavin was apparently a terrible hunter. According to several sources, the prince had been invited to go with her father on an afternoon hunting trip that had been arranged by Anifail the previous day. After an hour or so, they'd reportedly happened upon a spectacular ten-point buck that had been unaware of them, grazing in a meadow near the edge of the forest.

Before Bryn had even managed to line up a shot with his bow, however, Prince Gavin had nocked his own bow and quickly fired at the animal. His arrow missed the buck completely, instead connecting sharply with a small boulder. The arrow splintered on impact with an angry snap, sending the beast scurrying into the safety of the woods.

Though they'd seen two more deer, several rabbits, a covey of quail, and even a trumpeter swan in their travels, Gavin's ineptitude with a bow seemed to repeatedly alert prey to their presence and send them fleeing. The hunting party eventually returned to the castle empty handed, with her father muttering dark curses under his breath once the prince was out of earshot.

Aside from these stories about Prince Gavin, however, there was nothing. No talk of the girlfriend, or what her name was, or any other information Gwen might have found useful. Whenever people weren't talking about Gavin, they were talking about her, the aloof and undeserving princess he'd be marrying. Aside from depressing her a tad, skulking around and listening to whispered conversations had gotten her nowhere.

Gwen looked around her room critically. She was tired of sitting in this familiar spot, coming up with the same desperate schemes and rejecting them over and over again, getting nowhere.

Perhaps a change of scenery would help her thinking.

Days ago she'd been told by Anifail that she was not to be seen around the castle or the surrounding garden unless she wore one of three dresses that had been picked out for her. Doubtless this was so she'd make the proper impression if she encountered either King Alwyn or her betrothed.

Anifail hadn't said anything about what she should wear at the stables.

She couldn't very well ride in a dress, of course, but then again they hadn't expressly told her she couldn't wear her dress out there and then change her clothes, had they?

Tucking her riding leathers and other bits of clothing into a small laundry bag, Gwen left her bedroom and made her way to the servant's entrance. She gave the barest nod to the guards as she left the castle, trying to look as though there was nothing at all unusual about her taking a laundry bag with her.

It either worked, or the guards didn't really care in the first place. Neither of them bothered to give her even a cursory nod in return.

She maintained an easygoing, unhurried pace as she walked down to the stables, and spent some time considering where things stood.

The biggest obstacle to any plan she could think of was Rhosyn's situation. The more she thought about it, the more likely it seemed to her that Rhosyn had been part of her father's plan all along. It made a lot of sense really, allowing her to form a strong friendship with someone and then yanking her away and using her as leverage. Rhosyn was the only person Gwen really cared about, the one person in the world who treated her kindly, who made her feel the tiniest bit normal. What better way could they have found to control her? Even the thought of life without Rhosyn filled her with a desperate sort of loneliness.

Gwen shook her head angrily and banished those sorts of melancholy thoughts, reminding herself to stay focused on the problem. She'd spent enough time feeling sorry for herself, and that's not what the situation needed. Instead, perhaps she should spend some time reviewing some of the ideas she'd recently discarded. Maybe she'd see something she'd overlooked.

She'd already threatened to torture Anifail, but he'd made it clear that Rhosyn would suffer for it, so that was out. Trying something similar with her father probably wouldn't work either, since Anifail had mentioned that Bryn didn't even know where Rhosyn was being kept.

Putting a small amount of her saliva into their drinks and poisoning them both was something she'd seriously considered, but there were numerous drawbacks with that plan, not the least of which was the fact that she still wouldn't know where Rhosyn was. Sure, eliminating them meant she wouldn't be forced to go through with the marriage, but Rhosyn would likely starve to death. Plus, doing something like that would make her a murderer, damn her soul, and turn her crystal dark. Scratch that plan.

She'd briefly considered finding out more about the geis spheres and how they worked. After all, if they contained compulsions that forced people to do something, there might be one that made people tell the truth, or do something they were told to do, and she could free Rhosyn that way. Or she could find some way to remove her own geis. Of course, she had no real idea where the spheres even came from, or who might make or sell them in the first place, so that approach didn't seem likely. This being the day before the wedding, there probably wouldn't be enough time anyway.

Sooner than she'd expected, Gwen arrived at the stables. She hoisted the bag over her shoulder with a sigh, and then made her way into Rhosyn's living quarters so she could change out of her dress and into her riding clothes.

Once that was done, Gwen went to work.

She was actually quite proud of the job she'd done maintaining the horses, and keeping the stables tidy and organized for when Rhosyn got back. It was a lot of work, much more than she'd originally figured it would be, but she'd done it. She'd even swept out and replaced the hay in the stables a couple of times, something Rhosyn hadn't shown Gwen how to do. Sure, she'd had to figure it out herself, and she may not be doing everything exactly right, but it was better than just leaving the horses to fend for themselves.

Rhosyn was probably really worried about how the horses were doing, she realized. Left in a dark room, all alone, she could probably do little else but sit around and worry herself sick about the dozen or so animals in her care. That bothered Gwen. As if being held prisoner by Anifail wasn't bad enough!

Perhaps she could convince him to pass along a message letting her know that Gwen was taking care of the horses while she was imprisoned?

No, absolutely not. She wasn't going to ask Anifail for anything. He was a cruel, beast of a man, and he'd likely pervert the gesture into something else to make her life miserable. Either that or he'd become suspicious of her intentions, thinking she was planning something. Best to stay away from him entirely.

Donning a pair of heavy leather work gloves, she fetched some brushes and a bucket and spent some time brushing out the horses, taking her time with each, inspecting for injuries, and making sure she was doing a thorough job. That scratch she'd noticed on Dolivar's foreleg was healing nicely she noticed, though she was still extra-careful when lifting his leg up to inspect it. After unwrapping the bandage, Gwen cleaned the foreleg, scooped up some salve with a bit of cloth and gently spread it over the affected area, wrapping more cloth around the foreleg when she was finished. It was difficult to tie the bandage properly with the thick leather gloves she was forced to wear, but she managed.

Gwen gave Dolivar an apple and some hearty pats high on the shoulder when she was done. Forgetting herself for a moment, she tried murmuring 'good boy' to him. When no words came out she sighed, privately annoyed by the fact that she kept forgetting about her voice.

It was time for a ride, she figured. That always made her feel better.

She decided to dress Tambi, a dappled mare Gwen had always rather liked, and who probably hadn't been ridden in ages. Tambi had been acting a little anxious as of late, so a quick run might be just the thing she needed.

Once she had her properly dressed and saddled, Gwen hopped on and eased the mare out of the stable-yard, over to the meadow entrance, past the gates, and down towards the trail Gwen usually took. Once there, Tambi seemed to know exactly where she was supposed to go, and she picked up her pace excitedly. Gwen quickly found herself relaxing, picking up on the horse's rhythm, enjoying the fresh air.

They galloped hard for a while, but soon the mare had relaxed into an easy canter, and Gwen began to focus on enjoying the ride. This had always been one of her favourite ways to think.

Difficult though it was, Gwen realized she had to stop thinking about trying to find Rhosyn, and start focusing on other ways out of this mess. If she stopped the wedding from happening without implicating herself, there was a good chance Rhosyn would end up going free anyway.

King Alwyn had the potential to be an ally. She'd liked him the moment she saw him, if only because he seemed nothing at all like her own father. Of course, King Alwyn actually wanted his son to get married to her, and seemed quite embarrassed when he'd been forced to share the fact that Prince Gavin had been secretly courting someone else. The last thing he was likely to do was encourage his son to call off the wedding and rush back home.

But how was she to take advantage of the fact that the prince already had a girlfriend? She couldn't talk to Gavin about her, or otherwise suggest he follow his heart. She couldn't write him a letter about the matter either, since it would land her in a ton of trouble if intercepted. What she really needed was something that sent that particular message without being obvious about it. Something to remind him of her.

Like a present, perhaps.

He was her betrothed, after all. Nobody would object if she sent him a gift, would they? Her father might even be overjoyed by something like that, believing she'd resigned herself to her fate and was actively trying to help his plans. She just needed to make sure her gift was something that seemed innocuous, but that reminded him of his girlfriend.

A book, perhaps. A fairy tale, or a love story. Oh, and she even knew of the perfect one! It was one of her favourites, a story about a peasant boy who fell in love with a rich merchant's daughter, and had to fetch three golden feathers from a roc's nest to prove his worth. In it, the young peasant boy never gave up, never stopped believing he might one day win the hand of the girl he loved.

The book itself was beautiful, too; embossed leather and gold leaf, with breathtaking watercolour illustrations. Just the sort of gift you might expect royalty to exchange. It was perfect!

True, he might not be influenced by it. He might end up treating the gift as he'd treated her on their first meeting — tiredly acknowledging it and then ignoring it completely. Or he might get the wrong message from it, and feel shamed into accepting Gwen and making the best of things. Still, it was something, and it probably wouldn't get her into trouble. If it had even a small chance of working, it was better than nothing.

Gwen tugged a bit on the reigns and slowed Tambi to a walk, and spent a long while thinking of things she'd need to do in order to get the book and make it presentable. She considered where she'd acquire a silk cloth and ribbon to wrap it in, and how to get it out of the library. Once she had some semblance of a plan sorted out in her head, she looked around and took notice of where she was.

The trail had widened until it had become a small, open patch of meadow she recognized. It was the same meadow Rhosyn had brought Darin to that one time, from what she remembered of their earlier conversation. It was an ideal spot to bring someone; lush, rolling hills encircled by an expanse of majestic, leafy green trees. As magnificent as the sight was during the summer, she knew it would be particularly breathtaking come autumn.

Tambi pawed at the ground, which made Gwen realize they'd stopped moving forward. Well, that was probably just as well. They were about half an hour's ride from the stable, which meant a half-hour back, and maybe another half hour dressing down the mare after the hour-long ride.

Gwen made a clicking noise, pulling on the right rein and slowly turning the horse completely around so they could ride back. It was still early afternoon, with lots of time to fetch the book. Getting it out of the library would probably be easy, considering how busy everyone else was preparing for the wedding.

How would she get the book to Gavin once she got it, though? She wouldn't ask a servant to take it to him, even if she could talk. Maybe she could approach the Rhegarian soldiers and servants, indicate her gift, smile and perhaps communicate her wishes that way? Guardsmen probably wouldn't know what to do with a silent princess who'd come bearing what looked like a present, and would likely fetch the king, or—

Tambi reared up suddenly and gave a terrified whinny. Before Gwen could react she found herself launched backward, out of her saddle and into the air, the reins torn from her hands.

Despite her momentary surprise, Gwen managed to get her elbows behind her as she fell. The jolt of sudden impact coincided with a flash of white, and the breath was knocked out of her as a sharp pain ripped through her hip, elbow, ribs, and shoulder.

Dazed, she lay there for a few seconds trying to remember how to breathe. The sound of a rapidly galloping horse gradually faded away, and everything became silent.

Gwen propped herself up and coughed, though it hardly made a sound. That was odd. She hadn't realized you needed your voice to cough properly.

Groaning, she slowly got to her feet, inspecting herself for injuries, scowling.

It had been ages since she'd been thrown from a horse, and she remembered now why she avoided it. Even with the comparatively soft ground of the meadow, falling and landing from that height wasn't exactly fun. Her elbow smarted, likely scraped and bruised, and her shoulder felt like it'd almost been yanked right off.

Gwen looked down the length of field that Tambi had gone. Though she'd appeared a little anxious lately, it wasn't really like her to do something like that. She was pretty calm and docile most of the time.

Brushing herself off a bit, Gwen sighed and contemplated how to proceed. Tambi wasn't too independent a thinker, so she probably wouldn't run far. That, or she'd run all the way back to the stables to be with the other horses, which meant a long, long walk ahead of her, which she hoped—

A trace of movement caught Gwen's attention.

Black shadows and patches of grey rock seemed to shift before her eyes, weaving between the trunks of elms at the very edge of the woods.

Huge, nightmarish amber eyes regarded her from about thirty yards away, and a pair of black lips pulled themselves back to reveal two rows of sharp, angry-looking teeth.

With awful certainty, she knew exactly what had spooked the mare.

A dire wolf.

Three foot high at the shoulder. At least twice her weight. Likely more.

Staring intently at her, the grey-black monster growled deeply, and Gwen suddenly felt like the whole world had slowed down.

Chapter 17

Standing there, looking the huge wolf directly in the eye, Gwen kept as still as possible. It seemed like her heart was pounding so violently the wolf would be able to hear it, despite the distance between them.

The monstrous wolf simply stood there at the edge of the trees, watching her, growling ominously.

Without moving her head, Gwen glanced around for something she might be able to use as a weapon. Being the middle of a meadow, away from most of the trees, there weren't any fallen branches or deadwood laying about, but she did spy a couple of fair sized rocks. One looked to be about the size of her fist.

She reached down and picked it up, her attention ever on the wolf.

Her action caused the dire wolf's growling to increase in volume before returning to a rumble. It continued to stare at her, bristling, waiting.

There was no point in running. Gwen had seen regular wolves attack prey, and she doubted she could run faster than a deer. A horse might be able to run fast enough to get away. Tambi *had* gotten away in fact, galloping like the wind and leaving Gwen behind. Not that Gwen could exactly blame her.

The wolf wasn't moving forward into the clearing, but simply stood there, teeth bared, growling menacingly in her direction. Perhaps it was waiting for her to run, to try to get away. If she ran, she didn't think she'd get very far. The closest trees she could see were about twenty yards distant, and quite near where the wolf stood anyways.

Spying a smaller rock that seemed much better for throwing, Gwen bent down to pick it up, provoking another loud grumble of anger from the beast. She found the prospect of picking up a third rock terrifying, but she couldn't allow her fear to paralyze her. If she had any chance of making it through this, she needed weapons, and....

And what did she need with stones, anyway? She *was* a weapon!

Gwen hurriedly pulled the gloves from her hands and tossed them to one side. Then, she slid out of her leather riding coat, grabbing it by the collar as it fell behind her. After a moment's thought, she took the jacket and quickly wrapped it as best she could around her left forearm. Those teeth looked sharp, and the wolf's jaws were probably strong enough to crush arm-bones without too much trouble, even with her jacket wrapped around her arm. Still, padding seemed like a good idea.

Without her jacket, her undershirt would provide scant protection, but the more of her skin she exposed the better off she might be. If it got close enough, she had only to touch the monster.

Gwen could feel her arms tremble, though she didn't know if that was because of the cool breeze on her bared shoulders, or from the panic she felt.

The thing was still there, in the exact same spot, still snarling and bristling. Gwen took a deep breath, wondering what would happen next. As she did so, she realized she was still holding the rocks she'd scavenged.

Without even stopping to think, she threw the smaller of the two rocks right at the beast.

The dire wolf leaped to one side, easily dodging her projectile. Its growling stopped a moment as it stared at her, considering. Then it began growling again.

Maybe she was confusing it a bit. She wasn't exactly behaving like normal prey would, after all, which could be why it hadn't run at her yet. Maybe it was used to chasing things and was waiting for her to flee. Perhaps if she acted more like a predator, it'd have second thoughts about attacking her.

Gwen bared her teeth at the wolf, unthinkingly attempting a loud growl as well, though it came out as a gentle wheeze.

The wolf's teeth disappeared a moment, and it cocked its head at her as though confused, considering her once more.

Was it beginning to think of her a potential threat? She bared even more of her teeth at it, taking a half-step forward.

Quite suddenly, there was a growl so loud Gwen felt it in her chest, and the thing bared its teeth at her with renewed ferocity, making sounds even angrier and more terrifying than before.

Oops. Now it seemed to want to prove it was scarier than she was. Hardly a difficult thing to demonstrate, under the circumstances.

Then again, there was something about her it didn't know.

Gwen was going to be attacked, and soon. Some abstract part of her brain already knew that. She forced herself to calm down and consider her best options when dealing with that terrifying reality. Her left forearm was padded, so she'd try to keep it between her and the wolf. If she could fend it off with her left, she could attack with her right and hit it with her other rock, or slap at it with her open palm, attempt to touch it with her skin. She could try spitting at the thing as well, and whenever possible she should try to brush up against it with her bared forearms or shoulders. Fur didn't protect against her touch, something she'd learned to her tremendous sorrow after petting Rolf when she was younger.

She just needed to hurt it. If the wolf started feeling pain, it might reconsider Gwen's usefulness as food.

Gwen licked her lips nervously. A bead of sweat trickled along

Gwen's forehead, and she wiped it away with the back of her hand. Then, an idea suddenly coming to her, she quickly wiped her brow with her jacket-wrapped forearm, attempting to get as much sweat from her forehead onto the leather as possible before once more holding it out between her and the wolf.

Go ahead, she thought. *Take a bite of that, wolf. I dare you.*

The huge wolf studied her a bit more between growls, as though assessing her behaviour. Then, without warning, it lowered its head and bounded to one side. Just as quickly, it reversed direction with its head back up and ears perked forward, its huge amber eyes never leaving her for even a moment.

Gwen stood her ground, though terrified and shaking, and held her fist-sized rock aloft.

A second later the wolf did it again, dancing in the other direction this time, eyes bright and alert, closely watching her reaction. It did the same thing a third time, and then a fourth, tongue lolling over its slick, bone-white teeth.

The fifth time, it launched itself at her.

Gwen barely managed to get her arm up in time. Her elbow was shoved into her ribs, and she felt herself stumble back a half-step. Her arm was yanked violently to one side, then the other.

Bringing her rock-clutching hand around as quickly as possible, she tried smashing it into the nearest bit of blurry black-grey fur she could see. She felt the rock twist out of her sweaty fingers just as she felt rough fur brush up against her hand.

The rock took the wolf in the flank with a thump, and then fell to the ground.

The wolf bounded back several paces, presenting its side but facing her, its teeth still bared.

Gwen's breathing was ragged now, and she quickly scouted the earth around her for another rock.

Unhurriedly, the wolf turned in place, fully facing her once more. Then, suddenly, it perked up as though sensing something. It was no longer baring its teeth at her, but was standing there with its nose in the air, as though something was different about how it smelled. At one point it appeared to glance back at its flank, then back to her.

Maybe she'd gotten the thing's attention, or hurt it a bit. Throwing rocks wasn't what normal prey did, after all, so maybe she was confusing it. Or quite possibly there was something about the smell of *chi'darro* that made it regard her as something other than food. Wolves had an incredible sense of smell, so if she didn't smell like prey or act like prey, perhaps she could convince this thing she wasn't worth trifling with.

Gwen bared her teeth at it once more, trying to seem more confident than she felt. The dire wolf stood perfectly still, watching her.

She'd lost track of where her rock had gone, and the only one she could see nearby was much bigger — easily half the size of her head, and oddly shaped.

Gwen bent down and picked it up, and immediately knew she wouldn't be able to hang on to it one-handed for very long, much less raise it to shoulder height and throw it. Instead, keeping her jacket-wrapped arm between the two them, she let her other arm hang as she clutched the top of the rock, fingers gripping it desperately. She might have enough strength to do an underhand swing, but it'd have to be soon.

Appearing to make up its mind about something, the wolf began its crouch-dance anew, pausing each time it finished. Its tongue lolled to one side occasionally, giving her the momentary impression it was playing with her, though the malevolence in those hungry yellow-orange eyes left her with no doubts as to what would happen if she lost this particular game.

Gwen could feel her fingers start to cramp from the effort of holding up the rock, and she quickly scouted around for another. Within moments she located another fist-sized rock a few paces away. But how to get it?

She could heave this one at the wolf, then run and pick up the next. It was her only chance. She knew her fingers weren't capable of clinging to this one for much longer.

Reaching her decision, she brought her arm around and heaved the rock forward at the wolf with everything she had, breath exploding from her lungs in what would have been a tremendous groan of effort if she were capable of making a sound. As soon as the rock left her fingertips, she turned and bolted towards her next projectile.

Out of the corner of her eye she could see the thing easily leaping to one side to avoid the large stone. As its paws touched the ground, and with an tremendously roar of triumph mixed with excitement, the thing flew towards her once more, quicker than she'd imagined possible.

Gwen leaped forward, landing in a crouch beside her rock so she could reach down to grab it, her left arm raised behind her in a gesture of warding. As her trembling fingers wrapped around the rock and pulled it from the earth, she spun around in time to see the wolf, not five feet away. It sprang forward at her, its jaws wide.

Swinging her projectile side-arm while leaping backwards, Gwen loosed her rock, and knew she'd missed the moment she let it fly.

A part of her brain screamed at her, and she noticed she'd lowered her jacket-wrapped arm too far, and wouldn't be able to bring it up in time

Thwip!

A broken howl of agony filled Gwen's world for a moment. There was a second whispered *thwip* sound, and the deafening howl was instantly cut off.

The dire wolf crashed upon its side, the thing's momentum carrying it forward and knocking Gwen's legs out from under her. The world spun, and she fell directly atop the wolf's massive shoulder.

Panic coursed through her as she rolled away from the huge beast, struggling to right herself, her breath coming in gasps. Once on her feet, she managed to stumble two steps away before falling once more to the grass, her hand reaching for something — anything — that she might use as a weapon.

Gwen rolled over onto her back, throwing her arms up in a vain attempt to stave off the beast, already knowing she was too late... that it was looming over her, its muzzle mere inches away from her.

It wasn't.

Sun, clouds, and azure sky. A bird casually flying by. Aside from a faint ringing in her ears, the only sound she could hear was that of her own ragged breathing.

She hastily propped herself up on her elbows and looked past her boots to the scene that lay beyond.

The enormous wolf lay a few feet away, unmoving. Two arrows with identical fletching were buried in its side, one near the base of the thing's skull, the other in its chest, just under its outstretched foreleg. Its eyes stared vacantly at her, mouth still open enough to display most of its terrifyingly large teeth.

Gwen blinked at it a few times, slowly rising to her feet. Then she looked around the rest of the meadow, and saw Prince Gavin.

Though she had to shield her eyes from the sun and could barely even make him out, she knew it was him. He was a little ways up the trail and standing up in his horse's stirrups, holding a bow with an arrow at the ready, facing the open meadow.

The two of them did nothing but stare at each other from across the field for several moments.

Then, calmly, Gavin wordlessly relaxed his bowstring and tucked his arrow somewhere on the other side of his saddle.

That done, he turned his horse in order to face her a little more fully. Still standing up in his stirrups, holding one hand to his waist and the other out to the side, he bowed low to her.

A second later, in a way that couldn't have been coincidence, his horse seemed to bow as well, lowering its head to the grass and bending a foreleg.

Even amid the rapid, terror-induced beating it was already doing, she could feel her heart give an extra-loud thump.

She stood there a moment, awkwardly, her knees still trembling.

Then, she returned his gesture with a very exaggerated and thankful curtsey of her own, hoping that it conveyed some small measure of the gratitude she felt.

When she rose, she watched Gavin sit back in his saddle and stow his bow. Though she couldn't make out his facial expression, his actions had an air of satisfaction about them.

Then again, maybe he deserved to feel some satisfaction. He'd made not one but *two* amazingly good shots with his bow, and in rapid succession! On horseback, and with a fast-moving dire wolf as a target no less.

And yet, what of that disastrous hunting trip he'd been on with her father? If he were capable of making shots like this, then surely he would have made similarly impressive shots while riding with Bryn, which meant—

Sudden understanding caused Gwen's heart to melt the tiniest bit, and her eyes to well up.

An expert archer, one capable of downing a savage beast with precision and ease, but who was unable or unwilling to kill a deer, or a swan, or any other non-threatening woodland dweller. One who went so far as to be a terrible shot on purpose, spoiling her father's opportunities and scaring the animals off so they might live another day. This beautiful, perfect man....

A man of conscience.

And they were alone now, finally! There was nobody out here but the two of them!

Both of Gavin's arrows were still firmly lodged in the side of the dead wolf, sticking up into the air. They looked to Gwen to be very well made — he'd be down to retrieve them shortly, she knew. It'd be just her and him. Finally, a chance to do something!

Neither of them moved, and simply stayed where they were, regarding one another from a distance — he astride his horse, and she beside the dire wolf he'd just killed, which lay on the ground a few feet away from her. The wind brushed the short green grass of the meadow playfully as Gwen stood there, waiting. Moments stretched themselves into minutes.

Then, inexplicably, Prince Gavin turned his horse completely around and slowly rode back towards the trail, away from the meadow. Before long his horse broke into a trot, and both horse and rider crested a hill and were gone from view.

Puzzled, Gwen simply stared after him.

What was he doing? Why wasn't he coming down there to make sure she was okay? For that matter, why wouldn't he come to retrieve his arrows? At the very least, wouldn't he come over to offer her a ride back to the castle? Surely he could see she was horseless!

Why would he simply turn around and leave like that?

A breeze brushed up against her bare shoulder, causing her to shiver slightly. Still puzzling over Gavin's actions, Gwen attempted to fold her arms to her chest to warm herself, and in so doing she realized her riding jacket was still wrapped around her left arm, which—

Oh.

Gwen suddenly felt like she knew exactly why he hadn't come over.

At the time, taking her jacket off had been one of those life-or-death decisions, a survival instinct. Now, Gwen was painfully aware of just how clingy her simple undershirt had become. The thin material had plastered itself against her like a second skin.

Having saved her, he was now politely excusing himself for the sake of her modesty. In addition to everything else, Prince Gavin was a gentleman.

Giving the terrifyingly huge beast one final glance, Gwen turned and ran across the meadow toward the last spot she'd seen the prince. She unwrapped the jacket from her arm, throwing it over her shoulders and hurriedly slipping her arms through the sleeves as she ran.

Her knees still felt weak from her ordeal, and she stumbled often, but she forced herself to maintain the breakneck pace. She had to get him alone... had to find a way to bring him back to the stables, where she could get some paper or a book to write on. She'd take a rock and scratch the truth about herself right into the stable walls if she had to. And if her geis wouldn't allow that, well, she'd write words of encouragement, tell him to follow his heart, something. Anything!

As she ran, she noticed a trace of wolf-spittle on the arm of her jacket, and she tried not to shudder.

He'd saved her from that monster. Forced to marry a princess he didn't love, he was still brave and good-hearted enough to save her, despite the fact his own unhappiness was guaranteed as a result.

And by saving her life, he'd unknowingly put his own life in danger. In a way, Gwen realized, he may have just killed himself. It was like something from one of those ancient tragedies in her father's library, the ones where everyone died at the end.

This story wasn't going to end like that. She wouldn't let it.

Breathless, Gwen finally crested the last hill and arrived at the trail where it met the meadow. She quickly looked about her, hoping to find Gavin patiently waiting there for her so that he might offer her a ride back to the stables.

She heard a soft whinny a little further up the trail, and her heart caught in her throat.

Exhausted but exultant, she forced herself along the trail as quickly as she could, and in practically no time at all she spied Tambi.

The mare stood there, looking very ill at ease, her reins loosely tied to the branch of a nearby tree. Gavin's work, probably. Spying a riderless horse might have been how he'd known she was in trouble in the first place. He'd caught her horse, and had left it here for her.

Prince Gavin and his own horse were nowhere in sight.

Gwen already felt faint from all the excitement and running, and a part of her knew her knees wouldn't be able to handle riding Tambi at a gallop for more than a few minutes. And even so, Tambi was likely still skittish from her own encounter with the dire wolf, and would have to be ridden carefully the entire trip back. There was no way she'd be catching up to Gavin, even if he wasn't that far away, or riding all that fast.

He was gone.

She'd lost her chance.

Chapter 18

Gwen stared at the familiar scenery beyond her window, delicately wiping away another trickle of moisture that she felt high on her cheek.

The three servants acting as her handmaidens likely didn't understand why she was crying. Then again, they weren't her friends, probably didn't want to be there in the first place, and so didn't ask. They might have even been warned not to go near her. The four of them had been alone in Gwen's room for the last couple of hours, and the three maidens had kept to themselves the entire time, chatting quietly with each other, throwing the occasional look in her direction.

Oh, how she wished Rhosyn was here right now. More than anything she just needed someone to hold her, and tell her this wasn't her fault.

She'd tried everything she could think of. She'd tried so bloody hard.

After getting Tambi back to the stables, she'd scurried back to the castle, cleaned herself up, and set about fetching the leather-bound book she was giving to Prince Gavin. Then she gathered a nice, fancy-looking cloth and some ribbon, and spent over an hour preparing her gift, tying the ribbon in a way that looked elegant and proper.

She'd even personally handed it over to a Rhegaran guard, who seemed to understand what she wanted despite the fact she couldn't talk, and who assured her that he would deliver the package to Prince Gavin himself and no other. Gwen had almost wept with relief upon hearing those words, and had left the guest wing of the palace with a smile on her face.

The book was returned that evening, unopened.

Additionally, the returned gift aroused the suspicions of her father, who confined Gwen to her bedchamber and posted guards outside of her door. She'd spent the whole night pacing, unable to sleep, trying to think of some new thing she could try. Now unable to even leave her room, it seemed there was very little she was able to do.

At one point in the evening, she found herself wishing she possessed the resolve to throw herself from her tower.

Was she a coward because she couldn't muster the courage to do that? Was she a terrible person because she couldn't give up her life for someone else's?

Her throat felt scratchy and dry, and Gwen turned away from the window to fetch herself a glass of water from the nearby pitcher. Her movements were noticed immediately by the three handmaidens, who went silent at her approach and seemed to regard her with a touch of worry and nervousness. Sighing, and somehow managing to feel even more miserable than she had a few seconds ago, she poured a glass of water and headed back to her spot by the window. As she walked over, she glimpsed her reflection in the mirror next to her closet.

She looked like everything she ever imagined a storybook princess to be, and was barely able to recognize herself, even when she wasn't wearing the thin, gauzy veil they'd brought her. It was a beautiful dress, one that covered her from head to toe with luxurious white fabric. And yet Gwen found she couldn't appreciate this dress, much less like it. She hated it, in fact — loathed how beautiful it was and how wonderfully it fit.

When she was younger she'd often wish for some dashing knight to come along and whisk her away from this place, or wistfully imagine herself in a gorgeous wedding dress, about to be married to a handsome prince. Now here she was, about to be married to a handsome prince, just like in a fairy tale. And it was horrible beyond words.

A light rapping at her door attracted the attention of everyone in the bedroom. Shortly after, the door was slowly opened wide enough to reveal a nervous-looking chambermaid. Her eyes fixed on Gwen, and she hastily bobbed her head, looking apologetic.

"Princess Gwenwyn, I've been asked to send for your handmaidens," she said, voice little more than a frightened whisper. "You're to come down in a few minutes. The king has announced your feast will be starting soon."

Gwen nodded in reply, feeling ill.

The servant girl appeared the tiniest bit relieved, bowing her head and turning to smile at the three handmaidens, who were already in the process of making their way to the door. Once they were beyond it, Gwen heard the chambermaid comment how beautiful the girls looked in their fancy dresses, a statement that was followed by hushed, excited whisperings as the girls made their way down the stairs.

Turning away from the door, Gwen set her water glass down on the table, noticing as she did that her gloved hand was trembling slightly. She bleakly considered her bedroom window once more.

I am a coward, she thought bitterly. *If I had been braver, or even smarter, I would have simply let that wolf kill me. At least that way, I wouldn't have been able to hurt anyone else.*

It seemed like barely any time at all had passed before there was a second, much more authoritative rapping at her door. Gwen turned and saw two hooded guardsmen standing just outside her room. One gestured impatiently for her to come away from the window.

As recently as a day ago, Gwen might have been able to briefly imagine that the guardsmen were actually the disguised sons of some noble come to save her, or a brave peasant boy and his plucky friend who had come to ensure this travesty of a wedding did not reach its conclusion. Now, she'd stopped dreaming of those sorts of possibilities entirely.

Nobody was coming for her. Nobody wanted to save her from this. They were probably exactly as they seemed, two unfriendly guards sent by her father to make sure she didn't panic and run off somewhere.

Gathering up her bouquet of flowers and her fan, Gwen swept past the guards, her face as expressionless as she could make it. The two guards followed her, staying back just far enough to avoid stepping on the train of her dress.

At the bottom of the stairs, Gwen was surprised to see that even the stone hallways leading to the main hall had been decorated with ribbons and colourful flowers. The drab, oft-times dreary-looking walls had been treated with whitewash, and looked better than at any time she could remember.

She slowly proceeded down the transformed hallway, taking as much time as she could, ever aware of the heavy footsteps of the two solders behind her. Soon the dull roar and chatter of a large gathering of people could be heard coming from somewhere beyond the well-lit greeting area ahead of her.

There were a few dozen people in the greeting hall, mostly castle staff hurriedly carrying things to where they were needed, or talking excitedly to one another, or making last-minute adjustments to their uniforms, or other things of that nature. For a moment she simply stood there, watching everything.

Gwen hadn't been told where to go or what would be happening. That had probably been intentional, so she'd be off-balance and easier to manage during the ceremony.

"Princess Gwenwyn," a familiar, smug-sounding voice called out. "My, you look positively radiant this afternoon. Goodness, doesn't she look radiant?"

Gwen tiredly turned her head to regard Anifail, her lip already curling slightly. Though he wore a tidy new captain's uniform, he still somehow managed to resemble a brigand of some sort as he stood there, smirk on his face, arm in arm with—

Oh Goddess!

Rhosyn had lost some weight, based on how the dark blue dress hung from her shoulders, and despite the application of some makeup Gwen was able to make out dark circles underneath her friend's red-rimmed eyes. She was holding Anifail's arm like it was some sort of angry snake that might lash out and bite her at any moment.

Tears sprang to Gwen's eyes, and without even thinking she strode forward towards the two of them, wrapped her arms around Rhosyn and hugged her fiercely. She could feel Rhosyn's shoulders shake periodically, and she knew her friend was sobbing. Well, so was Gwen, for that matter.

Just seeing that Rhosyn was alive and well was about the best thing to happen to Gwen all week.

Reluctantly they parted, and Gwen held her friend at arm's length. Through her veil, she could see Rhosyn give her a tearful, sad little smile. Then Rhosyn took a quick breath, and began moving her lips excitedly, at which point she seemed to realize something. A moment after that, Rhosyn's expression became desperately sad, and she began sobbing anew....

Silently.

"Yes, there appears to be something the matter with my escort tonight," Anifail remarked sadly, his tone completely at odds with the gleeful expression on his face. "She's been like this ever since I went to fetch her. Perhaps she has a cold. She did ask me earlier to tell you that she's desperately hoping everything goes as planned this evening."

Anifail's expression made the meaning of his words very clear.

Gwen turned back to her friend in time to see another teardrop spill over her cheek, and the two girls simply regarded one another.

Then, Rhosyn raised her eyebrows at Gwen, as if to ask a question. Sighing, Gwen squeezed her friend's shoulders and looked her in the eye, shaking her head sadly. Rhosyn's shoulders slumped slightly, and she regarded Gwen with an expression that was both mournful and sympathetic.

Some questions simply didn't require words.

Anifail coughed. "Sorry, getting a bit awkward here, all this silence. I noticed you were looking a wee bit unsure of yourself as well. Might it have to do with some trepidation on your part, Princess? Perhaps a spot of worry? After all, I don't imagine you've had that mother-daughter chat regarding the sorts of things that happen on your wedding night." He smiled cruelly, reaching out to take Rhosyn's arm and pulling her towards him. "Well, have no fear; I'll tell you exactly what'll happen. We'll all feast, and then there's the ceremony joining you and Prince Gavin in marriage. Seems a bit backward, but apparently that's how they do things in Rhegar," Anifail said, shrugging. "Once that's done, you'll be whisked off to a room made up especially for the two of you. Oh, and don't you fret too much about what you're supposed to do once you're there. Once the vicar proclaims you husband and wife, I'm quite certain you'll know exactly what to do."

Gwen noticed Anifail squeeze Rhosyn's arm as he said the word exactly. Yes, he was making absolutely sure Gwen was reminded what was at stake.

"Well, I suppose we'd better go find ourselves a seat, my dear. Something near the front, perhaps." A smirk appeared in the corner of his mouth. "Wouldn't want you missing out on your best friend's special moment now."

And with that, Anifail turned and strode through the large vaulted doorway leading to the throne room, followed closely by a miserable-looking Rhosyn.

Watching him go, Gwen continued to stand there in the greeting hall, feeling lost and as alone as ever, despite the dozens of bustling people flitting in and out of the room. Her head began to swim a little bit, which was when she realized she needed to focus on her breathing, and not the tight ball of misery that had lodged itself in her chest. She took a deep breath, and then another, trying to calm herself enough to keep the tears at bay. Tears weren't going to help anyone today, least of all her.

Unless....

What if she were weeping as she went to the altar? It wasn't at all seemly, and would enrage her father, but it would send a message to Gavin and perhaps spur him into action. He'd rescued her in the woods, after all. Perhaps if he saw that she needed rescuing *now....*

Gwen had barely put together the first fragments of a potential plan when a wide-eyed maiden hurried through the nearby archway and into the greeting hall. Upon spying Gwen, she immediately came over to her.

"Princess Gwenwyn," she said, curtseying low before her. "They tell me it's time for you to enter."

Indeed, she could now hear the soft strains of violins playing a familiar, joyful tune.

Gwen nodded to the maiden, who curtseyed again before scurrying off into a hallway on the opposite end of the room, presumably on her way to notify the kitchen staff that everything was about to start. The few people that were left in the room noticed the music as well, and hurried off one by one until she was the only one left in the hall.

Steeling herself, Gwen clutched the bouquet of flowers tightly against her waist with both hands and began walking towards the sound of violins.

Chapter 19

Gwen entered the throne room, which prompted an unexpected trumpet fanfare to play from somewhere she couldn't see. Uncomfortably aware that all eyes were upon her, she walked forward slowly and deliberately with her handmaidens, barely looking around at anyone. Instead, she focused on the decorations. Under the circumstances, it wasn't all that difficult to do.

The throne room was utterly transformed, even more so than the garden or hallways had been. Vibrant silk streamers of all colours criss-crossed along the ceiling above her, producing a pattern that undulated and shifted as you moved across the floor, appearing completely different depending on where you stood. Ornate tables and chairs had been set up everywhere you looked, and every table had at least a dozen people sitting at it. Deep red satin bunting lined the walls, framing brand new torches and lamps in expensive-looking silver wall mounts, the sheer quantity of which were illuminating the room more brightly than she'd thought possible.

Gone were the severe, dark wooden panels and archaic tapestries, as well as all the other decorations she knew her father preferred.

There was a large banquet table set up where the throne usually sat, right in front of the newly whitewashed stone wall. Her father and King Alwyn were both sitting at the table, as were several other people she didn't recognize. Given the empty seat beside her father, it wasn't hard for Gwen to figure out where she was supposed to go.

Many of the several hundred assembled guests murmured to one another as she made her way to the other side of the room. She couldn't actually make out any snippets of whispered conversation, so she had no idea if they were discussing her beautiful dress, how lovely she looked in it, or how unfair it was that someone as undeserving as Gwen was about to marry the well-liked and charming Prince Gavin, who even now was—

Gwen blinked, and for a moment her steps faltered slightly.

Prince Gavin wasn't in the room.

In the stories she'd read that had weddings, the bride was usually the last to enter. That was pretty standard, wasn't it? And yet, the chair sitting next to King Alwyn was conspicuously empty.

Perhaps she *wasn't* getting married today. Might Gavin have followed his heart after all, and fled the castle before they were to be wed? Or perhaps he'd left because of the various things he'd heard about Gwen? He was no stranger to most of the castle guards and other servants, after all, and had spent countless hours talking and laughing and visiting with them during his attempts to avoid her this past week. Maybe he'd been told something about her he didn't care for.

Oh, wouldn't *that* be perfect — her father's plans foiled by the very rumours Anifail had been spreading about her. The very thought of it actually caused the barest trace of a smile to find its way to Gwen's lips.

She continued on towards the main banquet table, the train of her dress sweeping the floor behind her as she made her way to her seat. Idly, she began to wonder how she'd even be expected to sit while wearing this awkward, detestable gown of hers. However, once she arrived at her spot she saw that a small bench had been arranged for her rather than one of the high-backed chairs on which her father and King Alwyn sat.

Gwen sat down in her seat, facing the assembled crowd, and she quickly checked it for familiar faces. Almost immediately she noticed Anifail and Rhosyn had been seated at the closest table, not twenty feet away from her.

Anifail smiled and nodded when he saw he'd caught her attention, and he raised a silver goblet towards her with a nod. Rhosyn did nothing, and merely sat beside him, staring through the table.

Choosing to ignore his presence, Gwen turned her attention away from Anifail's table and scanned the rest of the room. She noticed an altar that had been set up on a dais in the corner opposite of where she was sitting. It was being tended to by an ancient-looking vicar in red and silver robes, whose few remaining wisps of silver hair had been lightly oiled and plastered against his balding pate for the occasion. On the altar were two crystals, one of which she recognized as hers. The other, much larger crystal was Gavin's, obviously.

But what of the prince himself? Where was Gavin?

A few minutes later, as if in answer to her question, a second fanfare sounded. Not long after, Prince Gavin walked into the room, looking handsome and regal beyond words. He was wearing what appeared to be a high-ranking soldier's uniform, white officer's gloves and a dark grey coat, tastefully decorated with various lapel-pins and other trappings Gwen assumed were marks of distinction or otherwise represented his official rank.

The murmurs and whispers of those in attendance seemed to triple in volume, and Gwen's heart sank. Obviously he hadn't run off anywhere, and had probably just been delayed while getting ready for the ceremony. And now he had arrived — this unfortunate, beautiful man her father had consigned to death.

Oblivious to any reaction his appearance might have provoked from those assembled, he strode through the throne room and to the main banquet table, stiff-backed and solemn. Without a word, he walked around to his seat and sat down, his expression bleak.

He didn't so much as glance in Gwen's direction.

Once everyone at the head table had taken their seats, Bryn slowly stood up from his chair and held his arms out towards the hundreds of townspeople who had come for the feast, a sign he was about to speak. Chairs squawked noisily against the floor as everyone stood up from their seats, and complete silence fell over the room within moments.

"Fellow Calderians, honoured guests, I bid you all welcome! Today we celebrate a truly joyous occasion, one that sees my dearest daughter, Gwenwyn, wed to—"

Gwen stopped listening at that point, already more or less familiar with the sorts of things her father would be saying. In truth, she'd become rather adept at ignoring her father's ponderous speeches over the years, and was fairly thankful for her ability to do so on this particular occasion. She knew the hypocrisy of his words would be too much for her, what with this whole wedding being nothing more than an elaborate execution.

After five minutes or so of droning on and recognizing notable guests, he concluded his speech by thanking everyone assembled, resulting in dutiful clapping once it became clear to everyone he'd finished. Bryn then gestured to King Alwyn, who stood up from his chair as well, giving her father a brief nod of thanks before beginning his own speech.

"Well, we Rhegarians aren't much for ceremony when it comes right down to it," King Alwyn said, scratching his chin in a considering fashion. "I'll admit I was a tad nervous arriving here, but quickly found that the legendary hospitality of Calderia lives up to its reputation. And… hey, what am I doing talking about Rhegar and Calderia anyway? Soon both names will be but an old and dusty memory, as our two peoples unite as one and form a brand new, glorious nation!"

His words were followed by much more enthusiastic applause, as well as a few cheers. King Alwyn good-naturedly signalled for quiet, eventually calming the room down enough so that he might resume talking.

He was much better at this sort of thing than her father was, Gwen noted.

"My one lasting regret is that my beloved wife did not live long enough to bear witness to this blessed arrangement — my dearest son, Gavin, being joined in marriage with your very own Princess Gwenwyn, a sweet girl who is lovely beyond words, and who I will soon be proud to call my daughter."

There were more cheers, though they sounded a bit less enthusiastic than before.

"Now," said Alwyn once the cheers had died down, reaching down to pick up his wine glass and raising it in front of him, "let's start this feast, shall we? I swear, if I'm forced to wait much longer, why, I might waste away to nothing!" he announced, patting his ample stomach.

There was some laughter, then more cheering and applauding as everyone took their seat. King Alwyn met their cheers with an easy, relaxed smile, oblivious to the slightly vexed expression that had appeared on Bryn's own face. Possibly her father had wanted to announce the beginning of the feast himself, but Gwen suspected he was more annoyed by the slightly more enthusiastic responses Alwyn's words had elicited from the crowd.

Bryn picked up his own wine glass and held it out to Alwyn, and the two kings solemnly toasted each other before toasting all in attendance. The gesture was returned by several hundred raised goblets, followed by another cheer.

And with that, the wedding feast began.

Gwen merely sat there, not even bothering to remove her veil. She knew that despite the pangs of hunger gnawing at her stomach, she would be too anxious and upset to eat anything at all. She sat quietly, hands folded in her lap, her head bowed slightly.

The feast itself was probably like none the attendees had ever seen. Collections of truly extravagant dishes arrived at each table, and everyone was allowed to sample this or that from the platter of delicacies before the trays were whisked away by the quick-moving castle staff, only to be replaced moments later by a brand new platter loaded up with even more extraordinary something-or-others. A harpist played gentle melodies that were loud enough to be heard, but not so loud as to hinder conversation.

Plates of elaborately crafted food were placed in front of Gwen, and then removed from her place after a few minutes, untouched and barely noticed. She very quickly lost count of the quantity of dishes that had come and gone, focusing instead on her thoughts, or glancing around the room a time or two from beneath her veil. Nobody appeared to be paying her much mind, save for Anifail, who sat at his table sipping from his goblet, sending her the occasional disquieting grin. Every now and then he'd whisper something to Rhosyn, who merely continued staring through the table, looking glum. Despite how hungry she must have been, Rhosyn didn't appear to be eating.

Nor was Gavin, Gwen noticed. Untouched helpings of food were being removed one after the other from his place at the table as well. Though she couldn't actually see him with her father and Alwyn sitting between them, she suspected the prince was sitting quietly in his chair, looking bleak.

Of course he wasn't eating. Who could possibly eat when feeling this defeated, this trapped? Any hope of happiness he'd ever have was slipping through his fingers. He was forever losing his chance to be with the girl he loved.

If Gwen didn't think of something, and soon, he could possibly be losing much more than that.

"Ready to turn the burden of leadership over to these two youngsters?" Alwyn asked of Bryn at one point during the feast.

"You bet! I can't wait," said Bryn, stabbing at a platter of meat with his fork and depositing his spoils onto his plate. Then he sighed, putting on a rueful expression. "You know, I was never suited for ruling. Not at all."

"Nor I, actually. I'll be glad to give it up," Alwyn said with a nod. "Not enough hours in the day, everyone coming to me with their problems. I'm not as young as I was. I figure I'm about due for some rest and relaxation."

"I couldn't agree more," said Bryn with a sly grin. "Why, it seems every year I'm having to renegotiate trade agreements with the kingdoms to the north just to keep them from robbing me blind! Now that we'll now have access to a port and opportunities to trade with kingdoms overseas, I imagine we'll have a much easier time of it."

"Oh, to have something to actually trade again!" Alwyn laughed. "Being a port city, most of our revenue is based on excise and merchant tax. Rare is the evening that I fall asleep and don't have nightmares about being chased by a horde of numbers with big, gnashing teeth!"

The two kings shared a laugh at that, and they both entered into some light-hearted discussion involving the economics of trade. Gwen could see her father paying particular attention to King Alwyn's words, likely attempting to glean as much information from him as possible about how profitable Rhegar's port activities were.

An hour passed, and then another. Slowly, the nature of the dinner courses being brought out began to change, and soon Gwen found herself staring at a plate containing frozen grapes, as well as thin rectangular wafers of dark chocolate. A dessert course, she realized glumly. Pretty soon it would be time for—

"And now, honoured guests," Bryn called out loudly, standing from his chair, "we have come to the part of the evening that is the entire reason for tonight's joyous celebration! It's the moment I'm certain we've all been waiting for; when our two realms become one, to be ruled over equally by your new king and queen, King Gavin of Rhegar, and Queen Gwenwyn of Calderia, joined this very evening in a symbolic union, one which shall receive the blessing of the Goddess Eirene herself!"

The room erupted with cheering and hearty applause, and underneath it all Gwen could make out the sounds of violins playing once more. Her stomach cramped, and her breathing quickened.

Amid the cheering and the processional music, Bryn turned and nodded respectfully to King Alwyn, who stood up from his own chair and smiled contentedly. Then he leaned over to Gavin, who was still staring down at the table with his shoulders slumped forward in resignation, and he whispered something. Upon hearing his father's words, Gavin slowly rose to his feet, turned, and then the two of them made their way around the table towards the altar amid cheers and music that seemed to be coming from everywhere at once.

Gwen sat there, feeling helpless. Out of the corner of her eye she saw that Anifail was smirking gleefully in her direction, and so she made a particular point of not looking his way. Instead she watched as Gavin, straight-backed and moving stiffly, walked over to the altar with his father.

The vicar smiled at the two of them, then nodded and said something to King Alwyn, who turned back and returned to the banquet table, an even bigger smile on his face. The violin playing seemed to increase in volume.

"Daughter," Gwen heard Bryn murmur from somewhere beside her. She looked to her right side, and saw her father's hand was extended for her to take.

Staring at the hand, Gwen remained motionless, afraid to move, her own hands still folded in her lap.

Several tense seconds passed.

"Now," said Bryn darkly, his voice little more than a whisper, "or the unhappy little girl sitting next to Captain Anifail becomes considerably more unhappy."

Bowing her head, Gwen took his hand in hers and stood up from her seat. From there, the two of them made their own way around the banquet table, towards the altar.

They encountered some difficulty making it over to the aisle, as her father accidentally stepped on the train of her dress a number of times before realizing what the problem was. The gown had also been tied especially tightly in a few places, putting uncomfortable pressure on her back and ribs, she noticed. And to top it all off, having spent several hours wearing it, she now felt like she was practically roasting alive in this cumbersome, loathsome thing. Even the simple act of walking was turned into a chore by this stupid, hated dress.

Once she'd made her way to the aisle, Gwen raised her head a little and risked a quick look towards the altar through the pale gauze of her veil.

Prince Gavin was looking directly at her for what might have been the first time since he'd arrived at the castle. No, not looking, but literally *staring* at Gwen with wide eyes, seeming the tiniest bit awestruck, his lips parted ever so slightly. He rather looked like a man who'd forgotten how to breathe, and seemed unable to look away from her as she slowly stepped towards him.

Okay, maybe she hated the dress a little less.

Eventually, Gavin's stunned expression gave way to a sort of profound sadness. For himself, Gwen realized, and his girlfriend. Sometimes it seemed to Gwen that the only reason she existed was to ruin other people's lives, to cause pain and make people cry, or—

She'd completely forgotten to cry!

Desperately, Gwen tried to summon tears and found she couldn't, despite how thoroughly miserable she was feeling. It was as if all the nervousness that was packed away inside of her was somehow preventing her from doing so, like she was too anxious or too scared to make the tears come!

It seemed like she'd been crying at the drop of a kerchief lately, but now that it actually mattered, she couldn't.

Gwen began to panic, her thoughts racing.

Step by slow, faltering step, Gwen and her father crept towards the altar. She felt like both condemned and executioner all at once.

By the time she was a few paces away from the altar, Gavin was no longer looking at her. His eyes were downcast, and he was standing in that familiar straight-backed way of his. Bryn released Gwen's arm, took the bouquet from her, and pantomimed a quick kiss on the cheek inches away from her veil before turning around and heading back toward the table, leaving her to take the final few shaky steps on her own. All at once, she was standing side-by-side with Gavin.

Behind the altar stood the vicar, a venerable, gentle-looking man with a wide, friendly smile. He beamed down at them both.

"Dearly beloved," the old man began in an excited, slightly wavering voice, "we are gathered here today—"

Chapter 20

Gwen gritted her teeth as she stood there, listening to the balding vicar talk of love and happiness.

The old man's voice wavered with the trepidation and uncertainty of someone who was doing something very unfamiliar, likely due to the sheer number of people he was addressing. He'd pause on occasion, look around thoughtfully, and then go on to make yet another comparison between the union of the two kingdoms and of the young couple standing before him.

His speech had been well crafted, and he appeared particularly earnest at times. He also kept smiling at her and Gavin whenever he mentioned joy, or compassion, or purity. Perhaps he truly believed he was doing something wonderful here today — that he was the one responsible for bringing about the happiness of not just a princess and prince, but an entire kingdom.

Despite the pure sentiment that may have been behind his words, Gwen quickly found herself hating the sound of this frail old man's voice. Try as she might, she just couldn't seem to block it out, though she desperately needed to do so if she were to collect her thoughts and figure out something else she could do.

She'd already spent enough time cursing herself for forgetting about her fan. As they'd approached the altar her father had taken her bouquet of flowers away, and with it had gone her paper fan, as well as the small piece of sketching charcoal hidden away in its folds. If she'd been thinking clearly, she might have tucked the fan away in her glove or something earlier in the day. Now it was gone, hidden in her bouquet, which was now Goddess-knew-where.

Still, there was a good chance she'd be able to get Gavin alone now, perhaps once the ceremony was over. Gwen didn't know if her father was hoping she'd poison Gavin with a kiss right there in front of everyone, but there was no way she was going to let that happen. She'd keep her veil on, pretend to kiss him, and then they would go to the room that had been made up for the two of them.

Then again, that was what Anifail had told her would happen, so it might be a lie.

Whatever. They couldn't make her kiss him. How could they? She and Gavin were about to become king and queen. Who could force them to do anything they didn't want once that happened?

Now there was an interesting thought, actually. Once the ceremony was done, she'd be co-ruler of a brand new kingdom. Sure, she still wasn't able to talk, so she couldn't simply order Rhosyn to be released, or for her father and Anifail to be arrested, but talking wasn't the only way to communicate what you wanted, was it? And paper fans and charcoal weren't the only things you could write with, after all.

It was an intriguing possibility, she realized. Maybe she wasn't supposed to clue in to the fact that in order for her father's plan to work Gwen was going to be bestowed actual power, and might be in a position to help herself. Maybe they'd believed her too stupid to realize something like that. All she needed to do was get married, get Gavin alone, and then find some way to communicate with him.

Of course, Bryn and Anifail had always been a couple of steps ahead of her, so maybe they'd already considered that possibility. Still, what could they possibly hope to do about it? Was she perhaps missing something? Once they were married, she could do what she wished, and not even her father would be in a position to stop her.

They'd still be married, of course, and something like that couldn't exactly be undone. Still, at least Gavin would be alive. Much, much better than the alternative.

The vicar's words caught Gwen's attention, and his wavering, annoying voice interrupted her thoughts once more.

"It is the promise between two people who love each other, who trust each other, who honour one another, and who wish to spend the rest of their lives with each other. It enables the two separate souls to share their desires, longings, dreams, joys and sorrows. Their their hearts free of malice, and—"

Gwen gave an inaudible little gasp as another realization struck her.

Maybe they didn't actually have to be married after all.

Malice! It was the key — the Goddess herself would bless this marriage, but only if there was no malice in their hearts!

Her eyes darted to her crystal, laying there on the altar. Just like at the chapel service, they would wait for her to hold it aloft and then invoke the Goddess through ceremony and incantation, at which point Gwen's crystal would probably glow just like it did during service. Out of habit, she had always tried to think nothing but good, pure thoughts when attending service, always privately afraid that thinking an unkind thought might cause the light in her crystal to flicker the tiniest bit.

But what if she did have malice in her heart?

What if her crystal *didn't* glow?

The wedding would be called off, quite obviously. If her crystal remained dark, both King Alwyn and Gavin would wonder why, perhaps even suspect treachery. In point of fact, there was treachery taking place, and lots of it, so if Gwen could just find a way to prevent her crystal from glowing they might become suspicious, start asking questions, and perhaps uncover some of her father's plan in the process.

Closing her eyes tightly, Gwen concentrated on the most terrible, horrible thoughts she could think of, directing them all towards the young man standing beside her. She pictured Gavin burning, bleeding, shrieking in agony. Gwen envisioned him in her mind's eye, visiting unspeakable horrors upon him in her imagination, and picturing herself as the source of his torment.

She cut him, stabbed him, tore off his limbs and ripped his still-beating heart from his chest, laughing merrily all the while. Some of the things she dreamt up were startling both in how specific and how horrific they were, and more than once she found herself having trouble believing these thoughts were actually coming from her own mind. They were frightening in their fury and intensity.

Deep down, she began to wonder if she was a horrible person after all.

Yes, she thought, furiously. She was a horrible person! She had to believe she was. If the Goddess was going to believe it, she had to believe it, too. Gwen renewed the intensity of her hate-filled thoughts, the vicar's words receding into the background. The seconds stretched themselves into minutes.

After a while, she felt a gentle nudge against her arm, and she opened her eyes. The vicar looked at her a little strangely, and she saw her crystal was being held out for her to take.

Gwen stared down at it for a moment, then took the proffered crystal in both hands. Gavin already had his, she saw, and was holding it about mid-chest. She couldn't tell if he was staring down at it, or simply hanging his head.

At the instruction of the vicar, they both turned to face those in attendance. A moment later two small children seemingly appeared out of thin air, placing two small satin pillows on the floor before them so they might have something to kneel on. Both Gwen and Gavin slowly went to their knees and held their crystals aloft.

"Oh Eirene, Goddess of Wisdom and Courage, creator of all things and mother to us all," the vicar intoned solemnly.

Gwen focused on her crystal a moment, then closed her eyes and bowed her head, as though in prayer.

I'll kill him, she thought viciously. *Once married, I'll take off my gloves and grab Gavin by the arm, and I won't let go! I'll burn the flesh from his bones! I'll force him to endure suffering that no man has ever experienced, suffering that would make the heavens weep! I will ensure that his shrieks of agony echo through the walls of this castle, and grown men speak of the day they heard his screams in hushed whispers! And I'll laugh! Do you hear me, Goddess? I will destroy this gentle, innocent man you've sent here, and I'll enjoy* it!

A part of Gwen that wasn't thinking furious thoughts could still hear the vicar's voice reciting his prayer, beseeching the Goddess to make her will known. She closed her eyes even more tightly, focusing as hard as possible on the violent images of pain and suffering her mind was offering up.

Beside her, she thought she could hear Gavin murmuring something under his breath. It sounded a bit like *please*.

Gritting her teeth, she concentrated on her angry, scarlet thoughts, her fingertips practically digging into the hard surface of the crystal as though attempting to pulverize it. All the while, in the very back of her mind, Gwen silently pleaded with Eirene to save Gavin from this predicament they both shared, begging that she be spared having to fulfill any part of her father's cruel plan.

Deafening cheers and applause erupted from somewhere beyond her tightly-shut eyes, and jaunty, triumphant music began to play. Gwen opened one eye, but the familiar warmth in her hand told her she needn't bother. She'd received the blessing of the Goddess. Her crystal was glowing.

So was Gavin's.

There had been no malice in his heart, just as she had none in hers.

She hadn't really meant any of those things she'd thought — some part of her had known it even as she'd been thinking them. Despite the ease with which her imagination had provided her with vivid, torturous images, she knew deep down inside that she wasn't truly capable of such things.

The tears wouldn't come now, either. She was too tired to cry.

Gwen felt her shoulders slump a little, and she was suddenly more exhausted than she could ever remember being. She lifted her gaze to the ribbon-filled ceiling, looking through them and into the heavens.

How could you, Goddess? How could you allow this to happen? How could you not see?

The Goddess of Justice was said to be blind. Today, perhaps she'd decided to lend her blindfold to the Goddess of Wisdom and Courage.

Both she and Gavin slowly rose from their knees and turned to face the altar. Chances were Gavin still wasn't looking at her at all, but Gwen couldn't really tell, having chosen to look away from him as well.

The balding vicar busied himself with smiling hugely at them, his gaze periodically flicking towards the jubilant crowd, looking as though this were the most exciting thing to ever happen to him. Quite possibly it was, she thought. He was most likely country vicar with a small congregation, hand-picked by her father to oversee a seldom-performed royal marriage ceremony. She imagined that every country vicar probably dreamed of something like that happening to them.

At least one person's dreams weren't being dashed to pieces tonight, Gwen mused bitterly.

She'd find a way, with or without the help of the Goddess. There was still time.

The cheers that had erupted at the sight of the two glowing crystals hadn't abated in the slightest, though Gwen suspected their cheers were more for Gavin, or simply the prospect of someone other than Gwen or her father ruling over them. Whatever their reasons, the cheers went on long enough that the vicar was eventually forced to raise his hands and motion for quiet.

Reluctantly, the cheering transformed itself into a low, excited rumble of approval.

"And now, fellow Children of the Goddess," the vicar said, his voice cracking slightly, "you share with me the honour of having been witness to this extraordinary event, blessed by Eirene herself! I present to you King Gavin and Queen Gwenwyn of Rhegar-Calderia. Husband... and wife!"

When the vicar uttered that final word a strange feeling filled Gwen, and a familiar sensation of pins and needles washed over her. Alarmed, she looked down to inspect her arms, then turned to her left and—

All at once, everything seemed to stop.

Gavin was suddenly so beautiful that it hurt her just to look at him. In fact he almost seemed to glow, as though he were some magnificent statue the sunlight had caught in just the right way.

The crowd continued to roar approvingly, but to Gwen the room may as well have been silent and empty. All she could register suddenly were the sights and sounds being provided by this achingly irresistible man standing next to her. She had to force herself to breathe just being this near him, and was almost overcome with the need to throw herself at him... to press herself against him, wrap her arms around him and kiss—

Oh no!

The geis. This is what Anifail had been talking about, back when he'd smugly suggested that she might know what to do. This was the second part of her geis, the one Anifail had put on her weeks ago. The vicar had said *husband and wife*, and suddenly she was so enamored with Gavin she could barely think. The final trap in her father's plan had been sprung!

Gwen shut her eyes tightly, trying to clear her head. She could hear people talking and cheering all around her, and she vainly attempted to block out the voices and focus on her thoughts, a task made more difficult by the blood she could feel thrumming through her temples, as well as the sick and anxious feeling that had taken residence in the pit of her stomach.

There were butterflies there in her stomach, too.

She realized that at some point her gloved hand had been shoved into Gavin's, and that both of their arms had been raised above their heads to even more deafening cheers. Even through the glove, just having her hand held by this man was enough to make her knees go weak.

Her arm was eventually lowered, and then she found herself being led forward by her new husband, who now had a firm grip on her hand. Gwen's eyes fluttered open involuntarily, and she saw that the world around her was lifeless and dull save for Gavin, who resembled some sort of god made up of colour and sunshine. He was a bright, shining jewel amongst the dirt and grime that was anybody and everybody else in the entire world.

She wanted him, wanted him more than anything. Gwen wanted to kiss him so badly her arms trembled, and her skin seemed to tingle. Visions of the two of them together appeared in her mind's eye, unbidden, and the thoughts and feelings those visions inspired made her ache in delicious ways…ways she'd only read about in books and stories. And he was hers, she realized. Her heart practically leaped out of her chest at the thought. They were husband and wife! Gavin was hers and nobody else's, and… no!

There was more chattering around them, but she could barely even register where she was, never mind the voices around her or who they might have belonged to. Her hand still gripped his, and he gently led her here, then there… through an adoring crowd and to a place where the voices and cheers became even louder. Everything became a blur of motion except for him, for it didn't seem there was any room in her world for anything or anyone else suddenly, like he was everything that mattered, or could possibly ever matter. She'd try focusing on where they were, or what hallway they were walking down, or a nearby face, and she'd eventually discover herself focusing on Gavin instead… how handsome he looked, or how fluid his movements seemed. In fact, Gwen barely even noticed when her veil became caught on something and was pulled off her head.

She almost tripped on an uneven floor stone, which made her realize she hadn't been paying any attention at all to her feet or what they were doing. It honestly felt like she was floating, whirling through this crowd and that, down a hallway, light-headed and dizzy from the sheer intensity of what she was feeling. Every now and then she'd realize what was happening and attempt to shut everything out and think, but it seemed to last no more than a couple of steps before she was once more overwhelmed by the very notion of Gavin and how unbelievably perfect he was.

Down another hallway they went, encountering fewer and fewer faces along their way. Gwen knew every nook and cranny in the castle, and yet she found it so difficult to concentrate that she hadn't the faintest idea where they were right now.

She briefly glimpsed a guard she didn't recognize who was standing at attention, and who gave the two of them a crisp salute as they breezed by. A second one did the same, and then a third, until at last they came upon a large, dark, wooden door. Twisting the handle with his free hand, Gavin pushed the door open. Then, head bowed, he led her through into the room beyond, seeming to pull her along with a little less gentleness than he'd displayed during most of their trek.

Then, Gavin let go of her hand.

Gwen caught herself almost stumbling over her dress as she was practically hurled forward towards the huge expanse of plush, silky pillows on the luxurious bed that had suddenly appeared before her. She righted herself, then looked around the room with wide eyes.

A bedroom — one full of spectacularly opulent furniture, elegant drapes, and other decoration that spoke of both excellent taste and a tremendous amount of wealth. One of the castle's old storage rooms, she realized… probably in the area of the castle where the Rhegarans had been staying. Had they brought all of this stuff with them all the way from Rhegar just to furnish a single room? For a wedding night?

Gwen didn't recognize a single stick of furniture around her, but everything was wonderful and perfect, like in a dream. The bed was positively huge, and was practically littered with down-filled pillows and other soft, silky things — bedding and other comforts fit for a king and queen. And they were alone, finally! And here she was, a queen, standing in this bedroom with her new husband, a king. This beautiful man who was hers to love and cherish and— … no no no!

She had to keep her head, for both their sakes! She *had* to!

Though the look on his face suggested he wished to slam the door shut behind him, Gavin carefully eased it closed. The soft sound of the door lock clicking into place had a feeling of finality to it.

Eyes closed, Gavin slowly rested his forehead against the massive wooden door, as though mourning the loss of something that lay on the other side.

"Well," he said bleakly, his deep, gentle voice making Gwen's knees weak despite its tone of bitterness and regret, "I suppose we're married now."

Chapter 21

The two of them remained frozen in place — he by the door with his forehead pressed against it, she still standing by the bed, torn between rushing over to him, and getting as far away from him as she could. Gwen felt like she was being pushed and pulled in several directions at once.

Her gaze never left him, not for a single moment.

There was a long, uncomfortable stretch of silence.

Gavin sighed.

"This is really awkward," he said, finally, turning and giving her a look that was both apologetic and distressed. "Look, I know this isn't exactly something you were hoping would happen, and it's probably not what you wanted at all. You don't really want someone like me, and I understand that."

Oh, how unbelievably wrong he was. Gwen fought to remain standing where she was, holding herself as still as possible.

"I'm not even a very good prince, really," he continued, running his fingers through his hair in a way that seemed self-conscious. "And

I… look, a girl like you could do so much better than this. I know that. You probably wish I wasn't even here right now. It's okay, you can tell me. Just saying it might make you feel a little better, to be honest."

He stood up a little straighter and looked at her expectantly for a moment, as though waiting for her to say something.

Still unable to make a sound, Gwen could think of little to do but force herself to refrain from throwing herself across the room at him, something that seemed to require more effort as time passed.

Gavin sighed once more and looked back to the door.

"Let's just talk, okay? I'm not going to make you do anything you don't want. Really, I mean it. Nobody should be forced to do something they don't want." His expression hardened. "All this supposed power we have, and yet we're powerless to change things. Slaves to what is required of us, or what is necessary. Game pieces moved around a board, like we're commodities, no matter whose lives end up getting ruined in the process."

The way he said those particular words caused a memory to bubble to the surface of Gwen's thoughts.

Gavin had a girlfriend.

Jealousy stabbed at her heart like a white-hot sword being driven clear through her chest. She discovered she hated this unknown, faceless girl, and with a ferocity that frightened her. Part of her was already frantically making plans, coming up with ideas regarding how she would find this girl, and what she'd do to her for daring to put herself between Gwen and this man, her husband! Why, she'd—

Gwen shut her eyes and took a deep breath, forcing her thoughts to quiet. It was like these feelings were coming out of nowhere now, like she was suddenly forced to feel things that didn't even belong to her!

"I'm probably ruining things for you, all of the dreams you had. You can tell me so," he continued. "I don't mind, really. You probably wish I'd just go away, or something, and that's fine. I'll understand.

It's good to say these things. Just tell me that's what you wish. That I was someplace far, far away."

These things he said weren't helping at all! She desperately wanted to tell him — to show him — how wonderful he was. It was like his gentle, self-deprecating words were somehow making him even more perfect in her eyes, despite his protestations.

"It's just that someone like you shouldn't have to do anything like this, or settle for someone like me. You're incredible! Goddess, when I saw you in that field, squaring off against that monster of a dire wolf, I just… wow. I've never seen courage like that before — never met *anyone* who didn't run at the sight of one of those things. And you faced it down with nothing more than a couple of rocks! You're amazing, Gwenwyn, not to mention beautiful, and it's not…." Gavin closed his eyes and sighed once more. "You deserve so much better than this. Better than me, anyway."

Why couldn't he just stop talking? Doing anything else would be infinitely preferable. Looking out a window, bemoaning his situation, sitting down and running fingers through his tousled brown hair, walking over to her and confidently wrapping his arms around her, finally letting her see the charming grin that had become the talk of the castle, then slowly bowing his head and leaning in close, as he— … no, no, *no!*

He was still standing by the door, and hadn't moved away from it. Though it felt like torture being so far away from him, the part of her that was still able to think clearly was very thankful. She was trying not to look at him, but it seemed like such a hard thing to do.

Gavin cleared his throat.

"I don't understand why you haven't said anything. Are you upset? Or angry? You can tell me; I just want to talk, honest. That's all I want to do right now."

That wasn't all *she* wanted to do right now.

Gwen gritted her teeth. It was maddening! Here he was, sounding as if he'd require hardly any convincing whatsoever to flee the kingdom, and she couldn't say anything. Her geis of silence would only be broken if she kissed him, something she was desperately trying not to do!

She had to find another way to communicate with him — one that could preferably be done at a great distance. Aside from getting dragged in here and standing around like some lovestruck dimwit, she hadn't done anything at all.

Tearing her gaze away from him, Gwen surveyed the room, looking for anything that might help her. She spied a dresser with a half-length mirror that looked like polished silver, and a nearby table loaded with plates of cheese and meats, and various wines sitting next to brilliant crystal glasses.

In the middle of the table, acting as a centerpiece, was her bouquet.

Gwen practically ran the half-dozen paces it took to get over to the table, grabbing the collection of flowers and digging through it, finding the paper fan in practically no time at all. She could write to Gavin!

Or could she? What if the newest geis prevented that, too?

Desperately, she opened the fan and pulled out the sketching charcoal she'd left in there, tearing a large swath of paper from the fan itself and smoothing it against the table, preparing to write. Then, with a trembling hand, she touched charcoal to paper and wrote *You are in danger!* in bold, clear letters.

She could write it! The geis wouldn't stop her!

Quickly, almost giddy with relief, she sat down in the nearby chair, leaned over the table and began scrawling a longer message.

"What are you doing?" Gavin asked softly from somewhere over her shoulder, his voice sounding alarmingly close.

A tremendous surge of excitement filled her chest. The charcoal Gwen was holding snapped in half, though she hardly noticed. Her eyes were closed, and she felt warm and tingly all over, practically in a swoon from the knowledge that he was standing near her.

He asked something else in a soft, gentle tone, but Gwen didn't really hear a word he'd said. She was too busy fighting off the impulse to whirl around in her chair and grab his shirt, to pull him down to her and—

Gwen bit her bottom lip savagely in an effort to maintain control, realizing that both her hands were clenched tightly, one of them gripping the tablecloth as though she feared falling out of her chair. Being this near him was excruciating!

Relaxing her fingers, she picked up one of the broken pieces of charcoal and continued writing with a shaky hand.

I am poisonous! You must leave right away!

She put the charcoal down, feeling exhausted, yet thrilled by what she'd just accomplished. She'd done it; she'd beaten the geis again! It wasn't exactly her best work, what with her unsteady hands and all, but it would do.

Exultant, she stood up from her chair, half-turned towards him and held up the paper in both hands for him to see.

Gavin's brow furrowed as he studied what she held in her trembling hands, and after a moment he looked a question at her. Then he looked back to the paper, seeming a bit distressed.

"Uhm," he began apologetically, "I'm very sorry, but I was never taught to read."

Gwen felt her jaw drop, and she stared at him open-mouthed.

No!

She sat down heavily in her chair, the paper falling from fingers that suddenly felt numb. Her thoughts raced, and she tried to focus on what she could do, her mind drawing a blank because of how close he was standing, not more than a few feet away.

"But that's what I mean, right there! You're so much better, so much smarter than I am. You deserve a husband who can make you happy. If you don't wish to see me again, you can say so. Just let it out! I mean, look at me. I'm just some guy who isn't even literate, and who hates being a prince. I don't know anything about ruling people, or anything, really. I don't have anybody I'd call a friend. I hate sitting at court. I hate pomp and pageantry. Most days I stink of horses.

I spend too much time with them, probably because I enjoy their company better than most of the people I'm around."

Gwen felt her lower lip begin to tremble.

Oh please stop talking, please, please, please....

"I'm not particularly clever, or even funny. I'm okay with people, but I'm just, I'm me," Gavin said, crouching on his heels so he'd be eye-level with Gwen as he spoke. "And that's okay. I'm happy enough with who I am. But what I'm saying is it's not okay for someone like me to be forced upon someone as—"

She couldn't stop it.

Before Gwen even realized what she was doing, she was upon him — her gloved fingers clutching the sides of his head, her own head tipped to one side, her lips desperately pressing against his.

Emotions of every colour exploded inside of her, and she discovered a tender yet fiery joy she'd never even known existed. In her stomach, entire fields of butterflies took flight in the brightest summer sunshine possible, fluttering through her and filling every part of her — every hair, every thought, every inch of her skin. It was a rapturous moment she prayed would never end, all dizzy, and wonderful, and warm.

And somewhere in there, mixed in with everything else, there was a feeling of pins and needles.

Her geis was lifted. The spell was broken.

Bliss transformed into horror as she realized what she was doing, and she violently threw herself away from him, half-collapsing back into her chair, aghast at what she'd just done.

Gavin reeled backward, looking stricken, his eyes wide. He opened his mouth as if to say something, but a quiet choking noise was all that came out, and he staggered away from her and fell heavily to the floor, looking as though he'd just been kicked by a mule.

She hadn't been able to stop it!

Gwen sat there helpless as Gavin made another urgent-sounding croak, and attempted to rise, his hand pressed against his chest, just above his heart.

The room became a tear-filled blur of colour and light as she lurched to her feet, her hands clasped over her mouth. Her foot snagged the hem of her dress as she stood, causing her to fall to the floor as well, at which point she simply lay there on the cold floor, sobbing, hand pressed against her stomach as though it pained her.

And it did hurt. It was beyond pain.

Gwen wanted to be sick — wanted to vomit up this terrible feeling that had taken up residence inside of her gut. The more she thought about what she'd just done, the more intensely she seemed to feel everything. Though the geis had been lifted, something seemed to rob her lungs of the air necessary to make any sort of sound at all.

And she simply lay there, sobbing noiselessly. She could do nothing else.

Damned. With a cold feeling of certainty, she knew she was damned — could sense it. This was what it felt like to be damned.

Slowly propping herself up from the floor, she looked over to where she'd last seen Gavin. He'd managed to stumble over to the bed before collapsing onto his side, facing away from her. His arms had wrapped reflexively around his chest, and she could see his shoulders shuddering convulsively.

Poisoned by her.

Gwen realized she had never watched someone die before, and just as that thought struck her, something seemed to click inside her head.

Murderess.

A killer.

She'd tried everything she could think of, tried so hard to avoid this outcome, but it happened anyway. And now she was damned. Unclean. A murderess.

It was utter despair, like little snakes squeezing the life out of her heart with every shuddering breath. Every horrible thing she'd ever experienced up to this point had been a picnic under a cloudless sky in comparison.

Bleakly, she wondered how she might go on like this, and very quickly she realized she no longer wanted to.

The torturous guilt, the unbearable burden of what she'd just done would quickly overwhelm and crush her, like grain under a millstone. She wouldn't — couldn't — go on like this.

Nothing at all mattered any more.

Brushing the tears from her eyes, Gwen scouted the room, and before long her gaze fell upon the nearby table containing the trays of meats and cheeses. Eventually, it rested upon the ornamental carving knife sitting next to a roasted lamb shank.

Gwen stared at the knife, her near-silent sobs becoming less and less frequent, eventually stopping entirely.

Nobody would profit from this horrible thing, the detestable actions of her father. She wouldn't be his puppet.

If *she* were dead along with Gavin, what happened to her father's plan then? Or, specifically, what if Gwen were found beside him, perhaps looking as though she'd been murdered? A young couple, king and queen, both murdered the same hour they were married? Suspicion, doubt… and with no new couple to rule the kingdom, things would likely revert to what they were before.

A stomach wound. That would be convincing. She'd heard once that stomach wounds were painful, but considering the pain in her heart right now, the prospect of a knife in her guts didn't seem all that bad. Maybe she even deserved to die in agony. Perhaps it was her punishment for not thinking of something in time.

It took hardly any time at all for her to reach a decision.

Steeling her resolve, Gwen pushed herself back up to her feet and slowly walked over to the table. She picked up the carving knife in one hand and inspected it.

Sharp. Not a stabbing weapon to be sure, but it did have a point, and the blade was almost the length of her forearm. It would do the job. She'd make certain of that.

Gwen turned her head and gave Gavin one last look. He was no longer convulsing, and didn't appear to be moving at all.

The room was utterly silent.

For a long while she simply clutched her knife in her hand, staring at Gavin's motionless form, thinking of everything that had led up to this point. If only she'd found the courage to allow herself to be killed by the dire wolf, or to leap from her window. If only she'd been more clever, or less afraid. He might still be alive.

Her fingers tensed around the handle of the knife, and as she raised it to chest height she stole one last look at the man she'd killed.

"I'm so sorry," she whispered, her voice choked with emotion.

In one fluid motion, Gavin whirled around and sat bolt upright on the bed, his tear-streaked face slack with disbelief, and he stared directly at her with red-rimmed eyes that were wide with confusion.

The ornamental blade tumbled out of Gwen's nerveless fingers and clattered to the stone floor, and she stared back at him in open-mouthed astonishment.

Chapter 22

"Are you okay?" Gavin asked urgently, standing up from the bed. "Do you feel unwell?"

"I'm...this...why were you—" Gwen couldn't seem to finish any of her thoughts, and her voice was little more than a hoarse whisper from disuse.

The two of them simply stared at one another, neither moving.

He looked *fine!* Blistering happened in an instant, she knew, but his lips, his complexion, everything looked fine! Aside from a bit of red around his eyes, he looked just as he had a few minutes ago.

What was going on?

She'd had some coloured balm applied to her lips earlier while preparing for the wedding — Gwen could still feel some traces of soft wax. But something like that wouldn't be enough to protect him from her, would it? Surely not.

Gavin's eyes focused on Gwen's mouth, as though his thoughts somehow mirrored her own, and his look of confusion intensified. Then he looked to the knife that lay at her feet.

"Why were you—" he began.

"What happened?" she blurted. "You fell, and I thought—"

Gwen looked away from him to the spot where he'd been laying a second ago. Her own look of confusion was probably the match of his.

Gavin looked to the bed, then back to her.

"I was... I'm sorry. I just—" He glanced at the bed again, wiping a tear with the back of his hand. "I was upset. I thought something terrible had happened. But you're not...I mean, I didn't...."

He looked momentarily distressed and his voice trailed off.

Silence once more dominated the room as they stared at one another, and Gwen, not trusting herself to stand upright, carefully lowered herself into the nearby chair and tried to think.

Was he hurt? He didn't look it. He did seem disoriented though. Was it from the poison?

"I don't understand," Gwen said, her voice sounding slightly raspy. She frowned, and attempted to clear her throat a few times, an activity that drew a renewed look of concern from Gavin.

"No! I'm...you need to—" he stammered. Then, closing his eyes, he gave a growl of frustration and looked to the ceiling.

What the heck was going on!? He was far less articulate all of a sudden. He hadn't sounded like this when speaking to her earlier, not at all! Was the toxin affecting his ability to talk?

"I'm...it's th—that I—" He sat down heavily on the bed and ran his fingers through his hair, like he was trying to think.

There was something familiar about the hesitation in his voice as he spoke, Gwen realized. It was almost like it was....

A compulsion?

Looking lost in thought, Gavin appeared to realize something, turning to Gwen a moment later.

"You wish me to tell you something about myself?" Gavin asked, his words sounding as though carefully spoken. "What I've been wanting to say to you?"

"Yes," she agreed, instantly.

"No!" he half-shouted, burying his head in his palms. Then he calmed himself, sat up, took a quick breath, and gave her an earnest look. "You *wish* me to tell you," he repeated, not making it a question.

Gwen's brow furrowed in confusion.

"I do," she said, nodding slowly.

Giving her a desperate look, Gavin waved his hands as though encouraging her to continue speaking.

"I...wish for you to tell me...what you've been wanting to tell me?" she managed to say, haltingly. She had a feeling she looked about as confused as she sounded just then.

Gavin closed his eyes and fell backward into the bed, groaning as though exhausted, his hands covering his face. At first Gwen thought it was because he was even more frustrated than before, but when he finally removed his hands from his face, the expression she saw on it was one of profound relief.

"Oh, thank the Goddess!" He sat back up on the bed, turned to her, his expression serious and alert. "Okay, this is hard to explain, but you're in danger. You can't do that again. Ever!" He gave her a slightly forlorn look. "Despite how much I really, really want you to. Are you feeling unwell? Dizzy? We need a towel, or something to wipe your lips, just in case."

His voice trailed off as his gaze darted around the room, eventually falling upon the tablecloth. In the blink of an eye he'd jumped up from the bed and dashed over to the table next to her, yanking away the cloth that had been draped over it. Food and silverware fell to the floor, and all the while Gwen sat immobile, trying to piece together what was happening.

"Here, quickly!" he said, holding the cloth out for her to take. "Look, I know this seems strange, but I need you to wipe your lips. And try not to touch them with your tongue when you do. Or swallow. Try not to do that either!"

She stared at what he offered. The white of the tablecloth was almost indistinguishable from the white officer's gloves he'd worn during the ceremony, the same gloves he still wore for some reason, which—

It hit her, very suddenly, and everything coalesced.

He was behaving exactly as she might *if she'd poisoned someone!*

And then Gwen was light-headed and dizzy, her thoughts becoming a whirlwind of revelations. She felt her muscles suddenly relax, and she practically melted into the cushions of her chair. At that moment, though it seemed impossible, she knew why he was acting this way. She *knew* why he hadn't died.

Unable to help herself, Gwen began to giggle.

Gavin somehow managed to look even more distressed than before, and the look on his face caused Gwen to laugh even harder.

"Euphoria! Quickly, rub this on your face!" he said. "And...spit! You need to spit into the towel! I'll get some water, or wine — something to rinse with! We've got—"

She was now laughing so hard tears blurred her vision. She could barely make out the form of Gavin as he grabbed decanter and goblet, made a botch of pouring and turned to her in exasperation.

"You've been poisoned! This is one of the effects," he cried. "Look, this is going to sound very strange, but my father sent me here to kill you! He has designs on your kingdom, and wishes to merge it with ours and rule over both. That's been his plan all along, this whole time! For years he's been planning this! You see, ever since I was a boy, I was forced to eat—"

"—a horrible blue-green herb," she managed to say through her laughter. "You've been fed it every day."

Speechless, Gavin simply stared down at her, his eyes wide. His newest expression just made Gwen want to start laughing all over again, but she eventually managed to control herself.

"I—" Gavin began, fixing her with a stupefied look. "My father said knowledge of it had been kept secret! You...your people know of the herb? You have an antidote? Immunity?"

"The herb is called *chi'darro*, which I suspect is some sort of foreign word meaning *tastes like chalk fried in rancid butter*, but I can't be certain," she said, grinning. Her relief was probably making her the tiniest bit silly, she realized, but she didn't really care. She'd been so serious, so miserable, for so very long. A little silliness seemed a bit like medicine all of a sudden.

Gavin blinked at her.

"You're...you...*how could you know what it tastes like?*" he asked, looking even more uncertain and amazed. Then his expression changed to one of dawning realization. "You've been...but you can't have, can you? It's just—"

"I've been given it my whole life. My father's plans sound almost identical to your father's. He sent me into this marriage to poison and kill you. I didn't want to. I foiled him once before, and managed to warn off one other prince, but my father made extra certain I couldn't do anything this time around," she said, feeling herself growing hoarse. She fanned a gesture in front of her neck apologetically, swallowing and clearing her throat once again. "I haven't been able to talk for weeks, thanks to something called a geis sphere, or I would have tried to warn you."

He watched her intently as she spoke, and after a while his confused look became one of thoughtful understanding, and he seemed to nod to himself. Then, Gwen saw the tiniest amount of suspicion cross his face, and his brow furrowed.

"You kissed me," he accused. "Is this some sort of trick? Why would you have kissed me if you didn't want me dead? And you had a knife, just now! What exactly were you planning on doing with that?"

Gwen bridled at the implication at first, but quickly realized how strange and unlikely things might appear from his perspective. This development was about the last thing she'd been expecting; he'd likely been taken completely by surprise as well, and was merely being cautious. Understandable, really.

"When you thought you'd killed me," she asked, "did it feel like you'd be able to live with yourself, Gavin?" She took a breath. "I had the knife because, because I…."

She shrugged.

Gavin appeared to consider that. "And the kiss? Why would you kiss me if—"

"I didn't *want* to kiss you. Well, actually, I suppose that's not exactly true. It was a compulsion, part of that geis sphere I mentioned. It took effect when we were wed. It, uh," Gwen looked away a moment, feeling heat rise to her cheeks. "It made me really, really want to."

She watched him raise a brow to that, consider her, and then he grinned like sun after a storm. In that moment, Gwen understood why Gavin's grin had become the talk of the castle.

"You know, It occurs to me to wonder if I might have been hit with something similar," he said, a playful glint in his eyes. "Honestly, ever since I laid eyes on you, I've really, *really* wanted to kiss you as well."

Gwen felt her cheeks redden further. Then she remembered something, and her eyes narrowed.

"Oh, and what would your girlfriend think?" she asked tartly.

Somehow, Gavin managed to appear even more bewildered than he had just a few short minutes ago.

"What?"

"Your father already mentioned the girlfriend you left back home," she said, realizing she sounded accusatory. "He told my father and me all about it. That someone special you are in love with back in Rhegar? What would she—"

"Gwenwyn?" he interrupted, already shaking his head. "Do you have a boyfriend? A special someone?"

"Well no, obviously," she said, giving him a look. "I can't, because I'm… I—"

"You're like me," Gavin said, lowering himself into a crouch before her, shaking his head once again. "No, there's no girlfriend back home. My father is a wretch, and a liar. A waste of skin. Like I said before, he brought me here to kill you. I found out about his plans a long time ago. He became rather upset I wasn't willing to play along with his grand scheme. Eventually he had to put me under a *wish* compulsion just to keep me manageable. I've been trying to get around it for years." Gavin took a quick breath before continuing. "Even though I was bound to do exactly as he wished, I tried everything I could think of to confound his plans. Wearing my riding leathers when we first met, acting aloof, refusing to look at you, all so you might feel uneasy, pressure your father into calling the wedding off, or perhaps choose to run away rather than acquiesce to an arranged marriage."

Gwen sat there, stunned. It was almost as if they'd been leading identical lives!

"So, if you were trying to get around your compulsion, why was it that when I wished that—"

"Whoa, whoa, careful! Please!" he said quickly, holding his hands out toward her. "Don't use that word, I can tell it's still active. I literally have to do what my father wishes."

"But, I'm not your father!"

"Yes, but last night he was in his cups, celebrating. I don't think he was thinking too clearly. He called me to his quarters late last night and rather drunkenly went over his plan — told me he wished for me to go through the wedding ceremony without fuss, and once that was done I should bring you back to the bedroom with all haste, and, uh—" Gavin flushed. "He told me I should do the sort of thing brides wish for their husbands to do on their wedding night." He took a slow, careful breath. "I think he meant it as a joke, or to torture me further, but he actually used the word *wish*. I don't know if he knew he'd said it or not, but I could feel it! So, I figured if I got you to wish for something—"

"Wait, you were trying to get me to wish to never see you again!"

He nodded somberly. "I knew if you said it, I'd be able to leave the castle. I'd grab my horse and ride somewhere, someplace far away, where no-one would find me. In truth, I'd probably just end up dying in the forest; I can't go very long without the herb. I tried giving it up once, but just that once. It was pretty awful." Gavin gave her a look. "But at least you'd still be alive. I mean, you didn't deserve to die."

Gwen thought about how desperately, how earnestly he'd tried getting her to send him away. And all that time, attempting to convince her, trying to coax her into saying those words out loud, he knew he risked his own life.

She couldn't even describe the thoughts and feelings that warred for her attention all of a sudden.

"However, the problem right now is that we've only solved half the puzzle," he said, running his fingers through his hair in a way she was beginning to find familiar. "I'm still under my father's control; I can sense it. I still have to do as he wishes, unfortunately. I probably have to do what you wish as well, at least for the moment. Right now I just need you to avoid saying the word *wish* to me until we can figure out some way around this compulsion."

"Like if I were to say to you: I wish for you to ignore the wish compulsion?" she asked.

"Don't—" he began, his arms raised as if trying to shield himself. Then he gaped and stared at his outstretched arms as though they were completely unfamiliar. His expression changed from one of anxiety to bafflement, then surprise, and finally wonder.

"Did that do it?" Gwen asked, feeling faintly smug.

"It's...gone!" he gasped, staring at Gwen as though she'd just performed a miracle.

The look of utter astonishment on Gavin's face was enough to cause Gwen to collapse back into her chair in another fit of giggling. It felt good to laugh, she realized. She hadn't laughed about anything in such a long time.

Gavin remained crouched on his heels a few feet away from her. He inspected his arms periodically, as though there was something new and surprising about them. Then he'd look at her and smile good-naturedly, and Gwen suspected he was mere moments away from laughing as well.

Then, suddenly, his expression became serious. He stood up.

"My father has people watching this room. Your father might as well, actually. We're blind to what might be waiting for us, but we probably have the element of surprise. We're going to need to come up with some sort of a plan. He glanced around the room. "Likely our only assets are here with us, whatever we can find and make use of."

"Rhosyn," she said.

He looked over to her, a question on his face.

"My lady-in-waiting. She's being held hostage to ensure I cooperate."

"Just one more thing we need to remedy," he said. "Do you know where she's being kept?"

"No, but I had a thought during the ceremony. We could leverage the fact we're now king and queen to our advantage, use that power. I don't think either of our fathers counted on that. Or this." She gestured to indicate them both.

"I'll bet they didn't," he said, pacing to one side, looking thoughtful. "The first thing we're going to have to do is gain the support of some strong arms, and-"

There were many ways that they could go about this whole thing, she realized. Gwen herself had already come up with one or two notions of how they might be able to work this situation to their advantage. With both their fathers being so secretive about their respective plans, the two of them would definitely have the element of surprise. They had time to come up with something, she knew.

But as for right now....

Gwen realized that she was watching Gavin intently as he paced in front of her. He was animatedly talking over some of the possibilities they could pursue, staring through the floor as he spoke, seemingly lost in thought.

She began peeling off her gloves.

"—are loyal to the Crown, not my father," he said, wagging a finger excitedly. "Which could help us, of course. The real problem is that the only orders Father's knights will accept are written ones. I believe that's how my father wished to control me — how he'd continue to rule once he'd made me king. I was kept away from books of any sort, and forbidden to read them, so that when it came to laws—"

"Gavin?" Gwen said softly.

"—he'd be the only one who could pass them, because I can't write." He looked at her and she saw realization dawn. "But you *can* write! And because we're king and queen now, our word is law... which means we—"

"We'll figure it out, Gavin. We have time," Gwen said, slowly rising from her chair.

"Yes, but once we figure out how we can go about this, we'll—"

"Gavin?" she repeated quietly.

"Hmmm?" he asked distractedly, turning to face her.

Once he actually saw her, he no longer looked distracted in the slightest. If anything, he looked almost exactly the way he had when he was standing by the altar, wide-eyed and staring.

She closed the distance between them in a few unhurried steps. By the time she'd stopped, Gwen was standing about a foot away from him with one hand raised in front of her, her palm facing him, her fingers spread. She looked him directly in the eye at first, and then moved her gaze down to his own hand, saying nothing.

The two of them simply stood there, facing one another.

Swallowing hard, Gavin slowly raised his own hand up. Then, spying the white officer's glove he still wore, he quickly shed it before starting the whole process over...gradually raising his arm and lifting his hand up, fingers spread, mirroring her own gesture.

They stayed like that a few moments, hands inches apart. Gwen felt her lower lip begin to tremble, and she was filled with a strange mix of uncertainty, nervousness, and anticipation all at once.

Gwen slowly eased her hand forward, towards his, noting that Gavin's own hands were shaking slightly.

Carefully, delicately, their fingertips touched.

And all of the butterflies in Gwen's entire world took flight all at once.

Closing her eyes, Gwen felt fresh tears spilling down her cheek, and some part of her realized she was smiling. Her shoulders shook slightly, and she felt almost like she was laughing and crying at the same time.

Contact. The touch of another. And not a fleeting touch, either, but gentle yet insistent, almost as if to reassure her that this feeling wasn't going anywhere. Actual warmth under her fingertips — it was a feeling that was almost too good to be real. She savored it as though it might disappear any second.

Tiny shivers scurried back and forth along her shoulders, and she found it difficult to keep the trembling from reaching her arms.

She opened her eyes to look at Gavin. Mouth half open, he was staring at their fingertips pressing together as though enraptured by it. The beginnings of tears had begun welling up in the corners of his eyes as well.

Her father's plans, his father's plans, the various plans the two of them would have to come up with...none of it mattered in that moment. Everything else in the whole world dissolved into nothingness next to one, simple truth.

He was like her.

They could touch.

There was time, she knew. The Goddess of Wisdom wasn't blind after all — She'd known exactly what She'd been doing. Eirene had indeed blessed them both, blessed this union. All of the talking and planning they had to do could wait for a little while. Right at this particular moment, however, she was alone in a room with someone who couldn't be hurt by her poisonous nature, possibly the only other person in the entire world. Someone who could perhaps understand what she'd gone through her whole life, and in ways nobody else possibly could.

Her life wasn't a tragedy at all, she realized. It was a fairy tale.

And she had found her prince.

They both stood there for several long minutes, touching fingertips, marvelling at the feel of it.

Gwen raised her other hand, and Gavin matched her actions, the fingertips of their other hands now touching as well.

"That compulsion, the one your father put on you," she whispered. "The wish compulsion. Are you sure it's completely gone?"

"I'm sure," he said, his tone slightly husky.

"Husband?" she said, smiling shyly, slipping her fingers between his and clasping his hand firmly but tenderly. "I wish for you to kiss me."

For a second it appeared as though he could barely draw breath, and he seemed startled. Then, after a few moments, he smiled down at her, and Gwen knew she'd devote every waking moment doing whatever was necessary in order to see that smile again and again.

"Well," he said, his voice little more than a whisper, "perhaps there might be some traces of it still hanging around."

He slowly tilted his head towards her, slow enough to make her ache.

Their lips touched.

It was tiny earthquakes in her tummy, in her fingers, all over. It was like nothing she'd ever dared to dream before. It was pure, breathtaking joy.

When the kiss finally ended, Gwen was engulfed by a lingering sense of wonder, and quickly found herself very much looking forward to his next kiss. Then, realizing that she needn't wait for him to do it, she kissed him right back.

It was then she discovered she could kiss while smiling, and that was wonderful too.

And that night, though they'd scarcely spoken a word to each other until that day, the two of them made a great many of their heart's desires come true.

Chapter 23

Their plan was so simple it seemed ridiculous.

Gwen continued to hover near the bedroom door, feeling a touch nervous. A few minutes ago she'd sent Faryl, one of Gavin's knights who had been standing guard, running down the hallways calling for a healer at the top of his lungs. Alwyn would learn of it shortly. If Bryn also had people watching their room, as both of them suspected he did, then it probably wouldn't take long for him to make an appearance as well.

The prospect of seeing her father was both exciting and terrifying.

She briefly wondered how Gavin was making out with his side of things, but refused to allow herself to become anxious about it. There likely wasn't anything to be worried about at this point; if things had gone wrong on his end she'd have heard about it by now. If things had gone as planned, however, then it was mostly over anyway.

"Gwenwyn?" she heard her father call loudly through the door just before he rapped his knuckles loudly against it. "Daughter? What is the matter? Is everyone okay? I've brought a healer and his assistants. I'd heard that something terrible had happened!"

She rubbed her eyes thoroughly to make it appear she'd been crying, briefly inspecting her work in the reflection of a nearby silver bowl. Then, after giving the lone figure sitting beside the bed a quick nod and a reassuring smile, Gwen slowly opened the door and walked out of the room, her head bowed.

Her father stood in the antechamber with a small retinue of healers, as well as a few important-looking advisers hovering on the perimeter. Bryn's expression was both alarmed and solemn, oozing paternal concern. If Gwen didn't know her father as well as she did, a part of her might have actually believed he was worried about her, or cared.

Upon seeing her, Bryn looked the tiniest bit relieved, at which point he barked orders to his retinue.

"Quickly, inside! What are you just standing around for?" Bryn roared, gesturing at the open door. "Something must be wrong with Prince Gavin; attend him!"

The small group of healers hurried inside, leaving Bryn and Gwen standing in the antechamber. He waved away the remainder of those he'd brought with him angrily.

"Speak, Daughter," he said, once everyone else was out of earshot.

"What would you have me say?" she asked, her voice little more than a whisper.

Bryn chuckled. "That's good enough. Well then, the deed is done. You've kissed him. You'll do and say nothing more unless I tell you, Gwenwyn, if you know what's good for you."

Gwen turned away from him, head still bowed, hoping she looked morose and defeated. As she had guessed, it didn't take him long to start gloating.

"Well, in addition to being newly widowed, you're now Queen, Daughter!" he said, his tone both amused and contemptuous. "How does it feel? You really should try to enjoy it while it lasts. We'll be attending service tomorrow, you and I, and if the Goddess doesn't approve of your actions, yours could be the shortest reign in history."

She continued to stand there, keeping her face as impassive as she could.

"Of course, what you did may not be criminal, and you might continue to receive Her blessings. I've got plans for that eventuality as well," he said, quiet laughter in his voice. "Later, once this is all sorted out, I'll be sure to tell you all about what is going to happen if Eirene still considers you fit to be Queen. You may prefer banishment, now that I think about it."

A commotion outside the antechamber attracted Bryn's notice, and he hurriedly resumed his play-acted role of anxious father. Within moments Gavin's father, Alwyn, burst into the room, leading his own retinue of physicians and servants, his expression almost as panicked and worried as Bryn's.

"What's the matter?" Alwyn demanded. "I'd heard something had happened, someone calling for a healer! I've brought my own personal physician, just in case he might be of some—" His attention fell on Gwen, which brought him to an abrupt halt.

Keeping a straight face was decidedly difficult just then. Gwen could almost see the exact moment Alwyn's artificial look of confusion became a very real one.

"King Alwyn!" Bryn said, "I myself have only just arrived. I was woken by calls for a healer, and I came immediately. I fear—"

"Where's my son?" Alwyn shouted, his eyes never leaving Gwen. "What have you done with my son?"

One of Bryn's healers returned from the bedroom, his brow furrowed in confusion. Bryn immediately began wringing his hands, giving the man a look of anxious concern.

"Is my son-in-law well?" he asked. "Is there anything wrong?"

"Uh, I don't exactly know," said the healer, thumbing toward the bedchamber behind him. "King Gavin isn't in there."

"Oh, Goddess! How could this—" Bryn did a double-take. "Wait... what?"

It took all her self-control not to burst out laughing right there.

"I said he's not in there," the healer said with a shrug. "And the fellow who is in there seems to be perfectly fine."

As if on cue, a second figure emerged from the room, looking tentative and apologetic. He held himself awkwardly, likely due to the fact that instead of his normal knight's uniform, he now wore a tasteful white nightshirt and a pair of black trousers from Gavin's wardrobe. He looked around, bowed to Alwyn, and then stood in place.

She looked back over to Alwyn and her father. It was plain neither of them knew what to make of this development, and each of them took turns staring at her, then the knight, then the room from which he'd just emerged.

Unable to contain herself any longer, Gwen covered her mouth in an attempt to stifle her laughter. Both Alwyn and Bryn's attention fell upon her, at which point she regained control, stood up a bit straighter, and smiled at them both.

"Yes, I'm so sorry, this is all a bit awkward, but I can explain. Entirely my fault, this whole situation. You see, I've always loved military clothing, and I absolutely adore the uniforms of the Rhegarian knights; they're so much more interesting than our drab Calderian ones. Perhaps it was a silly wish, but I desperately wanted to see how my new husband might look wearing one. Gavin was agreeable, and so we invited in the two knights who were standing guard outside of our room, and your knight Roderick here," Gwen bowed her head towards the nightshirt-clad fellow, "was kind enough to allow Gavin to try his uniform on for size."

The knight, Roderick, gave Alwyn a second apologetic bow.

"And then," she continued, "though I feel silly to confess it, I was overcome. The mere sight of my dearest Gavin wearing that uniform, well, it caused me to feel the slightest bit light-headed and dizzy. My husband ordered both knights to stay with me and then immediately left the room to fetch some help, though that was quite some time ago, and I fear he must have gotten himself turned around or something. We waited, and eventually I sent Faryl, the other knight, to fetch some help instead. Roderick, gentleman that he is, offered to watch over me until help arrived." Gwen smiled at the nearby healer. "Thank you for arriving so promptly. I do feel much better now."

"Enough of this!" Alwyn shouted. "Where is my son?"

"I'm sure he's about the castle, somewhere. In fact...oh *look!* There he is now!"

Both men turned to find Gavin entering the antechamber, an easy smile on his face. There was a sword at his hip, and he had nearly a dozen knights in tow.

Gwen smiled over at her father, who was staring at Gavin and the knights, then at her. He half-opened his mouth as though about to say something, then closed it again.

"Gavin!" Alwyn shouted, striding forward. "I *wish* for you to explain what in the seven hells is going on here this instant!"

Gavin flinched slightly, shying away from his father's rage as if out of habit. Then, as though remembering something, he relaxed, and his gaze quickly sought out Gwen.

She gave him a reassuring smile.

Grinning back at her, Gavin stood up straight and considered Alwyn, then took a slow and cautious breath.

"Nah," he said finally, abruptly walking past his father and towards Gwen.

Alwyn's eyes bulged at that, and he began sputtering incoherently. Gwen wondered if he'd fly into a fit of apoplectic rage.

"You...your voice," her own father said, staring at her disbelievingly. She watched as he swallowed, gathering himself. "How can you...if you haven't *kissed* him, why—"

"Gavin, my darling!" she smiled, pushing past her father and holding her arms out invitingly. "Oh, I know it's only been a short while, but I've missed you so!"

And with that, with both their fathers watching, the two of them shared a long, lingering kiss.

The silence was thunderous. When Gwen broke the kiss and turned back to them, both fathers resembled a pair of astonished statues.

"Oh look, dearest!" Gavin said, grinning as he pointed at the stationary figures. "Bookends!"

Gwen giggled and kissed Gavin once more for good measure. Then, she turned her smile upon her father.

"Oh, and I want to thank you, *Dad,* for your most excellent taste when it comes to suitors. I do admit I was a bit dubious about the whole arranged marriage thing at first, but now I'm completely sold on the idea! Why, Gavin and I barely had any time to get to know one another before our wedding day, but we've since discovered we have so many things in common. Same passion for horseback riding, same love of the outdoors." She grinned slyly. "Same *diet*."

She watched as Bryn looked at Alwyn, and Alwyn looked at Bryn. Soon their looks of dawning comprehension were replaced with mighty scowls.

"Yes, that's right," Gavin said, his tone cheerful. "Both of you had come up with the exact same plan. I'm sure the two of you will have much to discuss shortly, having so much in common yourselves. And, Father, you'll also be delighted to know that Gwenwyn has been teaching me reading and writing, since you always seemed too busy to bother with such matters. Why, I've even learned how to write my name! Would you like to see?"

Still smiling, Gavin reached into his pocket and pulled out a ragged piece of fan paper, holding it out before his father.

Alwyn stared at it, and his eyes narrowed.

"A royal decree?" He glared at Gavin and set his jaw. "I *wish* for you to explain this at once!"

Gwen clicked her tongue disapprovingly, shaking her head in mock disappointment. "You don't catch on very quickly, do you? Your son no longer has to do what you *wish*. If you want an explanation, you might want to try reading that paper he's got there. Most of the writing is mine, but Gavin did sign his name completely on his own. A beautiful job, too — much better than my own first attempt."

"Well, I did have some help practicing it earlier," Gavin admitted. "And I'm afraid that poor tablecloth is never coming clean."

Alwyn stared at them each in turn, then stared at the paper being held before him. After reading it, he looked even more confused.

"—rescind all prior orders from...*rescind?* You don't even know what that word means!" He ran frustrated fingers through his white hair, his eyes growing bigger the more he read. "I'm... I'm no longer in command of my knights? But this is nonsense! You can't just—"

"I already have, actually," Gavin interrupted, smiling. He looked to one of the Rhegarian knights standing nearby. "Honestly, they seemed pretty happy about it, too. Maybe even a touch relieved. And not just those knights that came with us, either. Even now, a sizable group of them are going around and spreading word of this to Rhegarian and Calderian knights both as we speak."

"Sergeant Niven," Alwyn roared, turning his ferocity on the knight standing next to Gavin, "you will cease and desist this absurdity at once!"

The knight stiffened slightly, but said nothing and continued to look forward.

"That's *Captain* Niven now, actually," Gavin said, laughing. He gave the knight in question a quick nod. "It would appear I have things well in hand here, Captain. If you would be so kind as to leave two or three knights with me, and then take the rest to go look into how Trevor and the others are faring, I would appreciate it."

"Majesty!" he said, thumping his closed fist to his chest in salute.

Alwyn stared open-mouthed as the small group of Rhegarian soldiers walked past him and down the hallway.

"Amazing things, words," Gavin said, idly inspecting the paper he held. "All I had to do was become king, show a bunch of words to the head of my father's personal guard, and suddenly he's doing everything I ask. I had no idea writing was so useful. And my signature...isn't it good? Although—" Gavin frowned, inspecting the paper critically, then looking over to Gwen. "Are you absolutely certain the 'i' has to have a heart over it?"

"Well, I think it looks nice," Gwen said.

"Hmmm. I might have to make a slight change to that later," Gavin said, rubbing his chin thoughtfully.

"It's your royal signature, Darling. You can't simply change it."

"Are you saying a king can't even change his own—"

"Treason!" Bryn snarled, now red-faced and outraged. "You think I'm going to stand around idly while you attempt to wrest control of my own kingdom from me?" He closed the distance between Gwen and himself. "This is a bloody coup!"

Gwen felt her stomach tighten, felt all of the old fears and anxiousness well up inside of her. And then she felt a comforting hand on her shoulder, a gentle reminder that she wasn't alone in this. Her fears abated. She looked up at Gavin, who gave her a quick chuckle.

"It's hardly a coup if we're king and queen now, is it?" he asked. "And as for bloody," Gavin gave Bryn a significant look, his hand now resting upon the pommel of his sword. "Gwenwyn told me all about her life here in the castle. If you would prefer things bloody, I could most certainly arrange it."

Bryn hastily retreated a step.

She wasn't facing her father by herself, Gwen realized. Never again would she have to weather the storms of his anger alone, nor Gavin his father. Neither of them was alone any more. He was her strength, and she was his.

Gwen touched Gavin's shoulder lightly and smiled up at him.

"Now, now, you can't do something like that, Husband. What would Eirene think?" Gwen looked thoughtful, tapping her lips with a finger. "Besides, why get your own hands dirty? They both had the same plan, and both acted like pushovers in front of each other, hoping to appear weak. Both probably had some way to get rid of the other eventually. We could always put them out to sea on the same boat, see which one of them comes back."

"Ooo, I hadn't even thought of that!" He grinned. "Wonderful idea, Darling!"

"Why, thank you, Love!"

She watched as Gavin turned back to their fathers. "I guess the point is there's really nothing you can do about it, is there? Your plan failed. There's a new king and queen ruling the two kingdoms, and we've already taken a few steps towards ensuring things stay that way. We're not monsters, of course, amusing as Gwen's plan may sound. No, we'll probably just lock you both in a room while we take care of some remaining details here and in Rhegar, make sure there's a clean transfer of power."

Bryn hadn't moved in a long while, and looked utterly stunned. Alwyn remained speechless, gaping at them. Gwen was content to simply stand there, watching both men, grinning.

The silence was broken by scuffling and muted yelling coming from beyond the antechamber door, and as the noise grew in volume, a bedraggled Anifail staggered into the room, having been shoved forward by two large knights.

"You have no right!" Anifail said, struggling to right himself. "I demand to know—"

It was then he saw Gwen and Gavin standing together, and he froze. She watched him calculate what was going on, grinning at him once she saw understanding dawn.

And then Gwen looked past Anifail and focused on the two figures beyond him, and her grin disappeared entirely.

Rhosyn was walking with the assistance of the fellow Gavin had called Trevor the first day they'd met. Trevor was being attentive and wore an expression of concern, but Rhosyn was haggard, and the nightshirt she wore was little better than rags. Her eyes were rimmed in red, and her cheek discoloured by the weal of an enormous bruise.

Gwen realized she was clenching her jaw.

"Any problem finding my wife's lady-in-waiting?" Gavin asked, his tone hard and level.

"None, My King," said Trevor. "She was in the same room as this fellow here. We found her next to his bed, standing, near exhaustion, her arm chained to the top of an oak nightstand in a manner that prevented her from sitting." He gave Rhosyn a worried look. "She hasn't said a word yet, nor made any sound."

Teeth still tightly clenched, Gwen strode forward, not stopping until her face was inches away from Anifail's. Though every part of her wanted to lash out and strike him just then, she instead raised an upturned palm between them expectantly.

"There's no way you'd just leave it lying around someplace," she said quietly. "Let's have it. Now."

Anifail gave her a slight sneer, and jutted his chin out at her.

The two of them remained frozen in place, locking stares. After a few moments, Gwen allowed her face to light up in a beatific smile, and she clapped her hands together excitedly.

"Oooh! I've just thought of a lovely new game!" she announced loudly. "It's called *How many holes can we poke in Anifail before he empties his pockets?* Who wants to be the first to play?"

Anifail snarled a curse, attempting to shake off the knight who held his arm. Gwen gestured to the knight, who let go of him, at which point Anifail slowly reached into his vest pocket and pulled out a small spherical object Gwen recognized as a geis sphere. He held it out before him, and fixed Gwen with a look of contempt.

Gwen held her open hand out underneath his. He dropped the sphere onto her palm.

As soon as she had possession of the sphere, she spun in place and dashed it against the stone wall next to her. It exploded with a *pop*, ballooning luminescent dust that very quickly settled to the floor.

The sound of Rhosyn's sob could be heard immediately. Then, as if hearing her own voice had just made things worse, she let out a cry and buried her face in Trevor's shoulder. Though seeming very surprised by this, Trevor instinctively hugged her, and began patting her lightly on the shoulder while glaring about the room in a protective manner.

Watching Trevor, Gwen felt an immediate sense of gratitude. She wanted to comfort Rhosyn herself, but she wasn't properly covered up — no gloves, no sleeves, none of the stuff she usually needed to safely embrace her. As much as she wanted to just then, she couldn't risk giving her friend a hug, which made her glad there was someone there who could do what she couldn't.

The two of them made quite a cute couple, actually.

Anifail gave a snort of derision, which brought her attention back to him.

"Queen," he laughed, taking a moment to spit on the floor. "You think you've won. I've got friends everywhere. I've got resources your feeble little mind can't even comprehend! You're not smart enough — not ruthless enough — to hold on to the crown. Not even by half! You don't have the nerve for it. Honestly, Princess, you'll never be more than what you are already — a scared, frightened, pathetic little girl. So go ahead. Enjoy this *victory*. Enjoy your time play-acting as queen. Once you've proved to everyone you're nothing more than an inept, empty-headed little doll, those of us who know how real power works will be right there, waiting. Waiting for you to make a mistake." He smiled cruelly. "One. Single. Mistake."

Gwen caught the barest hint of a growl coming from Gavin, and he seemed about to step past her towards the blonde man, but Gwen waved him away. Once again she stared at Anifail, who continued to stare back defiantly, a smirk on his lips.

He was doing what he'd always done, she realized — attempting to make her feel timid and fearful, so she might become timid and fearful as a result.

This was her first day as queen, the very first day of her brand new life. A life with Gavin. A life where she didn't need to feel afraid, or weak, or fearful, or ashamed. She wasn't about to let someone as worthless as Anifail set the tone for that new life.

Gwen smiled sadly. "Oh Captain, you're absolutely right. I'm not ruthless at all. I'm just a frail, weak little girl who's lived in fear for most of her life. I have no experience when it comes to running a kingdom, or being queen." She gave a light shrug. "I suppose my new husband and I are just going to have to pick it up as we go. We'll probably make a right mess of things, but I suppose eventually we'll just have to trust ourselves and our judgment, do what feels right. Learn." Gwen surreptitiously licked her lips and looked over at Rhosyn, who was now quietly watching from the protection of Trevor's shoulder. "You know, Captain, I feel as though I haven't properly thanked you for taking such good care of my lady-in-waiting these past few weeks."

And with that, Gwen threw herself at Anifail, wrapped her arms around his neck, and planted a big, wet kiss on his cheek.

Anifail staggered back, alarmed, and then became frantic, letting loose a piercing scream as he fell to the floor. Foul-smelling smoke had already begun to appear around his face and neck as he thrashed, screeching inarticulately and pawing at his cheek.

Gwen glanced over at Bryn and Alwyn, who both watched Anifail. Nobody seemed capable of anything more than simply standing in place and staring at the spectacle.

"Hey, look at that!" Gwen said, smiling happily at everyone assembled. "Maybe I'm just a teensy bit ruthless after all."

Gavin shook his head in mock sorrow as he watched Anifail writhe in agony.

"Not even married a full day, and she's already kissing other men," he remarked sadly, his voice completely at odds with the smile that was threatening to take over his entire face. "You know, you should be more careful about doing that sort of thing right in front of me, Darling. I could be the jealous type."

"Oh, don't be silly, Dearest. You know you're the only one for me." Gwen smiled, reaching out and taking his hand in hers. She sighed happily. "After all, we were practically made for each other."

About the Author

Aaron Kite is a writer/artist who likes putting slashes between occupations and who very rarely refers to himself in the third person. He was born on the exact same day that São Paulo Metro was inaugurated in Brazil, which the authorities claim is pure coincidence.

He has been interviewed by *Science Magazine,* the *Calgary Herald, National Geographic,* and this shady fellow named 'Jimmy' who kept pointedly asking him about his success as a writer with questions like "Got any spare change?" and "C'mon, really, do ya? I gotta catch a bus."

Aaron was one of the founding members of the amateur writing group "Starting Write Now", as well as countless side-projects which he'd mention by name if the government would finally get around to granting him immunity. He lives in Calgary, Alberta, Canada, which really ought to have another sub-section to it, because another comma there would look really slick.

At present he has three finished novels — *Two Cats,* and the sequel *Jade Mouse,* as well as the standalone (but with sequels percolating in his brain) novel *A Touch of Poison*. He's currently in the middle of writing the novels, *Ten Arrows* and *Revenant*, as well as about eleven or so other books that are all in varying states of doneness. When writing, he likes to disable his spell-checker and make up words, as is illustrated by the use of 'doneness' above.

He's allergic to cats, and thus he tries to arrange it so he's living with one whenever possible, probably just to prove a point of some sort.

Books by Five Rivers

NON-FICTION

Al Capone: Chicago's King of Crime, by Nate Hendley

Crystal Death: North America's Most Dangerous Drug, by Nate Hendley

Dutch Schultz: Brazen Beer Baron of New York, by Nate Hendley

Motivate to Create: a guide for writers, by Nate Hendley

Shakespeare for Slackers: Romeo and Juliet, by Aaron Kite, Audrey Evans, and Jade Brooke

The Organic Home Garden, by Patrick Lima and John Scanlan

Elephant's Breath & London Smoke: historic colour names, definitions & uses, Deb Salisbury, editor

Stonehouse Cooks, by Lorina Stephens

John Lennon: a biography, by Nate Hendley

Shakespeare & Readers' Theatre: Hamlet, Romeo & Juliet, Midsummer Night's Dream, by John Poulson

Stephen Truscott, by Nate Hendley

FICTION

Black Wine, by Candas Jane Dorsey

88, by M.E. Fletcher

Immunity to Strange Tales, by Susan J. Forest

The Legend of Sarah, by Leslie Gadallah

Growing Up Bronx, by H.A. Hargreaves

North by 2000+, a collection of short, speculative fiction, by H.A. Hargreaves

A Subtle Thing, Alicia Hendley

Downshift: A Sid Rafferty Thriller, by Matt Hughes

Old Growth: A Sid Rafferty Thriller, by Matt Hughes

Kingmaker's Sword, Book 1: Rune Blades of Celi, by Ann Marston

Western King, Book 2: The Rune Blades of Celi, by Ann Marston

Broken Blade, Book 3: The Rune Blades of Celi, by Ann Marston

Cloudbearer's Shadow, Book 4: The Rune Blades of Celi, by Ann Marston

Indigo Time, by Sally McBride

Wasps at the Speed of Sound, by Derryl Murphy

A Method to Madness: A Guide to the Super Evil, edited by Michell Plested
  and Jeffery A. Hite

A Quiet Place, by J.W. Schnarr

Things Falling Apart, by J.W. Schnarr

And the Angels Sang: a collection of short speculative fiction, by Lorina Stephens

From Mountains of Ice, by Lorina Stephens

Memories, Mother and a Christmas Addiction, by Lorina Stephens

Shadow Song, by Lorina Stephens

YA FICTION
The Runner and the Wizard, by Dave Duncan

The Runner and the Saint, by Dave Duncan

A Touch of Poison, by Aaron Kite

Out of Time, by D.G. Laderoute

Mik Murdoch: Boy-Superhero, by Michell Plested

Type, by Alicia Hendley

FICTION COMING SOON
Kaleidoscope, by Robert Fletcher

Cat's Pawn, by Leslie Gadallah

Cat's Gambit, by Leslie Gadallah

King of Shadows, Book 5: The Rune Blades of Celi, by Ann Marston

Sword and Shadow, Book 6: The Rune Blades of Celi, by Ann Marston

Bane's Choice, Book 7: The Rune Blades of Celi, by Ann Marston

A Still and Bitter Grave, by Ann Marston

Diamonds in Black Sand, by Ann Marston

Forevering, by Peter Such

YA FICTION COMING SOON
My Life as a Troll, by Susan Bohnet

Mik Murdoch: The Power Within, by Michell Plested

YA NON-FICTION COMING SOON
Your Home on Native Land, by Alan Skeoch

The Prime Ministers of Canada Series:

Sir John A. Macdonald
Alexander Mackenzie
Sir John Abbott
Sir John Thompson
Sir Mackenzie Bowell
Sir Charles Tupper
Sir Wilfred Laurier
Sir Robert Borden
Arthur Meighen
William Lyon Mackenzie King
R. B. Bennett
Louis St. Laurent
John Diefenbaker
Lester B. Pearson
Pierre Trudeau
Joe Clark
John Turner
Brian Mulroney
Kim Campbell
Jean Chretien
Paul Martin
Stephen Harper

www.fiveriverspublishing.com

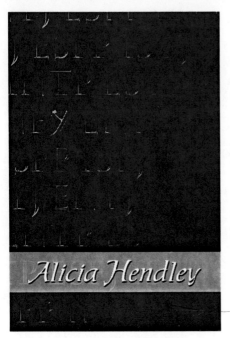

Trade Paperback 6 x 9, 314 pages, ISBN 9781927400296
$31.99

eISBN 9781927400302 $9.99

by Alicia Hendley

June 1, 2013

After the fallout from the Social Media Era, when rates of divorce, crime, and mental illness were sky-rocketing, civilization was at its breaking point. As a result, prominent psychologists from around the globe gathered together to try to regain social order through scientific means.

Their solution? Widespread implementation of Myers-Briggs personality typing, with each citizen assessed at the age of twelve and then sent to one of sixteen Home Schools in order to receive the appropriate education for their Type and aided in choosing a suitable occupation and life partner.

North American society becomes structured around the tenets of Typology, with governments replaced by The Association of Psychologists. With social order seemingly regained, what could go possibly wrong?

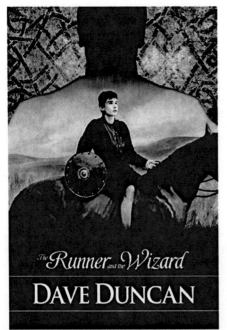

Trade Paperback 6 x 9, 100 pages, ISBN 9781927400395
$11.99

eISBN 9781927400401 $4.99

by Dave Duncan

October 1, 2013

Young Ivor dreams of being a swordsman like his nine older brothers, but until he can grow a beard he's limited to being a runner, carrying messages for their lord, Thane Carrak. That's usually boring, but this time Carrak has sent him on a long journey to summon the mysterious Rorie of Ytter. Rorie is reputed to be a wizard—or an outlaw, or maybe a saint—but the truth is far stranger, and Ivor suddenly finds himself caught up in a twisted magical intrigue that threatens Thane Carrak and could leave Ivor himself very dead.

Trade Paperback 6 x 9, 504 pages, ISBN 9781927400166 $37.99

eISBN 9781927400173 $9.99

by Ann Marston

August 1, 2012

Triumphing over adversity and evil, Kian dav Leydon brings the fabled Rune Blade Kingmaker back to the Isle of Celi after it was stolen, so the Isle will be ready when and if invasion comes.

A re-print of Ann Marston's Book 1 of the much beloved Rune Blades of Celi series.

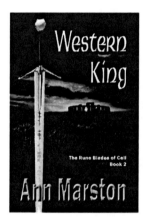

Trade Paperback 6 x 9, 440 pages, ISBN 9781927400272 $37.99

eISBN 9781927400289 $9.99

by Ann Marston

June 1, 2013

The wanderer Red Kian has ruled Skai as Regent, but now it is time for him to step down. War clouds are gathering. Maedun sorcerers have taken the continent, and Saesnesi raiders are pillaging the islands.

But Kian has three sons. One is a prince of Skai blood, one is a wizard touched by Tyadda fire, and one is a dreamer who longs to unite the Celi against their enemies. Who will inherit the rune blade known as Kingmaker? Who will have the power to confront the Black Riders who bring darkness like a cloak to cover the land?

The answer will surprise you. Just as it surprises them.

Trade Paperback 6 x 9, 372 pages, ISBN 9781927400470 $28.99

eISBN 9781927400487 $9.99

by Ann Marston

December 1, 2013

A kidnapped Princess and a clanless man share a terrible secret--the dark powers of Maedun are preparing a new assault on the shinning Isle of Celi.

Using stolen Celae magic, the sorcerer Hakkar plans to rip down the veil of enchantment drawn about the island kingdom. Only the great sword Kingmaker can save the land. Until it, too, is shattered.

Brynda, daughter of Keylan, must teach her Rune Blade to sing death's song--or Maedun's Somber Riders will slain all Celi for their own!

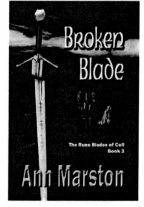

CPSIA information can be obtained at www.ICGtesting.com
Printed in the USA
LVOW12s0021190714

395015LV00001B/13/P